Rainy Day Women

An Au

By Kay Kendall

Author of Desolation Row: An Austin Starr Mystery

Rainy Day Women
An Austin Starr Mystery

Print ISBN 978-1-941071-17-5
eBook 978-1-941071-18-2

STAIRWAY⹀PRESS
STAIRWAY PRESS—SEATTLE

www.StairwayPress.com
1500A East College Way #554
Mount Vernon, WA 98273

To Bruce

The word supportive doesn't begin to give you enough credit.

Chapter One

I STOOD, CAREFUL not to make any noise, afraid to waken the sleeping ogre. If his constant twitches were any indication, he was only dozing. If he woke up, he'd be a real beast and leave me no peace.

My bare feet inched along the floorboards. I knew where the squeaky spots lurked and avoided them. Dim light from the hallway showed objects to avoid—chairs, tables, other hazards. By dodging and zigzagging, I managed to evade every potential noisemaker.

What did it matter if my escape took ten minutes? Breaking free was what counted.

I reached the door and turned back to check on the huddled figure. He still breathed heavily. Suddenly his body shuddered.

I froze. The smallest sound could disturb him, yet I would lose my sanity if I failed to escape.

Decades ticked by. No other movements came from the bed. This was my chance.

I took a deep, silent gulp of air and turned to glide down the hall. My release was not yet a done deal, but I could taste freedom.

I walked faster, bolder. I was halfway to ultimate liberation when a board creaked underfoot. I halted and whirled back toward the bedroom.

Tonight I was lucky. All stayed quiet except for my heart,

thudding loud enough to sabotage my escape. I feared he might hear it. But nothing indicated that my breakout wouldn't be a success.

I moved again. First my right foot, then left, then right. My focus was tight. Total. I could win this round. I would. I must.

Exhaustion would kill me if I didn't succeed.

I was so intent on reaching my goal that I failed to notice the tall, silent figure looming in the shadows. Only when he sprang forward did I realize I was done for.

"Ooh!" I gasped.

He wrapped his arms around my neck and pulled me to him. I pressed my face into his broad shoulder to muffle my sounds.

"I did it." I giggled into the fabric of his denim shirt. "Finally, finally, I managed to leave Wyatt's room without waking him up."

"Well done, sweetheart." David's voice was low and warm. "Now let's celebrate. I've got just the reward for you."

I lifted my head and caught a fleeting smile on his handsome face.

"Come see what I have to show you. If you're good—very, very good—you can play with it."

My giggles bubbled up again. David played this game when he felt romantic—which, alas, was too rare these days. The demands of his doctoral research overwhelmed him.

He pushed me across the threshold of our bedroom. "See what pleasures await you in my kingdom." He shut the door soundlessly behind us, and his voice grew deeper, louder.

"Shh." I placed my finger against his lips. "If Wy wakes now, he'll be up for hours. Then all my stealth and conniving will have been pointless. I know I'm a bad mother, but one more night without sleep, and I'll just—"

David sucked my finger into his mouth and made suggestive motions.

"Stop it. What kind of mom am I that—"

"What kind? Wonderful but tired."

"My mother wouldn't agree."

"Forget about her." He grabbed my finger and sucked it again.

"You're not taking me seriously." I laughed in spite of myself.

"But I will take you seriously. Put the emphasis on *take*." He pulled me across the room and threw me on the bed.

I squealed, pretending fright, while he tugged off my sweatshirt. As he reached to unhook my bra, the peal of the phone shattered the moment.

I started up from the bed, but he grabbed my arm. "Leave it."

"I can't. Wyatt will wake up unless one of us answers."

David released my arm. "I give up. But I'll get you yet, my pretty." He twirled a pretend mustache. "And it'll be soon, one of these, er, weeks."

I adored David when he was like this. Although he was making jokes, I knew the interruption to our lovemaking had upset him.

The phone had already rung four times. I dived toward it, crashing against the night stand. Rubbing my sore shin, I picked up the receiver.

"This is the Starr residence." There was only silence. "Hello? Hello?" I strained to hear and made out a sniffling sound trickling down the phone wires.

A welcome, familiar voice quavered across thousands of miles and into my ear.

"Austin, I'm in so much trouble."

"Larissa?" My nerves jumped to full alert. "What's wrong?"

More sniffs. "I'm so sorry. I didn't think I'd fall apart like this. I just need to tell you what's happened." Her cries became hiccups, and she stopped speaking.

My mind spun a rolodex of catastrophes, searching for reasons my friend, always upbeat and sunny, had gone into a tailspin.

Calculating the time difference between my Toronto home

and her temporary one in Vancouver, I figured it was seven in the evening out on the western edge of Canada. Only a disaster made her call when long distance rates were astronomical.

"Tell me what's wrong. You're scaring me to death."

I checked on David, saw him point at the clock and make faces at me.

"Hurry up. Come here," he mouthed.

My heart shredded. How could I meet the needs of both of them, my husband and my friend? I couldn't.

Little by little, Larissa's hiccups slowed, then stopped altogether. When I sensed she was about to speak, I turned my back on David and gave her my full attention.

She choked out a sentence. "Shona died."

"Shona who?"

"A grad student I knew here."

"I'm sorry." I didn't know what else to say—people died every day.

Hmm…that wasn't too sympathetic. But David's hand stroked my neck, and I wanted to melt into his arms. Still, I couldn't abandon Larissa. Not yet anyway.

"I'm sorry," I said again. "Shona must have been important if you're this upset." Shona's name wasn't familiar. I thought I knew all Larissa's new pals.

"You don't get it." Larissa's voice was shrill in my ear.

Apparently not.

Before I offered a snide reply, Larissa added two details in a whispery voice that had me shivering, even though the night was muggy with humidity.

"Shona was murdered. And I'm the Mounties' prime suspect."

Chapter Two

I GULPED A deep breath, forcing my voice to sound gentle. "Murder? You? Impossible."

Larissa's sobs filled my ears, breaking my heart into smaller pieces. When she tried to talk, her words were unintelligible.

"Oh, sweetie, calm down and give me details, okay? I can't help if I don't know what's going on. Maybe deep breaths will settle your nerves."

I offered this advice as much for my own benefit as for Larissa's. My body was shaking clear down to my toes. I dropped to the floor with a thump.

As her sobs gradually subsided, I tried to reach through the wires and pull up her spirits. "We can work things out. Together, like always. The Mounties will soon realize their mistake. No one in his right mind would think you could commit murder." I threw my assurances out into the universe as a prayer.

"No, everything is worse than you can imagine." She laughed, and the sound verged on hysterics. "But you *can* imagine. You went through all this before. You had to stand by David when he was accused of murder." Her voice broke. "Now you'll need to do that for me." The word *me* ended on a high-pitched wail.

I stood, but my knees buckled. David moved over to me, but I waved him away.

I focused on Larissa's words. She'd released them in a torrent.

"I've been interviewed twice by the Mounties already. Once at work and once at their headquarters. The second time was much worse than the first. And they're being so mean to me."

"You're joking."

"Do I sound like I'm joking?"

These words were slung in staccato fashion, and her tone grew snide. Yet this was a welcome change. Maybe she could pull herself together. Anger was better than being pitiful.

I struggled to maintain my calm. "I know you're not joking. Wish you were, though." Larissa was the only friend I'd made since moving to Canada from Texas. If anything happened to her, I'd be bereft. "Why are *you* a murder suspect?" I paused. "And who is Shona?"

"Good gosh, where should I start?"

"In your last letter, you sounded like you were having a ball out there."

"I was. It all just went down so fast. My summer job was going along great. Then Shona got killed."

"*Who* is Shona?"

"Sorry, I forget you don't know her. She's a—was—a grad student in the chem lab."

Larissa's new job at the University of British Columbia had surprised me. Chemistry and Larissa didn't make a good compound. I started to say that, but changed my mind, deciding to reassure her.

"That's better," I said. "Keep feeding me details—I need all the details. Now, tell me how this Shona died."

Larissa groaned. "Looked like an accident at first and—"

"Where? In the lab?"

"No, right before our women's lib meeting started."

She stopped to blow her nose, and I was left hanging. What was *with* this women's lib? When did Larissa get involved? She'd always said we didn't need it—she and I had already evolved into strong super women. Of course she laughed after saying stuff like that, but still.

Her sniffles stopped. "Sorry," she said. "My nose runs nonstop when I'm crying."

"Never mind. What's women's lib got to do with this?"

Larissa ignored my question and my short-tempered attitude. "The police say someone poisoned her." She hiccupped. "And so, here I am, grieving over Shona's death, and they suspect me for her murder. See what I mean?"

"Yes, but—"

"You've been down this road before. You know what I should do, Austin, what I should say, how I should act. I didn't kill anyone. You've got to help me. You were able to prove David's innocence."

Larissa's torrent of words, plus her demands, flooded my brain. I couldn't think. I couldn't speak.

"Naturally, I don't expect you to do that for me, but you're the best person to give me moral support. I really need you. To talk to, I mean. But if you wanted to, really wanted to come out here to Vancouver, then I wouldn't say no. Not that you have to. I mean, you have your family and all, but I could sure use some propping up."

"You got it, you know that. But dang, we can't talk long enough long distance. Where are you calling from? Who's paying for this call?"

Again she ignored my question. Instead, she whimpered. Every woeful sound tightened the muscles in my neck.

"Can't your father—"

"Papa flew out two days ago. Now Aunt Raisa is putting him up too. Thank heaven she didn't kick me out when the police zeroed in on me. He's here for as long as it takes."

"That's a relief. He'll straighten everything out. But you still haven't told me why *you're* a suspect. No one could look at you and think you'd kill anyone. It's preposterous."

Larissa gave one of her famous snorts, always so bizarre when made by such an exquisite creature. I loved the sound, especially now. It showed she was calming down, reining in her emotions at least a little.

She gulped air before she continued. "But listen, I did get some good news today. Shona's murder isn't the only one the cops need to solve because—"

"How's that good news?" That didn't make sense.

"Another UBC student was killed about the same time as Shona," she said.

"When was that? You still haven't told me."

"Did so. Happened six days ago. I told you that already."

I wasn't going to argue with her, but she hadn't noted the time of Shona's murder. "Six days? Why didn't you call right away if this is so urgent?"

"I told you. I just found out I'm a suspect."

Hope glimmered for an instant. Maybe Larissa's situation wasn't as dire as her sobs indicated. I glanced at David, lying on the bed with his eyes shut. He opened one eye, patted the bed, whispered, "Come on. Still time for a quick snuggle."

Larissa was saying, "Vancouver doesn't have many suspicious deaths, so—"

"Any connection between the two murders?" I couldn't help myself; I had to interrupt.

"Not likely. Some guy got killed at the nude beach down the cliff below campus."

"Nude beach? The University of British Columbia sanctions this place?" I tried for a spot of levity, and when she laughed, my jaw unclenched.

"Heck, no. Wreck Beach is on Crown land, so the university officials have no say. Someone told me the second murder would slow down investigation of Shona's. This helps me because, well—my lawyer said the police here don't often handle two high-profile murders at once, not in the fancier parts of town and—"

"I bet the two murders are related. I b—"

"My lawyer says the Mounties say absolutely not. They're wildly different. Anyway, that buys me some time." Larissa's voice ended on a shrill note.

Lawyer? She already had a lawyer. Why did she already have one if she only now discovered she was a suspect? I slouched against the wall.

"Listen, I know it won't be easy for you to get away. There's Wyatt and David. Your graduate work." She cleared her throat. "But can you please, please come out to Vancouver? How soon do you think you can leave?"

"But surely your father can—"

"Papa's agreed to buy your ticket." She whimpered. "Please say you'll come, Austin."

The pressure inside me zoomed so high that I felt I would pop like a two-penny balloon.

"I want to help, Larissa. You understand that, don't you?" I wouldn't leave her in the lurch if I could help it. She meant too much to me.

"Yes, I know," Larissa squealed. "No way I'd ask if I weren't so scared. And I'm sure it would be only for a couple of days. You'll get me settled, and then I'll be fine."

I was speechless, rare for me. We stayed silent for a moment, and my thoughts pulled me back and forth. Should I go, support Larissa in person? Should I stay with my family? I twisted the phone cord so tightly around my hand that my fingers were in danger of falling off.

I heard David leave the room. Now I could speak freely. "Let me talk to David first. I can't answer yet. Let's talk again tomorrow night, okay?"

"I'm all right with that." She pronounced each syllable precisely and slowly, giving her speech a formal, distant air. I felt guilty at disappointing her. "I assumed you couldn't give me an answer right away. I know you'll do your best."

I shook my head, an effort to clear my thoughts. "In the meantime, you still need to tell me more about Shona's death. Like where exactly she was killed and—"

A dial tone hummed in my ear.

"Damn it." I kicked the table, forgetting I was barefoot. "Ouch."

I heard footsteps behind me, and then David loomed up beside me. "What's going on?"

I looked at his dear face and blinked back tears. "Larissa must've run out of coins to feed the payphone. That happened the last time we talked too."

Except then we'd only been shooting the breeze, and now my best friend might be accused of murder.

Chapter Three

DAVID AND I stared at each other. I stood with my back against the wall, my hand covering my mouth, my eyes popping wide.

He broke the silence.

"Larissa's a murder suspect, and she wants you to fly out to Vancouver?" He turned away to straighten a stack of books on the nightstand. "Naturally you said you couldn't possibly do that." He shifted back around and waved a book at me. "Right?"

I swallowed. "Not exactly."

"Austin, you're my wife. I need you here. You know how much pressure I'm under."

"Believe me, I know."

"Besides, *nobody* is gonna believe Larissa killed anyone."

I raised a brow. David should know better than anyone that the authorities would consider anyone a murderer.

But I understood why he didn't want me to go. My own graduate studies placed third behind the needs of my guys. Having no time for myself depressed me, but David didn't want to hear about that. Especially not now.

He slammed the book on the table, and several other books fell to the floor.

"Shh. You'll wake up Wy."

We stood still, waiting to hear our son's cry. When none came, my shoulders relaxed.

"Should we talk about this now or wait until the morning?" I forced my voice to sound conciliatory.

David marched across the room and wrapped me in his arms. "Sorry, babe. Not fair to take my nerves out on you. Let's sleep now and talk it out tomorrow. I'll feel more human then."

We shared a kiss and got into bed. He spooned against my back and relaxed into sleep faster than I expected him to.

Not me, though. Peaceful slumber was impossible. I flipped and flopped, got up for a glass of milk, tried to read. And made such a ruckus that David plopped a pillow over his head.

He didn't complain. He knew how much Larissa's phone call had upset me.

I didn't have to imagine how she felt. I recalled the horror of David's time in jail and how it affected us. Now, a whole year later, we still struggled with the shadows cast back then. Sometimes I wondered if we'd ever emerge.

Imagining my normally confident friend standing in—no, engulfed by—similar shadows, I wanted to cry. To beat my head against the wall.

Her father would help her, of course. His devotion was total, a joy to witness. His own life had prepared him for facing the worst that hard-fought military battles and evil Soviet minions could fling his way. Dr. Klimenko, who doubled as my Russian history professor, could handle ferocious foes. Yet could he deal with the subtlety of the Canadian justice system?

I pictured him smashing his leather-clad fist on a magistrate's desk and yelling *po-russki*, in Russian, at a hapless Canadian bureaucrat. None of that would help Larissa's cause.

What she needed was someone calm and consoling to support her. To buck her up when events overwhelmed, assuring her she'd get through whatever was thrown her way.

What she needed was a good, stalwart friend.

What she needed was me.

A vision of my clogged schedule appeared in my mind's eye. Today was Monday, and every day in the coming week held a long to-do list. I had a household to run and research to do.

And Wyatt, what about him? I couldn't possibly leave him with David. With the deadline for defending his dissertation hanging over him, David was too busy to cope with an infant. I gnawed on my thumbnail, knowing I shouldn't even be thinking about leaving. To consider for even one second flying across the country to comfort Larissa was nuts.

Still, the idea wouldn't leave my mind.

Hence the flipping and flopping instead of sleeping.

When David was jailed for murder and I'd tried to find the real killer, I hadn't been a mother. And I'd learned the hard way that getting involved in a murder case brought unexpected dangers.

I sat up in bed, careful not to wake David, and was staring out the window when my thoughts took a sharp turn toward the light. I was viewing a trip to Vancouver the wrong way. I needn't play sleuth again. I only needed to go support a friend.

The two sides of my brain immediately roared into an argument with each other.

See, said one, the danger won't be great. Any comparison between what I'd done for David and what I'd do for Larissa wouldn't hold up. I could safely take Wyatt to visit Auntie Larissa.

You're crazy, the other side said. You may fool yourself, but you don't fool me.

The war inside my brain made my head ache.

The last time I noticed the bedside clock it said three thirty. I must have slept because three hours later, the danged thing rang and woke me up. I trudged down the hall to check on Wy. Hallelujah, he still slept. I lumbered into the kitchen, rubbing tired eyes.

I was making coffee when David walked in and strode to where I stood at the stove. "What're you muttering about? You had a restless night, didn't you?" He slapped my bottom, then ruffled my already-tousled hair. "Did you worry about Larissa all night?"

I wrinkled my nose and ducked my head, shielding my face so he couldn't read it. He was too astute.

"I've been trying to figure out a way to help her. Just moments ago, I had a breakthrough and—"

"Bet I know what it is."

"Sure, Mr. Smarty Pants. Tell me." I reached up to smooth his beard and then burrowed into his chest.

"You still want to fly out to Vancouver, even though you know I'm against it." He drew back from me. "Furthermore, you're going to ask me to babysit while you're gone."

Oh, he thought he was so clever.

"Am not. I wouldn't do that to you."

"No?" His eyebrows lifted.

"No." I backed up and looked him straight in the eye—easy to do since he was only an inch taller than me. "My plan is"—I hitched a breath—"I'll take Wyatt with me."

David stared at me. His mouth opened and shut without making a sound.

"Cat got your tongue?" I beamed. Victory. "See—you didn't know what my bright idea was." This was a game we played, each trying to prove we could read the other's mind. I'd won this round.

A muscle jumped in his cheek. "Look, don't be cute about this. It's not funny. How can you dismiss what happened last year?" He put his hands on his hips. "No way will my wife and son fly out and get tangled up in another murder case. You could run into some homicidal psychopath, and I think—"

What? He had switched arguments on me.

I spread my hands wide and smiled at him, attempting a beguiling look—or at least a pleading one. "This won't be like last time. I won't be in harm's way. I'll be there for moral support only. Wyatt will be safe. And so will I."

"Why can't you provide support over the telephone?"

I cocked my head, wrinkled my nose, shut my eyes. Hoped I demonstrated my pain. Yes, I was trying to work the situation.

"Look, here's my logic," I said, lowering my tone and slowing my words, hoping I sounded reasonable. "Phone calls aren't good enough. You should've heard her last night. Larissa's beyond upset. She needs me."

"I need you. Wyatt needs you. We're your family." He kicked the table leg.

Now we'd gotten to the nub of the issue. My rationale had to be clear and persuasive. "First, *you* don't need me right now. You're busy with your dissertation. If Wyatt and I leave, you'll be able to focus and get tons of work done."

I ticked off one finger and then another.

"Second, Wyatt will still have me. Third, my trip won't cost anything. Larissa said we can stay at her aunt's house, so no hotel costs. Then we'll be back in a jiffy, gone only long enough for you to miss us. And besides"—I ticked off a fourth finger—"Larissa is family too."

Would he leap to agree? When he didn't—and really, I'd doubted he would—I played my top card. "Okay, here's my backup plan. But be warned: bringing Wy with me will work out better than my other idea, but you can choose."

"Choose from what?" David frowned.

"I'll ask Mother to fly up and babysit while you study."

"Damn it, Austin," David yelled. "You know that I—" He stopped abruptly and burst out laughing. "You're really determined if you're willing to ask your mother."

"Darned right."

"What makes you believe she'd agree? Since we've been in Toronto, she hasn't deigned to visit, even though your dad wants to."

"Won't know until I try." I turned on the full wattage of my smile. "Shall I ask her?"

He stroked his beard and chewed on his lip. Then he pulled me to him and wrapped his arms around me.

"I've suspected your mother, in her heart of hearts, was glad when I went to jail. Regardless of my innocence, I bet she wanted me to stay behind bars. Then maybe you'd leave Canada, return to Texas, and forget your unsuitable, draft-resisting husband."

I pulled away and flounced to the other side of the kitchen. "Isn't that a little unfair?"

"No. I wasn't the future your mother mapped out for you. She'd give anything to get you back in Texas and remarried to some oil millionaire."

"Maybe, but remember this. She also drummed into me stuff about whither-thou-goest and making marriage and family the be-all and end-all of a woman's life." I pointed out the window at our neighbors hurrying off to work. "So I'm right here. I followed her grand scheme, just took a little detour north. If she's not happy, she needs to blame herself."

"Your logic is right on, but your mom won't see that." His mouth twisted into a big grin. "Nix this idea. Your mother would only add to my stress."

He shut his eyes for an instant, shook his head, and turned away. He poured a cup of coffee before he said, "Look, here's my biggest objection. You will not be able to stop yourself from nosing around, playing sleuth again in Vancouver. It's your nature. No matter how many times you promise, you'll forget, just like that." He snapped his fingers.

He walked closer and stopped two feet away from me. "You know I'm right."

His gaze bored into me, and I found it difficult not to look away. Still, I forced myself to hold my eyes steady and kept my voice assured. "I promise I will not play detective, not this time. Cross my heart and hope to die." I mimed crossing my heart.

David didn't laugh. He scowled. "Not funny, sweetheart. You nearly died from giving me support last year. You'll forget about your promise. I know you will."

"But I promise, I do promise. *This* time is different. I wasn't a mother before. That's made me more, uh, serious, I suppose. More cautious. I won't be cavalier with my actions this time. I did learn my lesson, truly I did."

He shrugged and clomped to the kitchen table, lowered himself onto a chair and shook his head. I felt a flicker of remorse, watching his struggle. He picked up his cup of coffee. But instead of drinking it, he stared into its blackness.

The wall clock clicked.

Clicked.

Clicked.

I needed to let David come to his own decision. I was impatient—wanting to hurry him along—but I didn't tap my foot or fidget. Well, not if you didn't count the two toes on my right foot that I surreptitiously crossed for luck.

The screech of a chair against the floor made me jump. David stood. "Okay, you win. Go and take Wyatt with you. But I am not happy about this."

My stomach tightened. I diagnosed a slight case of guilt. "So why are you giving in?"

"I don't have time to argue, and I know you won't give up. Besides, our boy needs his mother."

As if to confirm David's words, Wyatt's good-morning cries came from down the hall.

"I'll be right back." I rushed out to get our three-month-old before his wails turned to a full-force gale.

And before his father could change his mind.

Chapter Four

LATER THAT NIGHT I huddled on the living room sofa and waited for the phone to ring. My watch said eleven o'clock. Meaning it was eight in Vancouver. Out there, long distance rates were about to drop, so Larissa was bound to call soon.

"Aren't you coming to bed?" David growled from the hall. "Here's our chance. Wyatt's been asleep for ages. Why are you still up?"

"Be in shortly," I answered. "Probably Larissa will—"

The phone rang and cut me short. "Here she is. Won't be long, I promise."

I should quit making promises. I sounded guilty ahead of time, ahead of my sin of breaking my solemn promise not to play sleuth in Vancouver. David was bound to sense the shift.

He grunted and slouched down the hall toward our bedroom. He'd spoken few words to me since he'd agreed to my trip.

I picked up the receiver and without further ado made my announcement. "Larissa, I'm coming."

Her answering squeal pierced my eardrum. "I knew David would come through. Thank him for me, will you?"

"Sure thing. But there's a snag. The only way I can come is to bring Wyatt." I paused. How should I put this? "Well, I, uh—you sure it's okay to stay at your aunt's house? Do you think I can find a reliable babysitter for a few hours a day?" There, I got it all out.

"Of course you can stay at Aunt Raisa's." Larissa clicked her tongue, which meant that she was thinking hard. "Now, let me see. Maybe I can pull a babysitter out of my hat—you know, like a rabbit." She giggled.

What a relief, hearing a moment of her usual high spirits. At twenty-one, only two years younger than me, she still sounded like a cute kid.

After a few beats, she let out a yelp. "Got it. Mrs. Mirnaya lives down the street. She's an old family friend. Bet she'll help out."

"But can she take care of babies?"

"Absolutely. She raised seven of her own and babysits for mothers in the neighborhood. Everyone loves her. She's the perfect image of a Russian *babushka*." She gulped audibly. "Not like my Aunt Raisa. She's something else again."

"What's that mean?"

Larissa had an outsider's view of the USSR. She was only half Russian, and she'd never lived there. Professor Klimenko married her Canadian mother when he fled to the Great White North for a safe harbor.

"A military commander's spirit lives in my aunt, but she's on my side. So, no sweat."

The description of Larissa's aunt piqued my interest, but I returned my focus to the issue at hand—the potential babysitter. "If the neighbors adore her, then let's try Mrs. Mirnaya."

"Check. I'll see her tomorrow morning. Tell me what to ask her."

We discussed babysitting arrangements until I remembered my goal—getting more details about Shona's murder. "Enough baby stuff for now," I said. "You must tell me about Shona. I want to mull over everything, let the details seep into my skull before I get to Vancouver. Come on, Larochka, tell me all."

I'd picked up the Russian diminutive of Larissa's name from her dad. I could only imagine how distraught he must be over her current predicament since his experiences with authorities—the

Soviet kind—had not been pleasant.

"Sure," she said, "but you'll have to wait while I run get more change to pump into this payphone. Call you right back."

Hanging around, waiting, fried my nerves. And David was expecting me, maybe even sleeping by now. Curses.

I sat, a jittery mess, drumming my fingers on the coffee table. Five minutes later she still hadn't phoned back. Visions of horrible things happening to her rose in my head. My imagination ran around like wild horses without direction.

At the ten-minute mark, David reappeared in the doorway.

"What are you doing? You're not even on the phone. Clearly I'm not a priority to you." He whirled away and stomped down the hall. Our bedroom door slammed.

The phone rang. I clutched my forehead. Debated. Picked up the receiver.

"Go see your travel agent tomorrow." Larissa's voice was jubilant. "Papa's going to arrange for your airplane ticket. And Mrs. Mirnaya agreed to babysit."

"Way to go. No wonder it took so long. I got nervous waiting."

"Sorry, Austin." Her voice fell. "Listen, I've got change to talk for just a few minutes, to give you a sketch of Shona's...of her...death."

The line went quiet. Here was my chance. I could hang up now, get back to David.

Oh, heck. Two more minutes wouldn't hurt him. I plunged in.

"You said at first Shona's death was considered an accident. Can I assume this happened in the chemistry lab at UBC?"

"It's complicated."

Why was she being cagey?

"You're making me think Shona mixed chemicals for a dangerous lab experiment. If so, then can you simplify? I don't remember much from high school science classes."

"No, it was nothing like that." Larissa's tone was grim.

"Shona was in the student union when she died. At six in the evening. She ate leftovers from her bag lunch while she waited for me to join her at seven. We were going to a meeting of a women's liberation group together."

"So how does this make *you* a suspect? I don't get it."

"She drank poisoned tea from a thermos, and I'd made the tea. *That* makes me a suspect. The prime suspect, I'm sure." She laughed hoarsely. "This is difficult for me to talk about, especially on the phone. Really, I'd much rather forget about all of it."

"But you can't."

"I know that, silly. I'm trying to give you an inkling of how I feel. Let's wait until you're out here. I'll pour out all the details when I can see your face, Austin."

"Okay, I understand."

But I didn't understand, only pretended to.

"By the time I get to Vancouver, the RCMP will have solved the case, arrested the killer, and you won't have to worry about a single thing." The expression *whistling in the wind* popped up when I uttered those words. Larissa wouldn't believe them anyway, but they felt good as they came from my mouth.

We said our goodbyes and rang off. I stared down at my feet while my mind whirled like a psychedelic kaleidoscope. The few specifics Larissa offered about the murder left me with more questions than I'd had before. However, about one issue there was no question whatsoever: Larissa was incapable of killing anyone. The mere idea was laughable.

The circumstances looked bad, true. Even if the police determined that only Larissa had the means to poison Shona, surely no one had unearthed a convincing motive for Larissa to kill her pal.

And there couldn't be one, could there?

I pulled hard on the reins of my mind. I shouldn't gallop off in that direction, getting all involved and pondering the specifics of the murder. I'd promised David I wouldn't do that, if only he agreed to me going to *support* Larissa.

But, oh man, did I feel torn.

I turned out the lights and tiptoed down the hall past Wyatt's bedroom. He often howled like a banshee for an hour unless I stayed with him. Every so often he slept soundly. Tonight he was a lamb, thank goodness.

That left me only one upset guy to deal with. I opened the bedroom door and went inside to face David.

Chapter Five

DAVID SAT CROSS-LEGGED on our bed. He appeared engrossed in a mathematics journal—his idea of light bedtime reading. He did not look up.

I cleared my throat. "Hello, handsome."

He kept reading. When his hands raked through his hair, a few strands spiked up. Last year, jailers had shorn his hippie-length hair, and even after his release, he'd kept it short. I preferred this neater look, but wished there'd been a less fraught way to achieve it. Prison time left my husband with a sorrowful expression that threatened to become a permanent feature.

"Hey, you." I climbed into bed beside him and moved the journal away. He said nothing, only stared straight ahead. I moved his arm around my shoulders and nestled against his chest. His body remained rigid, unyielding.

"Sorry, honey. Didn't expect that to take so long and—"

"Even one minute was too long to wait." He tipped his head up and scowled at the ceiling. However, his arms did relax around me. "So what's happening now?"

"Looks like Wyatt and I can fly Wednesday morning. Professor Klimenko bought my ticket. Nice of him, don't you think, since we can't afford it?"

David sniffed and smoothed out the sheets with elaborate care.

"Now all I need to do is go to the travel agency and pick it up."

He sat up and loosened his grip on me. "You're leaving so soon?"

"Better go and get it over with, not have a trip hanging over our heads."

"Look, I'm sorry, babe. I wish I could be more supportive." He finally looked into my eyes.

He didn't sound sorry at all.

"You think I'm not worried about Larissa, but I am. It's just that I worry about your safety and what you're getting yourself into. Besides, the damned deadline on my dissertation is pressing down on me and—"

"Hush." I placed my hand over his mouth. "Naturally you're stressed. Your dissertation is a big deal. I feel guilty, but we owe Larissa and her father so much." I picked up his arm and put it back around my shoulders, where it belonged.

"When will you come back?"

Ouch. My return would be a sticky point. Well, honesty was my best approach. "Haven't thought about it. Who knows how dire Larissa's position is?" I looked up at him and smiled innocently, then leveled a beseeching gaze at him. "Don't you see, honey? I can't answer your question until I get there and judge for myself what's what. I don't know. I really don't."

His arm tensed against my shoulders. I didn't look at his face, but I knew he was frowning.

"Maybe a week," I said. "How's that?"

He released me and got out of bed, picked up his braided leather bracelet he'd placed on the nightstand, toying with it for a moment.

"All right, I suppose." He put the bracelet down and turned to level a penetrating look at me. His lips were pursed.

"For heaven's sake, don't pout," I said. "It's not becoming."

He laughed. "It's sure as hell becoming when you do it."

I stuck out my tongue.

"I'll miss you like crazy. Kind of used to having you and little

Wy around, with both of you whimpering and crying about one thing or another."

I reached behind me for a pillow and bashed his head with it. "Such a kidder. I'll miss you too, but we'll be back so soon, you'll hardly have time to miss us."

A smile transformed his face. "We'd better make time—"

"—while the sun shines," I concluded, and we grinned at each other like fools.

We thought we were as clever as television comedians with our little vaudeville-esque routines. Since he'd left jail, I used humor to lighten his moods. Sometimes it worked.

"I'll turn out the lights. Wait right here and don't go away." He got out of bed, crossed the room to turn on the radio and ditched the lights.

The radio tuned into Bob Dylan singing "Lay Lady Lay."

David got back into bed and kissed me for several luscious minutes. "I want to change Dylan's words and plead 'stay, lady, stay,' but if you feel you have to go to Vancouver and support Larissa, then okay. But I don't like it."

"Hmm." Hot breath on my ear made me nudge closer. "Do that again, will you?"

And soon we were wrapped up in each other, and the rest of the world fell away.

#

On Wednesday morning I stood in our tiny living room, surveying the few belongings we'd acquired in Toronto. The furniture was used and scruffy, but Indian cotton throws added color. Snapshots of Wyatt sat on bookcases made of bricks and boards. Books and papers spilled out of them, and more books were stacked around the room. This felt like home. It was our home. This was the first time I'd be leaving it.

My bags were packed, and soon Wy and I would be flying west. The lyrics from Peter, Paul and Mary's record circled in my head—except, unlike in their tale, I knew I'd be back again soon.

Long distance plane travel had never fazed me. In fact, I loved it. If I started Wy out early, maybe the four-hour flight from Toronto to Vancouver would set him up to be a great little traveler. Then we'd share many more trips with him—on happier occasions. I crossed my fingers.

The early sun filtered through the venetian blinds and lit all the places that I'd not dusted in months. I was fortunate David wasn't like my friends' husbands. They didn't tolerate slovenliness in their wives. My mother's voice barged into my head, shoved the folksingers aside, and announced, "I trained you better than this, Austin."

Damn it all, for almost two years I'd lived thousands of miles away from her, and still, *still*, Mother provided the soundtrack in my brain. She never praised, only admonished. I wished I could turn her off like I could our hi-fi. A shake of my head helped me refocus on the coming trip, but I knew she'd pop up again soon.

David had taken the luggage downstairs to our Volkswagen van, and now his footsteps came clomping down the hall toward our apartment. I plucked Wy from his playpen and slogged over to open the door for David.

"All set?" he said.

"Right." I held Wyatt against my shoulder and moved into David's arms to be held in them one last time before leaving.

"I'm so lucky you're my husband. Have I ever told you how much I love you?"

A tear ran down my cheek. He wiped it away.

"Not in the last ten minutes." He kissed Wy on the forehead and me on the lips. Wy took the opportunity to burp.

Spit-up stained my fresh blouse. Damn.

"Can you hold him please? I'll clean this off, and then we'd better go." I handed Wy to David and marched into the kitchen for a wet cloth.

Fifteen minutes later we were driving along the Gardiner Expressway toward Toronto's Pearson Airport. Wyatt gurgled happily on my lap, strapped into his plastic carrier. I held him tightly. The seat belt wasn't long enough to stretch across two of us, let alone the carrier. He played with my hand for a few moments before the car's motion lulled him to sleep.

I reached out and patted David's arm, feeling like the luckiest girl in, well, at least Toronto. Remorse and guilt nibbled at the edges of my heart because I was about to leave this dear man. At the same time, my heart rejoiced at the coming adventure. The sound of Peter, Paul and Mary singing "Leaving on a Jet Plane" swam in my head. Only an act of willpower kept me from humming along.

I hoped the tune I'd sing on my return would be upbeat. Something like "Dance to the Music" by Sly and the Family Stone would do nicely.

With my free hand I switched on the radio. John Lennon's wail of "Don't Let Me Down" stabbed into my stomach and twisted the knife. I shot a sideways glance at David.

At the same time he shifted his eyes from the road to look at me. "You won't, will you?"

"No, I won't let you down, honey." I punched the radio buttons, looking for a happier song for my send-off. That Beatles song was a guilt trip. The knife twisted another turn in my gut. Swell, a perfect metaphor for my flight out to help Larissa—guilt trip.

Chapter Six

A PINCH OF good luck met us at the airport. David found a parking spot close to the terminal's entrance, making it easy for him to escort us into the building. The staff at the ticketing counter of Canadian Pacific Air fussed over Wyatt while they checked us in. He responded with smiles and delighted gurgles, the star of our adventure.

David helped me lug our gear to the departure gate. We found two seats in the waiting area and settled in for the forty-minute lull before boarding. Strangers smiled at us, and some people—all of them women—came up to say how darling our baby was and how lucky we were to have such a "good" one.

Maybe our progress was too smooth. I fretted that our good luck was used up on boarding rigmarole—none left to carry us through tough spots ahead during the flight or when we landed in Vancouver.

David reached out to Wyatt. "Let me hold him. He'll keep you busy on the plane. Go buy something to read, use the ladies room, or just walk around by yourself."

"You're a darling." I beamed at him. "I accept your kind offer." I kissed his cheek, handed Wy over, grabbed my purse, and headed off to find a restroom.

I'd better say *washroom*, the correct Canadian-ese. Small differences between American and Canadian usage still hit me every day. I cast an analytical eye on the concessions that lined the hallway and saw no stores that weren't Canadian. Good lord, how mistaken those countless Americans had been. "No culture shock in Canada," they'd all promised. That was wrong, just plain wrong. If I'd known then how many adjustments I'd have to make to live in Canada, perhaps I would've rethought my move with David. I might have tried to convince him to ride it out in Texas.

But it was too late now. Way too late.

I pushed aside this too-frequent regret and tramped onward. When I noticed a long bank of payphones, I stopped, recognizing my chance.

I dug a dime out of my purse and stuck it in the phone slot. Maybe my old pal, Detective Sergeant McKinnon, would share a tip on how to help Larissa.

My luck still held; my mentor answered right away. Relieved he wasn't out catching bad guys, in a few terse sentences I explained the reason for my unexpected trip. DS McKinnon had met the Klimenkos when they'd sheltered me during David's time in jail. I knew McKinnon would be worried about Larissa.

He was silent for a moment after I explained the situation.

"In the first place, Austin," he said slowly, "I'm glad to hear from you. Second, in British Columbia, the Royal Canadian Mounted Police have authority to investigate murders."

"Okay, that's good to know. Even though you're not RCMP, do you have any advice for me? Is there anything special I should know about them?"

"Yes!" The word exploded through the lines and burst into my ear. "Stay out of their way, lass, and let the Mounties solve their case. You almost got yourself killed last time. I'm surprised that David's letting you fly out there."

Letting me? What was I, chattel?

I clenched my teeth. "I promised David I wouldn't interfere in this murder case. Besides, he knows how much we owe the Klimenkos."

McKinnon's hearty laugh hurt my ear.

"He believed your promise? Well, I don't. Like I said, be

careful. But if you hit a rough spot, call me. I'll be a sounding board, if you need one, and you're sure to need one. I know how headstrong you can be."

In the ensuing silence, I was sure his thoughts drifted back to our last exploits. I broke the silence to thank him and to promise yet again not to interfere.

Then I added, "By the way, sir, have you got contacts in the Vancouver branch of the RCMP?"

This time he howled. "See what I mean? You're foolish if you think you're going just for moral support. You may kid yourself and David, but you don't fool me. And I won't share any RCMP names, particularly because you're married to a draft-age American. You could really hurt David if you engage with the Mounties. Stay clear. Better if you run something by *me* should the need arise."

Glancing at my watch, I saw I'd been gone five minutes already. I rang off in a hurry and rushed into a nearby washroom, made use of it quickly, and ran back to the gate in time to hear the boarding announcement for my flight.

David stood when he saw me, his strong arms cradling Wyatt. Both of my guys smiled when they saw me dashing toward them.

"You cut that close," David said. "I got worried. Did you buy something to read?"

I took Wy from him and wiped drool off his soft, downy cheek. "I ran out of time."

"Oh?" David raised an eyebrow.

"I called McKinnon."

"Really?" Both his eyebrows were raised now.

"I told him about Larissa's problem. He said I shouldn't get involved. I told him about my promise to you. He wished her well. That was it."

"Interesting."

I tried not to read too much into that seemingly innocent comment. "I confess I did ask one leading question."

"And that was what?"

"Found out the RCMP investigates all murders in British Columbia."

He shook his head. "Going to have a hard time staying out of this, aren't you?"

I pulled a face. "You're right. But I promised. I will be good, and I will definitely not talk to the Mounties." He didn't need to know why that promise was easy to make and crucial to keep.

Evidently he believed me. He grinned. "In that case, look at this. Someone left behind an old copy of the *New York Times*."

Hot diggity. I loved the *Times*, even if it wasn't the current issue. I snatched it up and hugged David hard. "Thanks."

After we hugged and kissed some more, David helped us onto the plane. The pretty gate attendant was too busy flirting with a tall businessman in an elegant suit to worry about whether she should let David on the plane with us or not. "Sure, go ahead," she said, waving her hand airily when David asked if he could help us board.

He got us seated and stowed our gear. We were all set.

A pang pierced my heart when he said, "This is the first time we've been apart in almost two years."

Except for your ten days you in jail, I added to myself. "Wish you could come with us."

"Me too," David said. "Me too."

"Happy studying. Hope it all goes well."

"Be good, Austin. Take care." With a soft kiss for me and a noisy one for Wyatt, David was gone.

His departure felt more like a rupture, like someone had chopped off my leg. I looked around the cabin in a daze.

Wyatt and I had three seats to ourselves. I cuddled him to soothe him and skimmed the front page of the *Times*. Once we were airborne and he was fast asleep or happily sucking on his pacifier, I would devour the news from the States.

The plane took off on time, and Wyatt fell asleep on the seat beside me. I kept a hand on his tummy and dived into the newspaper. Even though it was a few days old, I was soon caught up in everything I'd been missing.

Armstrong, Aldrin, and Collins were back from their moon trip and cleared by NASA to rejoin their families. North Vietnam troops were attacking U.S. Marine bases along the DMZ. Police in Los Angeles were hunting suspects in the murder of actress Sharon Tate, the pregnant wife of film director Roman Polanski, and four of her friends.

After reading the whole front section of the *Times*, I folded the paper and put it away. The news was grim, and I'd had enough. For the rest of the trip, Wyatt and I dozed off and on. Aside from bumpiness over the Rockies and an elderly lady who wanted to chat, the ride was uneventful.

#

Rain pelted our plane as we landed in Vancouver. Wyatt and another infant two rows up screamed the whole way down. I felt sorry for the babies, who couldn't soothe their earaches. I rocked Wy and crooned, eventually distracting him. He was such an angel.

I was anxious to see Larissa and assess her situation, but watching two hundred people inching up the aisle, I knew my escape would take hours or at least seem to. By the time I struggled to the exit ten minutes later, loaded down with Wyatt and all our gear, the weather had grown even worse.

I covered Wy with my jacket and crept down the slippery ramp stairs to the tarmac. Rain cascaded onto my bare head while I dodged and weaved past puddles on the runway. Why had I packed my umbrella in my suitcase? Vancouver was famous for frequent deluges.

I dashed into the terminal, my hair and clothes soggy-awful. I wanted to shake myself like a dog. Wyatt wasn't as wet, thank goodness. Not if I didn't count his leaky diaper.

Larissa had promised to meet the plane, but she was nowhere

to be seen. We'd arrived on time, and Larissa was always prompt. Where was she? I couldn't run to the ladies room to change Wyatt until I connected with her.

I gnawed a ragged cuticle. What if she failed to show up? Another quick glance around came up empty. My tote bag grew heavy, and Wy's fidgets escalated by the minute. I adjusted my loads and paced the hall, searching every face.

A young woman carrying a baby pulled a toddler with her other hand. The presumed husband followed, gawking at shapely stewardesses nearby.

Why couldn't he help with the kids? I carried the weight of Wy's care, but at least David helped out occasionally. I wished he were with us, and I longed to call him, but we agreed to phone only when rates were cheapest. I had hours to wait.

During a second circuit of the terminal, I noticed another woman—pretty and petite, like Larissa. But Larissa didn't smoke. The stranger threw an empty pack of Players on the floor, then ground out a butt with her Earth shoe. Larissa would never behave like that.

The arm carrying Wy grew numb. He puckered up to scream, and I ducked into a washroom to change him. I wished I'd been able to bring his stroller along on the plane, but it was way too cumbersome. I wondered why no one had invented a baby stroller that was small and collapsible. Whoever did would make lots of money.

Back out in the hall, I cast a covetous eye on a vacant wheelchair. How easy it would be to plop Wy in it and push him around. I squelched my wild idea and stalked the terminal again. After five more minutes I finally spotted Larissa—half hidden by a potted plant, staring out a window.

"Yoo-hoo. Over here." At my excited shriek, passersby turned to stare. For once I simply didn't care.

Larissa rose slowly to her feet and lumbered toward me as if she were dragging a hundred-pound sack. She didn't hop up and down the moment we laid eyes on each other as I'd expected.

Her undying enthusiasm was one of many characteristics I loved, but today her aura was at best, restrained, and at worst, listless. When we were several yards apart, Larissa suddenly rushed forward and clasped me in a fierce hug. She didn't notice that I held Wyatt.

How strange.

Her body felt like a skeleton against mine. I disengaged gently and appraised her. Limp hair plastered her skull like seaweed. Her tie-dyed blouse was buttoned wrong, and her skirt had a torn hem.

My heart ached to see my vibrant friend looking like such a mess. The real Larissa must be inside somewhere. Mentally I dusted off my hands. I had a job to do—to help her escape this distressed shell, cheer her up, and maybe—just maybe—discover the proof that showed she was no killer.

Stop. You're here for support, not to play detective.

I summoned the willpower necessary to keep from speaking my mind, telling her how bad she looked. Instead I said, "Larissa, here's Wyatt. He's been missing your cuddles." My little guy gurgled at her as if on cue.

Larissa's eyes grew wide. "Oh goodness, look how he's grown, and so darling." She stroked his cheek, but her smile didn't show up. "I thank heaven you came, but I'm ashamed I called you away. I bet David's upset you left."

Her hands flew to cover her mouth while her eyes pleaded with me. "But I've got to tell you that I...I'm not in good shape." She began to cry.

At first I didn't know what to do. Never before had I been the one to provide comfort—it was always the other way around.

I dropped my tote bag and hugged her with my free arm. Larissa cried into my hair for a long moment before she pushed away.

I grabbed her hand. "You're anxious—anyone would be. But remember that your father and I won't let anything bad happen to you." I looked around. "Where is he? I expected him to be here."

Larissa sank onto a bench as if she'd run a marathon. She dried her eyes and sighed.

"Papa had trouble finding a parking place. He'll meet us at the luggage carousel."

"Fine, so let's get going. Buck up, my little buckaroo. Daddy always says that when I'm down in the dumps."

She managed a meager smile. "You used to say that sometimes, back in the good old days before anyone thought I was a killer."

I never dreamed she'd be this devastated by the murder investigation. In all the time we'd known each other, she'd been a resolute and strong dynamo, her toughness belying her delicate beauty.

Wyatt and I sat beside her on the bench. I turned him toward Larissa, hoping his cuteness would cheer her up. She scarcely looked at him.

"Okay," I said, "I'm not surprised you're upset, but something has changed since we talked. What's happened?"

Her hands twisted in her lap, then she fingered her shirt buttons. She reworked the buttons and said, "Oh damn, I'm such a mess. I can't do anything right these days."

Afraid she would cry again, I jumped in. "Don't beat yourself up. You suffered a blow, but you'll be fine. Now, I repeat: What else is bringing you down?"

Larissa lifted her head and glared. "The RCMP interviewed me for the third time this morning. They told me I could not leave Vancouver. They seem more convinced than ever that I poisoned Shona."

"What? What's changed?"

She cleared her throat. "A witness came forward to implicate me. I don't know who it is—the Mounties won't tell me. All I know is that someone is lying about me."

Chapter Seven

LARISSA HUNG HER head and mumbled. She talked so low, I had to ask her to speak up.

"If you really want to know," she said, glaring at me, "I'm scared out of my wits. *Not* just scared of going to jail—I'm also afraid of getting killed. Whoever poisoned Shona could kill me too. I'm in her women's lib group, we hang out all the time. I could be next." A sob caught in her throat. "And besides, I miss Shona. You don't know how much she did for me."

"Look," I said, "someone's trying to frame you. Maybe the killer himself. Or herself."

She nodded. "I thought of that. Or someone is simply mistaken."

"I don't know anyone in the RCMP out here, and DS McKinnon specifically warned me to stay clear of them. I'll call him and ask if he'll nose around for us if something particular comes up that we need to know about. How's that?"

Her eyes widened at McKinnon's name, and she smiled. "Do you think he'd do that?"

"I called him before I left Toronto. He wasn't keen on me barging into another murder case, so I promised him I wouldn't. I promised David too. But this is different. When I get a chance, I'll call McKinnon again. All he has to do is find out something about the witness, and we can take it from there."

"Thanks, Austin." She squeezed my hand, then she lowered

her head again. "Still, it's so awful. I wish you'd had a chance to meet Shona."

"She must've been wonderful," I said slowly, "if you liked her so much, but I don't know enough about the murder yet to have an educated guess about all the other stuff. You've got to tell me more—lots more. I don't have gobs of time either. David has a stopwatch running on this trip. So once we get to your aunt's house, we can really talk." I stood, a little clumsy from carrying Wyatt so long. "Let's go. March." I assumed the role of a drill sergeant.

Larissa sniffed. "All right. Sorry to be a wet blanket. I'm not good company, and I'm so embarrassed. I've wanted to see your little boy again, and then I didn't even see him when he was right under my nose."

Her distraction underscored how upset she was.

"No apologies," I said. "Remember how you always buck me up. Listen here, girl, I owe you big time."

"Yes, but I—"

"No quibbles." Struggling to hold Wy steady, I pointed at my tote bag. "Can you handle that? It'd be a big help."

"Of course."

"Now let's get going." I stepped off as briskly as I could, given how exhausted I was from the long flight and baby-tending.

We hiked through the terminal, rode the elevator down to the next floor, and found the luggage carousel. Professor Klimenko was waiting for us.

With courtly Old World politeness, he took my right hand in his good left one. I'd learned to ignore his injury, which he always covered with a black leather glove in the style of Dr. Strangelove. Yet I still obsessed about learning the cause of the injury. So far I hadn't devised a polite way to ask. He'd defended his Russian homeland against the invading Nazis during World War II and eventually got crosswise of the Soviet authorities, but I didn't know how he'd escaped to safety in the West.

But that was a riddle for another day. Today I needed to

focus my energy on propping up his daughter and if possible, finding one single, tiny clue that would free her from suspicion.

Surely that wouldn't cause me any problems. Not just one clue.

Professor Klimenko's greeting broke into my thoughts. "I'm pleased you and your son were able to come to Vancouver. Larochka needs all the support we can give her." He awkwardly patted her shoulder with his damaged hand.

I smiled at his tenderness—and to hide my tension. "I'm glad I could come, but the days will rush by, and I don't know how long I can stay."

"We understand, my dear. We're grateful for whatever time you have. We're staying with my sister-in-law. Raisa lives in the Kitsilano area, not far from the university. It is, however, a long, slow drive from the airport in rush hour traffic."

Larissa held out her arms. "I'll hold Wyatt while you find your luggage. Leave your bag too."

"Thanks. I'll be right back."

Easier said than done. After twenty minutes, all the other passengers from my flight had grabbed their suitcases and left. I had checked two bags in Toronto. Only one had arrived in Vancouver.

I approached a CP Air worker who lounged against the wall, smoking. "My suitcase hasn't arrived. What should I do?"

"File a report, eh, like everyone else."

My travel woes obviously didn't interest this man.

"Where should I do that?"

"Over there." He flapped a listless hand and seemed to feel he'd done his duty. He wandered off without giving my problem another thought.

I ran back to the Klimenkos, explained my situation, and returned to the so-called help area. Half an hour later, I finally finished the necessary paperwork. I grabbed the suitcase that held all Wyatt's baby things and lugged it to the Klimenkos. I could make do without fresh clothes, but if I didn't have diapers or cans of infant formula, that would have been a mess. Thoughts of wearing dirty clothes and borrowing toiletry items didn't amuse me, and I mourned my lost umbrella. Yet once settled into the Klimenkos' car, I relaxed.

Professor Klimenko drove, Larissa beside him in the passenger seat. I sat behind her and cradled Wyatt. I leaned my head against the window. The time in Vancouver might be six p.m., but my internal clock told me it was three hours later.

Larissa twisted around to talk to me. "Are you too tired to do anything tonight?"

"No, of course not." *Okay, I lied.* "I was able to snooze on the plane."

She faced the front again, and I shut my eyes. After a moment, they flew open. Despite being exhausted, my mind would not shut down.

We crept along in traffic. Mountains to the north, the ocean on the west, and all around were unusual trees, flowers, and houses. I'd expected British Columbia to be like Ontario. Instead it was a veritable California, Canadian style.

"What's that strange tree?" I leaned forward and tapped Larissa on the shoulder. "Over there." I pointed to a tall dark evergreen with limbs shaped like candelabras.

"A monkey puzzle tree," she said.

"*Araucaria araucana,*" her father added.

"Forget the Latin." I laughed. "Monkey puzzle will do fine. Everything's so green and flowery. I'm drowning in foliage. Back home in Texas the landscape is stark, so this lushness is peculiar."

Larissa laughed. Actually laughed. "Most people love it here. You think this is lush? Wait until you see the rose gardens at UBC." She was still chuckling. "I'm going to campus later, and you'll come too. I can't miss any of my women's lib meetings."

Professor Klimenko's head twitched toward his daughter. "You think that's wise?"

"Why shouldn't I go?" Larissa's tone was sharp.

"Your lawyer said to keep a low profile as the investigation proceeds." His tone grew harsh too. "It's one thing to continue your summer job but quite another to go on with extracurricular activities. Actually, I wish you'd quit that job, but since the police told you to remain here, you need something to do. But everything else you should drop."

"No, Papa. Austin and I will go tonight, and that's final."

Their loud conversation woke Wyatt, who'd been sleeping on my lap.

Larissa was an emotional person, given to wide mood swings, yet I'd never seen the Klimenkos fling so much as one cross word at each other. That had been a veritable shouting match by their standards. They quit speaking to each other, and even their back of their necks seemed to stiffen.

My nerves flared. I had to break the tension. "Look at those funny houses. They've got sparkles stuck in the walls."

"Pebble dash, the British call it," Professor Klimenko said. "A cheap yet functional way to build houses in this climate. Brick is expensive, and wood exteriors can't hold up to all the rain." He relaxed as he performed his role of teacher.

"Pebble dash sure looks cheap." I giggled. "Ugly too."

Larissa gave a little cough. "My dear Austin, how I've missed your bluntness."

"That's what I'm here for, entertainment."

"We appreciate your coming here." Professor Klimenko's tone was anything but merry. His seriousness chilled the mood again.

Shoot, I'd almost succeeded in cheering them up. I squelched the urge to punch his shoulder. Silence, thick and heavy with tension, filled the car. Once we finally swung into a driveway, I felt I was coming up for air. I inhaled a deep breath—the air was redolent with the scent of flowers—and hauled myself out of the back seat. With Wyatt against my shoulder, I faced Larissa.

"All right, let's get down to work. Lots of questions about Shona's murder are bubbling in my head. And only you are the answer lady."

Larissa opened her mouth and managed to say "right" before the limitless rain of Vancouver chose that moment to let loose again. She ducked her head, grabbed my tote and Wy's suitcase, and dashed into her aunt's home. I rushed after her, eager to hear what information she would cough up. I had waited too long to hear it.

Chapter Eight

THE HOUSE SURPRISED me.

First, its two stories were clad in that awful pebble dash stuff. Why had I shot my mouth off about it earlier?

Second, the interior was claustrophobic. Although relieved to escape from Vancouver's interminable rain, I gasped for breath. The air was overly warm, and the rooms were snug. Russian artifacts—*matrioshka* nesting dolls and painted wooden boxes and bowls—crowded every surface. Prints of famous Russian paintings filled the walls of the front hall and living room. Everything was neat and orderly.

There was just too much of it.

I was so overwhelmed by the visual assault that I didn't register the earsplitting opera music coming from a hi-fi. But Wyatt did. He burst out crying so loudly that he covered up the waltz from Tchaikovsky's *Eugene Onegin*. While I hurried to quiet him, a swinging door opened, releasing the aroma of seasoned meat from the kitchen.

The sensory overload whipped me back to the time, several summers earlier, when I'd studied Russian in Moscow. This home struck me as a cozier, larger, and more bourgeois version of the Soviet apartments of academics I'd visited.

A stocky, buxom woman bustled into the room. She wiped her hands on her apron before planting them on her hips.

"*Khorosho.* Good. Ready to put *pelmeni* to boil." She turned to me. "Larochka says you love our Russian dumplings, so I made for your visit. I her aunt, Raisa Lozovsky. Call me Raisa." Without waiting for my reply, she pivoted and left the room.

The smell of meat, onions, and garlic made my mouth long for these Siberian treasures—so much better than their Polish equivalent, pirogi. Just my opinion, mind you.

I tilted my head and looked at Professor Klimenko.

He said, "Please have a seat. You are tired from your journey." He gestured at a sofa, covered with stacks of books and papers. Larissa rushed to clean a spot so Wyatt and I could sit.

I plopped down, dropped my bag, and propped Wyatt against my waist. Larissa, her father, and I each began to speak, but we were interrupted by a ringing phone. Raisa ran into the room to answer it. She held a short conversation and hung up.

She pointed at her niece. "Message for you, Larissa. Your meeting moved to tomorrow. Otherwise, same time and place." She disappeared again.

Larissa's head fell to her chest, and she exhaled loudly. "How disappointing. Austin, I'm so eager for you to meet my women's group."

Since I'd just renewed my vow not to speak my mind too freely, I didn't admit I was relieved.

"Tomorrow will be fine," I said.

Why did she insist I attend her meeting? Didn't she have more important matters on her mind right now?

"Besides, tomorrow will be better," Professor Klimenko said. "Austin will be rested by then."

He was right. Transcontinental travel with my son had depleted my energy. I felt overcome with everything facing me— new places, new people, tending to Larissa, and caring for Wyatt. Thinking about what lay ahead exhausted me even more.

Raisa called us to dinner.

We gathered around a large dining room table. While the others ate the delicious-smelling food, I held Wyatt and fed him his formula. Finally, I got to tackle my own bowl of pelmeni, swimming in their steaming pool of beef broth.

"Raisa, these are the best pelmeni ever."

Maybe the trip wouldn't be so taxing. Good food always cheered me up.

"You're very kind to let my son and me stay here," I said. "I hope we won't be—"

"No trouble. They vouch for you." She waved her hand at the Klimenkos. "They need you here."

After the meal everyone busied themselves getting Wyatt and me settled. I put him down to sleep in a carrying cot that Raisa had provided and expected a few moments for myself.

Raisa had other ideas.

She said, "Larissa, why don't you take Austin to nice pub? Young people need time on own. I watch eye on baby."

Good grief, I couldn't leave Wyatt with this woman. Raisa was the first female not to fuss over him. She scarcely seemed to notice him.

Larissa looked at me and raised an eyebrow. "Okay if we hop down to the pub? Or are you too tired to go out?"

Excuses gurgled in my mind. "I don't want to bother you, Raisa, but many thanks for your kind offer."

"Not bother. I ran children's center in Vladivostok. Little fellow no trouble."

Interesno, as the Russians said. My curiosity was piqued, and I vowed to learn more about Raisa. Sometimes I was too nosy for my own good, a trait my Texas grandmother pointed out in less than complimentary terms. But I didn't care, and curiosity wouldn't kill me. Plus, David sweetly preferred to call me inquisitive.

I wondered when I could call him. I already missed him.

"Please, please, let's go," Larissa said, "unless you really need your sleep." She gestured with her head and rolled her eyes toward the door. Her message was clear.

Of course, I was too tired even to wiggle my toes, let alone go to a pub. Did these people think I was Wonder Woman?

Wonder Woman or not, I did know how to be a good guest.

"Sure. Let's do it." I turned to Raisa and gave her a pleading smile. "First let me show you where Wyatt's things are and how he likes—"

"Of course, *devochka maya.*"

She smiled back, and I felt warmed by her use of the affectionate Russian for *my girl.* For the first time, I felt warmth from and for this brusque, efficient woman.

Fifteen minutes later Larissa and I were ensconced in a booth in a smoke-filled bar that looked like an advertisement for Guinness. We were damp, having rushed down slippery, rain-washed sidewalks three blocks to the pub. The dim lighting was useful; I wasn't anxious to display my clothes. They were not just damp—like Larissa's—but also rumpled and dirty. And I had nothing else to wear.

"What'll it be, ladies?" A tall, dark-haired waiter loomed over us.

"A Molson for me please," I said.

"For me too," Larissa said.

For such a bruiser of a fellow, the waiter had a surprisingly gentle look on his face. The guy stood still and stared at Larissa. I'd witnessed that kind of fascinated male behavior often around my friend. Men couldn't help themselves because of her beauty. From the look on his face, however, he wasn't so much entranced as...well...*sad.*

"What's the matter?" I asked.

The guy's face reddened, but he continued to stare. He was good looking, maybe thirty or so, and more respectful than the men who usually ogled Larissa. He finally spoke to her.

"I hear you're in some trouble with the Mounties."

Her pretty chin quivered. "What have you heard? Who told you that?"

"You know how it is, gossip going around the bar. I feel bad for you."

He did look concerned. I'd give him that.

"Uh, I'm sorry," he said. "Didn't mean to bother you. I'll go get your beer."

"What's your name?" Larissa said.

"Gary."

He edged away from our booth, but Larissa put out a hand and touched his arm. "Wait, please. Can't you give me more detail than that?"

"I don't want to upset you." He hung his head, looked at his feet, then loped off.

Larissa and I stared at each other for several moments before either of us spoke. Then we talked on top of each other.

"How do you think——" I began.

"I don't like this at all," she said.

"But you know how people create rumors." I spoke fast to cut her off, to halt another downward spiral. "We're near the university. Lots of students must live in this area, so close to campus, and you said Shona's murder had been in all the papers." I leaned forward. "Of course this is awful for you, but really, it's to be expected. Pretty soon the Mounties will clear your name, and all this will be a horrid dream."

Larissa tossed her head and grimaced.

Gary returned with our beers. Again he dallied at our table, but this time he gave details about the gossip he'd heard.

"Two officers from the RCMP were in here yesterday, asking about you. Wanted to know your habits and what kind of person you are. They wouldn't say why they were asking, but after they left—they didn't stay more than ten minutes—guys here got to talking, and someone suggested maybe their questions had to do with the murder at UBC." He twisted the towel that hung from his belt.

"Thank you, Gary." Larissa's voice was composed, reassuring—sounding like the old friend I'd known so well back in Toronto. "I appreciate that you told me. Did they say anything else?"

He shook his head. "That's all I know. Sorry. I have other

customers, but I'll tell you if they come back in here. Good luck, eh." He left.

Larissa watched him walk away. "What a nice man. His eyes are extraordinary."

"You're right."

I spoke without stopping to think what her words implied. I was busy trying to think who Gary reminded me of. I snapped my fingers. "That's it, *Mannix*. With his dark hair and kind face, Gary looks like Mike Connors."

"Who?"

"An actor who plays a private eye on a television show. I forgot you never watch TV."

"Hmm, maybe." She still gazed in the direction of our waiter had gone. Her eyelids were half shut, and a small smile played around her mouth.

Then her comment about Gary hit me, one as unexpected as a compliment from my mother. For the first time in our friendship, Larissa had made a favorable comment about a guy.

She took a deep breath, bit her lip, and seemed to come out of her trance. "All right, all right, I've got to stop running away from the jam I'm in." She placed her palms flat on the table and stared straight into my eyes. "What do you want to know? I'm ready to talk."

Waves of relief washed over me.

She'd come to her senses at last. Here I'd been dreading having to get her comfortable with talking, and good old Gary had somehow provided the key to unlock her reserve.

Chapter Nine

I TOOK A sip of Molson. "Let's start at the beginning, Larissa. How did you meet Shona?"

She put her elbows on the table, clasped her hands, and rested her chin on them. Her gaze across the scarred table was marred by a tear trickling down her cheek.

"First I need you to understand something, Austin."

"What's that?"

"I *want* you to know everything. It's just that—" She stopped to sniff and brush away the tear. "Whenever I try to talk about Shona, I get upset. So by not talking about her, I protect myself from painful emotions. I'm afraid I'll go down too far and never come back up again."

I squeezed her hand. "I *get* it. But I'll be able to be more helpful if I know more. And besides, your whole life could become quite painful if you remain a viable suspect in Shona's murder."

Larissa shuddered. "Right, I know that. I just don't want to fall apart."

"I don't care if you cry or fall apart. Maybe you need to acknowledge and really *feel* the depth of your emotions after the loss of your new friend. That could help you move on. Tell me what you're able to talk about. Just plunge in."

She sat up straight and put her hands in her lap. "Okay then, here goes." She took a great gulp of air. "When I began working in the chemistry department at UBC, none of the grad students paid any attention to me. As a worker bee, I had no status. But after my first few days there, Shona would stop by my desk at least once a day and ask me about myself. She was really friendly when no one else was."

Larissa paused and shut her eyes. "Shona had so much personality. Whenever she entered a room, the air around her went *zing*. When she talked to me, she focused her energy on me and made me feel special. That was super important in my circumstance, friendless in a strange new city—never mind that I'd *chosen* to move here for the summer. Once she befriended me, then others joined in. After a few weeks, I felt like one of the gang in the department, when they'd all been so stand-offish before." She opened her eyes and focused on me. "Needless to say, I was grateful to Shona."

Larissa stopped to drink from her glass. I watched her closely, wondering how she was bearing up, forced to talk about her dead friend when she hadn't wanted to. She appeared to be emotionally unscathed, so I pressed on.

"Where was Shona from?" I asked.

"Didn't I tell you? She's American, from Seattle. Her folks still live there."

This information surprised me. I wasn't sure how important it was, but it changed my mental image of Shona.

"Did she come here with a boyfriend or husband who was evading the draft?"

I thought of my own situation. Most young Americans in Canada were protesting the war in Vietnam.

Larissa shook her head. "Shona got a teaching assistantship in the chemistry department to help pay for grad school, a deal she couldn't get back home. Of course, she was in no danger of being drafted, but she was against the war anyway. So was the boyfriend she left behind in Seattle."

"Have you met him?"

"No, and as far as I know, Jack never came up to visit her in

Vancouver. He'd wanted to marry her and keep her in Seattle. Even bought a diamond engagement ring, but Shona wouldn't be tied down. She said she loved Jack but insisted on keeping her relationship with him loose and easy. He, however, wanted commitment. He was distraught when she refused to get engaged, and then he broke off with her. As far as I know, she never saw him after she started grad school."

"That's interesting." I squinted hard at the ceiling, hoping to find inspiration there, when a new possibility occurred to me. "Wonder if he was hurt and devastated enough to kill her?"

Larissa chuckled, a happy sound that made me smile. "Come on, Austin. Isn't that a reach?"

"We need to find someone Shona knew who had a motive to kill her. *You* had none." I scowled and sucked in a breath. "What you had were means and opportunity."

"Thanks for the reminder."

Although her grin was rueful, little by little she seemed to be regaining her old self. My job was to push her farther down that track.

"What does this Jack do for a living? Is he a grad student too?" I wasn't done with the guy yet. He might fit into the group of suspects I was determined to find.

"Jack works in a lumber mill east of Seattle. He met Shona at the University of Washington, but dropped out before graduating. Big guy, lots of muscles, and gorgeous hair that could make him an honorary Kennedy." She laughed again. "That's how he looks in photos, anyway."

"Excuse me." Gary appeared at our table, looking down from his great height, tapping his watch. "Last call. Would you ladies like more beer?"

Larissa glanced at me. "Don't know about you, but I could use another."

"Okay," I said, "but only if we're fast. Time for me to go back and check on Wyatt, then call David."

Gary said, "You can't stay long anyway. Closing time in half an hour."

"So bring us two more, please, and make it snappy." Larissa's half smile undercut the command in her words. That tiny lift of her lips was enough to light up her face and potent enough to send Gary away singing under his breath.

Larissa could invoke ecstasy in males when she deployed only a smidgeon of her usual wattage. Had Shona possessed this power too?

Again Larissa's gaze followed our waiter as he darted away on long legs. In a low tone she murmured, "He doesn't look like a Gary. Seems more like a Garrett."

What a fine time for her to get a crush on someone. She rarely dated, despite many offers. Now, even in the pub's dim light, I noticed a flush spread from her neck up to her cheeks, making them glow.

Squelching a desire to push her in Gary's direction, I returned to my questions. "Tell me more about Shona. Did you two see each other just in the lab or—"

"Remember I said Shona introduced me to the women's group at UBC?" Larissa's former glow disappeared, and her words were edged with irritation.

"Right, I forgot that." Why on earth did she keep talking about women's lib? She'd never shown any interest in the movement before. Her interest was an anomaly, zooming in out of nowhere.

"Shona told me about the meetings and urged me to go." Larissa's face crumpled when she said Shona's name, but she didn't cry. She picked up a paper napkin and wiped water from the worn table top, then took a few deep breaths and pressed on.

"Shona worked in the civil rights and anti-war movements in Seattle and learned how things went. She said guys always ran the show and only allowed women to do grunt work. Women's consciousness-raising became her thing at the University of Washington, so when she moved up here, she formed a group at UBC too.

59

"When I arrived in May, the Vancouver group already numbered thirty, up from only ten. Now our meetings can hit a hundred or more. It's pretty cool."

Shona's activities and their implications jolted me, showing new possibilities. I spoke slowly, carefully. "So, you not only worked in the same lab with Shona, but you also attended group meetings with her too?"

"Right on."

"So maybe her women's activities had something to do with her murder?"

"Don't be silly," Larissa spat out. "All the women adored Shona. Her nickname was Shiny Shona."

Here was a tidbit worth chewing over. Anyone so magnificent was sure to provoke jealousy. And rampant jealousy could lead to murderous rage.

Chapter Ten

WE DASHED BACK to Raisa's house down streets made slippery by rain, racing to beat the next downpour. I needed to check on Wyatt. I'd been away two hours, the longest I'd ever left him with anyone other than his daddy. Once I was satisfied that Wy was coping well with his new surroundings, then I'd call David and tell him about my long day. I'd need to talk fast because, even late at night, long distance rates were sky high.

When we entered the house, all was peaceful and quiet.

No crying baby, no loud Russian music.

A moment later, Raisa descended the stairs. She wore a robe over a long nightgown and despite being dressed for bed, she immediately offered us tea.

"You must be chilled," she said and hurried into the kitchen.

"Any problems with Wyatt?" I called after her. I had to ask. Raisa was efficient and no doubt dependable, but was she attuned to an infant's needs?

"Of course not. *Konechno, nyet.* Why would *I* have problems?" She sounded incensed.

"No offense," I stammered, "but it's just that I never——" I realized I would be heading deeper into trouble if I continued. "Excuse me. I'll run up to see him and then come back for tea."

Without waiting for Raisa's response, I rushed up the stairs, but once there, I felt silly. Wy slept peacefully in his makeshift bed. I made sure his diaper wasn't leaking, tucked his blanket around him, kissed the top of his head, and returned to the first floor.

I made a quick mental recalculation of the ordering of my duties. The call to David must come after we drank our tea. Mother's voice echoed in one ear that I had to be a polite guest, while in my other ear David's whispered, "Don't forget about *me*."

Professor Klimenko joined us in the kitchen. We were chatting pleasantly over our tea, with me trying to warm up to Raisa, when the phone rang. Raisa excused herself to take the call, then returned to say the call was for me. "It's Canadian Pacific."

The airline was calling to report that my luggage was still lost. They were *so sorry*, but that was just the way it was. I'd get another update in a few days, assuming there was news.

Curses. I assessed my tired, rumpled skirt, spied a spot of baby spit-up. I couldn't borrow clothes from tiny Larissa, and even though I might fit into Raisa's Soviet-esque blocky ones, I didn't want to wear them or suggest doing so. I hung up the phone in dejection and stomped back to the kitchen to deliver the bad news.

"I can't go anywhere with you tomorrow. Not dressed like this."

"You'll be fine," Larissa said. "We'll clean your clothes tonight and do a quick ironing. That'll fix you up fast. I'll put in some hours at the chemistry department midday, and you can come with me if we can set up Mrs. Mirnaya for babysitting. How does that sound?"

"Maybe I should buy a few new things to wear before I meet your friends. I'm embarrassed at the impression I would make otherwise."

"Pish posh. Don't be silly." Larissa waved her hand airily.

"Easy for you to say." I feared I sounded testy but, well, I was. Even under ordinary circumstances, it was no fun being seen with and compared to gorgeous Larissa.

"Raisa, may I use your phone again please?" I asked. "My

husband expects a call, and I need to let him know that Wyatt and I arrived safely. I'll be sure to reverse the charges."

Raisa pursed her lips. "Konechno. Call straight. You do us favor coming here."

Professor Klimenko nodded.

"Khorosho. *Spasibo*." I said, shy because my accent was dreadful. My pronunciation of such easy words as *good* and *thank you* still needed work. "I won't stay on the phone long."

I went into the living room where at least the telephone's location afforded some privacy. Nervous caterpillars crawled around my stomach. David might grump at me now that I was *really* gone.

He answered on the second ring.

"Austin? Thank heavens it's you. I got worried. Was everything all right on the plane? How's Wyatt? How're you?"

"All's well, sweetheart." Joy flooded met at the sound of his voice. "The trip was uneventful, and Wy acted like a seasoned traveler. I miss you, though. How're *you* doing?"

David snickered—a sound I was relieved to hear. "Getting loads of work done smoothing out my dissertation, preparing my defense. I hate to admit it, but having the apartment to myself makes it easier to relax and get work done." He sighed loudly. "Still wish you were here, though."

We talked a few more minutes and then agreed to hang up for the sake of our household budget. I was in the midst of telling him how much I loved and missed him when he interrupted.

"Wait," he said, hurriedly. "Are you behaving yourself?"

"Of course. Why? What do you mean?"

"Don't be coy with me, Austin. You know what I mean— I'm referring to your habit of galloping into dangerous territory. You promised you'd leave the murder investigation alone."

"I remember, and I'm being good."

He snickered again. This time the sound wasn't so reassuring, not with that edge to it. "You haven't been there a full day yet. Even you couldn't get into trouble that fast."

"Want to make a bet?" I couldn't help myself, treading into a delicate zone. Perhaps he wouldn't find my kidding humorous.

"No, I do not want to bet." His tone grew demanding. "Leave the investigation to the Mounties. It's their job, not yours. Besides, you've got my son there with you. I want both of you back home with me soon, safe as can be. Understood?"

"Understood."

This conversation wasn't ending up as well as it had started.

"When shall I call again? How about two nights from now?"

"Fine," he said, "and then you can tell me about your return flight."

"That's a deal." I doubted I'd keep that promise. Curiosity was eating me up. Who knew what clues might innocently plop into my lap? If they did, I wouldn't be able to ignore them.

As David and I said our goodbyes, I smacked my head, remembering my idea to call DS McKinnon and ask him about the witness who had popped up to implicate Larissa. Maybe he could use his contacts to find out the details.

After hanging up, I checked my watch. Dang it all. Too late to call the detective. I'd have to figure out a way to call in the middle of the day tomorrow.

Chapter Eleven

THE LIGHT OF day showed clearly how awful my travel clothes looked. Even though they'd dried out overnight, they looked as if they'd endured ground fighting in Vietnam. Everything imaginable marked them *except* blood and guts.

Raisa had offered to wash and iron my skirt and blouse over night, but Larissa and I had returned so late that I hadn't been able to ask that of her. Now I regretted being so noble. At least Wyatt looked adorable in a clean little blue onesie with a bunny on the front.

After breakfast, Larissa and I took Wyatt to meet the famous Mrs. Mirnaya, beloved of all mothers on the block. To my delight, she was exactly as her publicity had said—like a dumpling of a Russian *babushka*, all bright smiles and apple-red cheeks. She fussed over and petted Wyatt enough to make up for Raisa's lack of appreciation of my darling son.

We spent half an hour with Mrs. Mirnaya, long enough that I felt relaxed leaving Wyatt with her. Her home was well stocked with toys for all ages of children. There were two playpens and a Jolly Jumper. Wyatt was the only child there that day, and I was sure Mrs. Mirnaya would dote on him. We agreed to pick him up in the late afternoon. Larissa and I were free to drive out to UBC and do our *rat killing*, as my Texas grandmother called it.

The sun beamed down on us as we traipsed back to Raisa's house to borrow her car. The two houses—Mirnaya and

Lozovsky—were on the same block on West Eighth. As Larissa backed out of the driveway, she explained the route we would take.

"The area called the University Endowment Lands begins only two miles from here," she said. "I'll drive over to Tenth. It leads right into University Boulevard."

She grinned at me. "What luck my aunt lives close to UBC. She likes the house because it's not far from the Russian Community Center, just east of here." She pointed behind us. "If I take you to the center, you'll be *forced* to use your Russian."

Five minutes later we reached University Boulevard. "Just look at this." Larissa smiled in delight. "The Endowment Lands begins right here."

"What is this? Where UBC begins?"

"No, the province made this land trust sixty-plus years ago to raise money to set up a university here. It's splendid having parkland on the edge of a big city. Toronto's got nothing like it."

Broad grounds stretched out on each side of the boulevard, like a manicured golf course bounded by trees. All the branches seemed to reach out, threatening to choke me. Why did overwhelming lushness upset me when everyone else seemed so delighted with it?

Tearing my eyes away from the vast greenness, I decided to bring Larissa back to our primary task. "Okay," I said, "so this is Vancouver's answer to Central Park, or maybe Houston's Memorial Park—one I'm used to." I held my breath, considering my next words. "So, yes, it's pretty, but tell me who I'll see in the chemistry department. Who there might have a motive to kill Shona?"

Larissa let out a small yelp. "Good grief. I told you that everyone loved Shona. *Everyone.* She didn't have an enemy in the world." She looked sidewise before turning back to the road.

"Perhaps so." I drew out the words. "But clearly she had one real enemy, the most vicious kind."

"Ouch. Take it easy, pal. I'm still feeling fragile."

"I'm sorry. I'm on edge—leaving Wyatt with people I don't know, wearing dirty clothes, and worst of all, feeling a timer running on my visit. David made that clear last night."

Larissa nodded. "I meant to ask you about that. How's he doing with you and Wy gone?"

I never knew how much to share with her about my marriage. I needed someone who'd listen to me rant and rave occasionally when David annoyed me—I figured that was normal. However I also figured Larissa wasn't the best one to tell. I wanted them to like each other, and so far they showed a polite acceptance.

Better hedge my response now.

"David reminded me of my promise not to hunt for a killer."

Larissa's howl filled the car. "Heaven help you. You're revving up your motor to interfere. Good thing he can't hear the questions you keep throwing at me."

I pursed my lips and said, "Providing moral support in your time of need is my main reason to be h—"

"Ah, come on, Austin. I *know* you."

"Sure, I admit I'd like to, well, uncover *one* big clue pointing to the bad guy. I'm burning with curiosity. "

"Don't get me wrong," Larissa said. "I want you to interfere. I just don't think you'll find any bad guys in the chemistry department." She turned into a parking lot. "And here we are." She found a parking spot and shut off the motor.

I reached out to grab her sleeve.

"What is it?" she asked.

"Here's my mission as I see it: the RCMP is on the case tracking down physical clues and checking alibis. That's hard for me to do since I don't know anyone or the lay of the land. But I can *judge* people. I can often tell when someone is pretending to feelings they don't have, people who aren't being straight with me. If I meet as many friends of Shona's as I can, my personal lie-o-meter might go *twang* and suggest a viable suspect."

"That's true. You seem so harmless, not like a cop. But still people talk to you."

She looked surprised, but I figured it was my Texas friendliness that got people talking.

I chewed on my lip. "*Motive*, that's what I'm looking for. Antipathy to Shona, despite how *shiny* and adored you say she was."

Larissa's eyes filled with tears. "I couldn't ask for a more devoted friend than you."

Before we collapsed into a maudlin heap, I punched her on the arm. "All right then, let's go dig up some suspects."

However, the weather didn't cooperate. Rain clouds burst open, and a deluge hit the car. I scowled.

"Let's sit tight. Maybe the rain will stop in a sec."

"Okay," she said, "and I'll tell you more about my job. You seem to think I work in the lab itself, but I don't. By saying 'lab,' we mean the whole area used by our group—all the offices, laboratories, and meeting rooms. For example, I'm part of the lab group, but mostly all I do is type."

"That clears up something I wondered about—how you could work in a science lab when you have no experience."

"My summer job came through a friend of Papa's, Dr. Adler. Five years ago he was a post-doc at Harvard under Dr. James Watson. Adler liked how Watson ran his labs. Have you heard of him?"

"Uh, I think so." I searched my memory. "Watson and Crick. Nobel Prize winners, I think."

"Smart girl. A few years ago Watson shared the Nobel Prize with Crick and Wilkins for discovering DNA."

"And your Dr. Adler worked with Watson?" I whistled. "That's impressive."

"I know nothing about the science, but here's what brought me here," she said. "Every afternoon Watson's whole group at Harvard takes a break and enjoys refreshments together. Adler saw how this boosted communication among the different parts of the lab and decided to run his own lab the same way."

"So where do you fit in?"

"I buy, prepare, and serve food and drink for Adler's lab breaks. That's all I do besides type for his grad students."

She bent her head until it rested on the steering wheel. "And that's why I'm a murder suspect. I'm the only one with access to the Earl Grey tea, which I myself buy from Murchie's."

I slammed the dashboard with my hand. "You're kidding me! Then lots of people could've poisoned Shona's tea. Focusing on you is preposterous."

Larissa looked up through wet lashes. "No, it would've been difficult for anyone else. You'll see when we're in the lab."

I shook my head. "You say this tea is so fancy that you lock it up, treat it like something precious, like diamonds, or dangerous like uranium? That's crazy."

"I simply did what I was told and—"

"Wait, wait. Sorry to interrupt, but don't other people drink tea? Why wasn't someone else poisoned too?" Questions swam in my head. I had to keep asking them as long as Larissa was willing to answer.

Her lips rose into a smile, fell, then rose again. "Shona was a speedy, hopped-up kind of woman. She'd sprint into the meeting room early and get to the goodies first. We all knew her habit and kidded her about it, but she didn't care. She'd just laugh and grab another cookie. Her metabolism was so high that even with all the sweets she ate, she was thin. Energy came off her in waves, and she lit up a room. Like I said, everybody loved her. Shiny Shona."

I tried not to roll my eyes, unsure I would've liked this Shona. Of course I couldn't say that to Larissa. Instead, I squelched my reaction by asking another question.

"Okay, so Shona always got to the break room first, yet I still don't understand why someone else didn't drink poisoned tea."

"My routine explains it. Each person has a labeled mug, and there's a firm rule not to use anyone's but your own. People squawk and kick up a fuss if their mugs are borrowed. The Mounties' theory is that I put poison only in Shona's mug before anyone else came in the room."

"Still seems like a stretch to me. So how did the poisoned tea get into the thermos?"

She shrugged. "They figure she poured her cup of tea into the thermos."

"Kind of convoluted if you ask me." I ran down the long list of questions I still needed to ask, choosing the most important one. "So maybe you had the means and opportunity to kill Shona—although I can't agree you're the only one—but what about *motive*? What's the RCMP say about that?"

"No idea. But clearly they think I could have a motive. Maybe you can ask them."

"I'm afraid to try. McKinnon says I can't talk to the Mounties safely. Anti-war activists tell David that our names are on some RCMP record somewhere. Everyone says they keep track of draft resisters in Canada and share details with the FBI, even though they're not supposed to. That's why I'll ask McKinnon to nose around for us."

"But you're here legally, with landed immigrant status."

"Believe me. I'd be trying to talk to the Mounties about this murder case if my situation were different. I have to keep a low profile because of the draft, the war, David and, well, you know." I shifted in the seat and rubbed my neck. "David hasn't received a draft notice yet—hasn't broken an American law either—but it's still horrible living under this cloud. You know how most people feel about draft dodgers." I spied a ragged cuticle and chewed on it.

"I'm sorry I upset you. I didn't mean to."

Guilt stabbed me in the throat. "Don't worry about it."

Larissa looked in the rear-view mirror and smoothed her hair. "I like working with Dr. Adler's group, and it's a shame everything has changed. I'm allowed to keep going to work because—"

"Of course you are." The words exploded from my mouth. "You haven't been charged with a single blessed thing."

"But now everyone in the lab is suspicious of everyone else. The RCMP made us scared of each other. I feel everyone watches me. Everyone knows I had charge of the tea."

Her fingers gripped the steering wheel so hard, I thought it would crack.

"Besides, I miss Shona."

I patted her shoulder. "Everyone always watches you, Larissa, silly girl. It's because you're gorgeous. Now, listen here. We'll get to the bottom of this. You'll see." I couldn't help but offer assurances that I frankly didn't feel. I wondered what else the Mounties thought they had on Larissa.

She rubbed her eyes and sniffled. "I've racked my brain trying to solve the tea mystery. Now I wonder if someone tried to frame me, but who would do that and why? Aside from Shona, I hardly know these people."

She gestured out the window. "We're in luck on one thing anyway. The rain's stopped. Now you can see how beautiful everything is. Oh, I was so bored with Toronto."

I peered through the rain-streaked windshield and noticed the luxuriant foliage, newly cleansed and brightened with rain. Even the hydrangea seemed to have grown thicker, giving them more energy to suffocate me.

The austere landscape of south Texas didn't hold so much greenery and variety. It had never threatened me. And the rain here in Vancouver, would it never stop? It was almost as bad as the snows of Toronto.

Larissa pointed to the passenger side window. "Look. See across the waters of English Bay to the mountains in West Van and North Van? This place is so gorgeous, like heaven must be."

At least the ridge of mountains to the north weren't so close they boxed me in.

"I was enjoying all this so much." Her tone switched, became doleful. "Then someone killed Shona."

Larissa twisted toward me and put her hand on her heart. "I swear that I'm not a murderer."

"I know that." I gasped. "Why else would I be here? And how come you feel the need to reassure me? I'm totally convinced of your innocence. These people have done a number on your head, don't you realize that?"

"Sorry." Larissa's short burst of a laugh held a hysterical edge. "All my instincts are off. I've never had anything this awful happen to me before. The proverbial charmed life," she said, ending on a wistful whisper.

"How can you say that? You lost your mother and then your aunt died. And if that's not enough, your father can't visit his homeland and may have KGB operatives looking for him."

She held up her hand. "Stop."

"All that does not add up to a charmed life."

Whenever I mulled over Larissa's background, I was struck by her strength of character. Now, for the first time, I realized her strength wasn't limitless.

"You're strong, Larissa. Other people would buckle under all that loss."

"Papa and I are a good team. He never lets me feel vulnerable, but I feel vulnerable now. Any minute I'll be arrested and hauled off to jail. Look what happened to your husband. Even a few days in jail would send me over the edge."

"Just stop it. That won't happen. Not if your father and I can help it. You're way ahead of the game. We haven't begun to rip into this case. Remember, it took us a week—*a whole week*—to figure out who committed the murder the Toronto police were so sure David had committed."

"Hmm, good point. Hey, I bet I know what you're going to say next."

"What's that?" I asked.

"Buck up, my little buckaroo."

"Right on, little buckaroo." I opened my car door. "Now let's go find us a killer."

Chapter Twelve

MY DIAGNOSIS OF Vancouver? The city suffered from a split personality. One moment the atmosphere reeked of fresh foliage and the sun shone off wet pavement that sparkled as though diamonds had been strewn along the sidewalks. You believed you were in one of the most beautiful places on earth. Even I recognized that, despite how much it bothered me. Then ten minutes later heavy clouds again blanketed the sky, and rain cascaded down your neck and flooded your shoes.

All that shiny green disappeared, walloped and drowned by every shade of gray imaginable.

When Larissa and I left the car, the sun peeked through the waning clouds.

Smiling up at the sunshine, she began a running commentary on the sites we walked past. After two blocks, she pointed ahead to a Gothic revival structure, heavy with gray granite. "That's the chemistry building, the oldest building on campus and—"

She never finished. The alternate personality of Vancouver whomped us. The heavens unleashed torrents, and we sprinted. In my hurry I dropped my purse, and had to stop and recover it from a puddle. Larissa rushed ahead and waited for me in the building's doorway.

I felt like a drowned rat. My only clothes were soaked again.

By the time I covered the last yards and gained the shelter of the entryway, I wanted to chew nails. "I can't meet your friends looking like this," I told Larissa.

I held back a sneeze and shivered. When I searched for a tissue, I found only sodden lumps in my purse. My favorite bag, made of macramé, had been marinated in dirty puddle water. I wished I'd left it back in Toronto.

Larissa watched my clothes drip and leave puddles on the floor, put a hand to her mouth, and tried to suppress giggles.

"Easy for you to laugh," I said. "You're not wearing soggy rags."

"Aren't they abysmal," she suggested. "Or maybe bedraggled? Running down the alphabet, how about catastrophic?"

I ignored her attempt at wit and wrung out the hem of my skirt. I opened my mouth to complain about her perverted sense of humor, but a loud commotion caught my attention.

A male student clattered down the long stairway nearby.

"Hey, Keith," Larissa called, "what's going on?"

He stopped on the bottom step when he saw Larissa. He straightened, gasping for breath. Looking over the railing, he said, "An experiment went haywire. There's a chemical fire."

"Is the fire under control?" Larissa's eyes widened, and she clutched my arm. Her grip was tight.

Keith stared at his shoes—the better to avoid Larissa's beauty? "I have trouble breathing when there's even a whiff of smoke. Asthma." He patted his throat. "I had to leave, but I think everybody else stayed."

"So we can go up?" Larissa asked.

"Um, I imagine so. The fire alarm hasn't been pulled. Like I said, I was choking and had to get out of there."

"What happened?" Larissa said.

"That's an odd thing." Keith coughed a couple of times. "Frank was mixing chemicals for an experiment with metallic sodium. He wasn't careful and got water in the beaker with the sodium. The mixture exploded, shattered the glass, and caused smoke to billow. You know how cautious and slow Frank always is in the lab, right?"

"Yeah, maybe." Larissa wrinkled her nose and shrugged. "I haven't talked much to Frank," she said. "If you say he doesn't usually make a mistake, then I believe you." She relaxed her grip on my arm. "Sorry, I forgot my manners. Keith, this is my friend Austin Starr, come to—er, to visit me."

He nodded in my direction and coughed.

Larissa said, "So it's safe to go upstairs? I need to get to work."

"Guess so." Keith cocked his head. "No, go on up. I'll go back with you." He coughed again, then recovering, he grinned at Larissa.

Larissa looked away. Her standard response to guys more interested in her than she was in them was to ignore them.

I still dripped onto the tile. "Uh, Larissa, excuse me, but can I just—"

She swung around to me. "Gosh, I'm sorry. I forgot how uncomfortable you must be. Let's dry you off a little. See you later, Keith." She started down the hall.

I followed her into the ladies room. When we were inside with the door shut, I said, "He's sweet on you, isn't he?"

"Maybe, I don't know—or care."

"But he forgot about his asthma and fear and wanted to return to the lab with you. Seems conclusive to me. He's smitten." I blotted my hair with a paper towel, then wrung out my sopping skirt. My blouse was plastered to my skin.

"All I know is Keith's the nervous type—though I'm not one to judge, given how I am these days." Larissa stared into the long horizontal mirror that stretched over a row of sinks, frowned, then drew a comb from her purse. Her thick brown hair had a tendency to curl when it was damp. On her, however, anything looked good, including wet, crinkly hair. Come to think of it, the top of a rag mop plunked on Larissa's head couldn't dim her beauty.

I also gazed in the mirror, groaning when I saw myself. "The first impression I make on your friends won't be a good one."

"Quit worrying. You're not here for a photo shoot. You're here to check out the lab, keeping me company while I file and type. Just relax and keep an eye on the inmates, see if anyone acts funny." She put her comb back in her purse. "Time I get to work. As long as I put in my five hours each weekday, I'm okay, but I don't like to trail in too late. Come on, let's get out of here."

I followed behind her, and my shoes squished at each step. I was physically uncomfortable, mortified at my appearance—and unhappy that my best friend was acting like a loon.

Well, perhaps I overstated the loon part. She was, however, indulging in wild mood swings and failing to focus on the predicament she was in. In short, behaving irresponsibly. That wasn't like her. Of course, I wasn't the happiest person on Earth right now either, so who was I to throw stones? But I hoped that all I needed in order to feel better was dry, clean clothes. Maybe when we returned to Raisa's house my luggage would have been delivered. I could only hope.

Larissa and I trudged up the long, steep staircase to the second floor. An acrid smell hung in the hallway, and when Larissa pushed open a door, a slight smoke haze hung in the air.

The room we entered held a pair of heavy wooden desks, with a chair beside each. In one of them sat a young man. A middle-aged woman was wrapping gauze around his hand. She looked up briefly.

"Hello, Mrs. Carson," Larissa said. "Is everything back to normal? We ran into Keith, and he told us about the accident."

The man whose hand was being bandaged flicked his eyes up at Larissa and then back down again quickly. This must be Frank, the student who caused the accident. He pressed his mouth into a firm, grim line. He had a beard, neatly trimmed and short. He didn't appear to be part of the counter-culture; he was too ship-shape.

Larissa looked at him. "How're you doing? I hope you'll be okay." When he didn't answer, she said, "Sounds like you're lucky you're not hurt worse."

Frank glared at his hand and issued a small grunt. He rose from the chair, leaned down to whisper in Mrs. Carson's ear, and left the room.

Larissa shrugged. "Guess he was embarrassed." She tossed her hair back from her face and sat at a desk.

"He'll be fine," Mrs. Carson said. "Frank's a diligent researcher, mortified at his mistake. Besides, I've dressed much worse wounds in my time, mostly from cut glass." She turned to look at Larissa. "You may look damp, but you," she addressed me, "have you been swimming, my dear? Most unladylike, I must say." She shook her head.

I cringed, but tried hard to hide my humiliation, mumbling about dropping my purse in a puddle and taking a while to retrieve it. I couldn't meet the woman's eyes. She was an immaculate specimen of femininity. Her hair curved in a pageboy style, as smooth as Wyatt's cheeks, and her clothes were ironed precisely. Nothing about her appearance was out of kilter. Only the ruffles on her skirt and the low scoop of her blouse kept her from looking like a prim schoolmarm straight out of a cowboy movie.

"This is my friend from Toronto, Austin Starr," Larissa said. "She and her baby have—"

"You have a baby? How marvelous." Mrs. Carson's face lit up like a flashlight switched on. "I love infants. How old is your sweetheart? A boy? Or a dainty, sweet little girl?"

I fingered the bodice of my drenched blouse, tried to pull it away from my chilled skin. "A boy. Wyatt is three months old."

"I'm waiting to have grandchildren, but my daughter just got married. I say it's her duty to give me a grandchild, but so far she doesn't listen." Mrs. Carson scowled. "My daughter says she wants to do her own thing. Doesn't want to live the life I've led. I tell her it's totally fulfilling to look after one's family, and if she keeps going the way she's headed, soon she'll be burning her bra."

I'd gotten pregnant so quickly and unexpectedly after my wedding that Mother hadn't had a chance to pressure me to reproduce. Perhaps I was lucky.

Mrs. Carson's voice yanked my mind back to the present. "Larissa, there's a stack of papers that needs organizing and filing. Work on those today. All of a sudden I have extra paperwork." She breathed deeply and passed a hand over her face. "The fire blanket had to be used after Frank's accident. You wouldn't believe the bureaucratic tangle that causes."

"Oh dear, I had no idea," Larissa said. "I'll get right to the filing. Austin won't be in the way. She can sit over there."

I considered the armchair she pointed to, upholstered in cloth, and then gestured at my wet clothes. "I can't. I don't want to mess up the furniture."

Mrs. Carson looked down her long nose at me for a moment, then snapped her fingers. "I know just the thing." She bustled over to a cupboard and pulled out a thick blanket, a regular one, more like my father's old army blanket from World War II days than what I imagined a fire blanket to look like.

She placed it on the chair's seat. "Even you can't harm this old thing. Sit on it until you dry off."

I started to protest, but she cut me off.

"Sit." She pointed to the chair and blanket.

Raised to be obedient and dutiful to my elders, I sat. The back of my blouse was so wet that I feared I might catch pneumonia. Wyatt's pediatrician said that germs had to be involved in catching a cold. The good doctor said an experiment had shown that putting children to bed wearing chilly, wet socks had proved not to cause a cold, but I doubted that was factual. If I didn't come down with the sniffles by the next day, I'd be surprised.

Larissa settled down to sort through mounds of paper, and Mrs. Carson began typing away at an IBM Selectric. The shock of seeing the Selectric sent me reeling back to a typewriter's role in the murder I'd been tangled up in the year before. Propelled by nerves, I jumped up and squished over to Larissa's desk. A book with a pink cover lay there, and I picked it up.

Larissa pointed at the book. "I brought that for you to read while I work."

Against the pale pink background was a cartoon drawing of a woman's head and shoulders. The woman looked scared or surprised. Big letters announced *The Edible Woman* by Margaret Atwood.

"I don't know this author."

"She's Canadian," Larissa said. "Margaret Atwood published poetry before, but this is her first novel. It's like nothing you've ever read. Everyone in my group raves about it. You *must* read it, Austin."

I decided to humor her, and if I tried the book and didn't like it—well then, no harm done. In her present situation, she deserved to be indulged.

Larissa caressed the book with her fingertips, then honored me with her most extravagant smile, offered with her head held high. "This book will raise your consciousness."

Squelching my annoyance—I disliked being preached at—I spoke as calmly as I could. "What does *that* mean?"

"Just read the book. I'll explain later."

Mrs. Carson looked up and sniffed. "Tripe, all that nonsense, but my daughter's always talking about it too. Ridiculous." She returned to the electric typewriter and pounded away again.

I knew that IBM Selectrics preferred a lighter touch, but I wasn't about to mention that to this opinionated, superior female.

I returned to my chair, nestled into its blanket covering, and settled down to read.

The story of Marian McAlpin, a young Toronto woman facing a crisis, hooked my interest. Although the details were different, Marian's worries felt all too familiar. How should she live her life? Should she obey society's demands? Did she have to obey all of them, or could she get by following only some?

I became lost in another world. For a short time, all thoughts of Shona's murder and chemistry accidents flew from my mind. As I delved further into the story, however, tension in my shoulders increased each time I turned the page. Suddenly, midway through the book, when a main character ranted about lice-ridden drug addicts and *draft dodgers up from the States*, my mood turned back to panic.

For heaven's sake, David wasn't a real draft dodger, not yet anyway. He simply was in Canada to protest the war and the draft—he called himself a draft resister. He'd never even received a draft notice. But who was I kidding? The only reason we were in Canada was David's determination not to fight in Vietnam.

Then the reason why I was so upset hit me. Whenever I realized that I wasn't doing what *everyone was supposed to do*, self-doubt smothered me. No wonder I identified with Atwood's lead character. Marian's parents had pushed her to marry Peter, but his personality was so strong that she feared he would consumer her. He would gobble her up, making her an *edible woman*.

I heard again the distant drumbeat of my childhood—Mother's constant repetition that only when a woman married and had children would she find fulfillment. I was musing on this, staring out the window at the falling rain when, out of the corner of my eye, I saw the door from the lab open.

Keith walked in. Maybe Larissa was right about him being the nervous type. He did seem edgy, jiggling a pencil from hand to hand. Every inch of his thin frame—reminding me of Ichabod Crane—seemed to quiver. Why was he so nervous? Was this the sign of a killer? I needed to talk to him again.

He beetled over to Larissa's desk and waited, tapping his foot until she looked up. "May I use the pencil sharpener?"

I laughed quietly. What a lame excuse to talk to a pretty woman. If he were brainy enough to be a graduate student in chemistry, surely he could come up with a better ploy. He was blushing like a grade school kid handing a Valentine to a popular girl, one too popular for him and far out of his reach.

"Sure. There it is." Larissa pointed at the pencil sharpener, screwed into the wood at a corner of her big desk. "Have at it." She returned to organizing files and didn't look up again until

Keith had shuffled out of the room, head bowed.

Wait, wait, wait. Neither he nor Mrs. Carson treated Larissa strangely, as if she were a murder suspect. They exhibited no fear around her. I'd point that out to Larissa as soon as I could. That should perk her up.

Mrs. Carson rose from her desk. "Hold the fort for a while, Larissa? I must go to the dean's office about this darned fire blanket." She opened a closet and pulled out a gray blanket. A smoky smell permeated the room. "Phew," she said. "What an awful stench. I'll drop it off and be back in half an hour."

Once the coast was clear, so to speak, I left my chair and sidled over to Larissa.

"Is there a way I can call long distance and send the charges to my home phone?"

"Sure." She pulled a pamphlet out of a drawer. "Use these instructions. It's not hard."

Several minutes later I had DS McKinnon on the line. When he heard I wanted information on Shona's murder investigation, he groaned. "Goddamn it, Austin. I knew your trip was a mistake."

"That's a first. You've never sworn at me before." I giggled.

"Not funny, young lady. And I apologize."

"Just get me some information and I'll forgive you."

"I will not."

"If you don't, I'll have to do all the digging myself, and then if I get hurt, it'll be your fault."

Behind me, Larissa laughed. "You're too much," she whispered.

"All right," I said into the receiver, "maybe I overplayed my hand."

"You have no hand to play," McKinnon growled. "You are too much, young lady."

"That's what Larissa just said."

"Is she there? How's she doing?"

I lowered my voice. "Not well. All shook up. Yesterday the

Mounties told her not to leave the city."

McKinnon whistled softly. "Okay, you win. I'll see what I can find out. Give me your phone number."

I gave him Raisa's number, thanked him profusely, and hung up.

After I settled into my chair, Larissa danced a little jig. "Thank you, thank you. I feel better now. The detective sergeant is our good luck charm."

"He certainly helped David in his time of trouble. In the meantime, before we hear from McKinnon, I want to nose around here. Tell me, do you think Keith could have a motive, you know, for, uh, Shona?" I tried to be delicate, but frankly, it wasn't my strong suit.

She shook her head. "I doubt it."

"But he's so nervous, like he's afraid he'll get caught at something."

"He's always like that. If you want to talk to him, ask him a few questions, go right ahead."

"At the least, maybe I can dig up facts or tips about someone else from him." I flapped my skirt in a useless effort to dry off and hoped my shoes would be dry when the time came for the meeting that night.

Good grief, I still had another command appearance today. But not if I could help it.

"Say, Larissa…" I began.

"Yes?"

"I'm afraid I'll be a no-show for your meeting. Just look at me. I've nothing to wear that doesn't look as if it came out of a missionary barrel." I cast a sorrowful look down the length of my torso and beyond, straight to my ruined shoes. "These rags are hopeless, and I'm terribly embarrassed."

Larissa's chin jutted out two inches. "I'll call Aunt Raisa and see if the airline delivered your suitcase. If not, we'll stop and buy you some new clothes. Then we'll go to my aunt's for dinner, and you can change before we come back out here again for the meeting."

My head sank to my chest. Her rational response defeated me. I wanted instant release from feeling cold and miserable, and there was no relief in sight for hours and hours.

"That will have to do, I guess." I stepped in the direction of the door, wanting to flee, and then remembered the dangerous tea. "Can you show me where you fix goodies for the afternoon snack? Is now a good time, with Mrs. Carson away?"

"I can't now. I forgot to type some important reports and want to finish them before I have to confess to Mrs. Carson. I'll show you in a little while."

"Okay," I said, "I'll go find Keith."

"Wait a minute." She grabbed my arm. "The Atwood book's great, isn't it?" Larissa sounded so eager, it was pathetic. "What did I tell you?"

How could I encapsulate my feelings about the novel in a few words? I settled on being vague. "We'll talk about it later. My hunch is Keith will have good information about Shona. I want to catch him before he leaves."

Wiggling my fingers in a goodbye-so-long gesture, I left the office, hoping I wasn't just whistling Dixie.

Chapter Thirteen

THE FATES—OR evil water sprites—had it in for me. When I drank from the water fountain in the hall, it shot water all over my blouse.

I squished down the hall and went in the door to the lab. Rows of tall, dark metal workbenches were laid out ahead of me. Seated on high stools were students absorbed in their research. Some looked up to see who had entered, then looked back down right away. A few did double takes, no doubt surprised to see a bedraggled female who didn't belong in their orderly world of scientific research. At least it must've been well-ordered before Shona's death.

I spied Keith across the room, seated near a bank of windows. My shoes made icky noises as I crossed over to his work bench. He glanced up and smiled, not jiggling any objects for my benefit.

"Sorry to interrupt," I said, "but can you spare a minute to talk? Maybe out in the hall. I don't want to disturb anyone."

"Really? What about?" His hand shook, and he dropped a pipette. "Damn."

"Basically about Larissa."

His shoulders lowered. "Sure, okay." He placed the pipette on a shelf, adjusted a lever on an apparatus I didn't recognize. "Let's go," he said.

Once we reached the hall, I fought for an opening. I finally said, "Larissa and I've been good friends in Toronto. I'm here for moral support because she's been, um, agitated about Shona's murder." I waited, hoping he'd show a reaction to guide my inquisition.

"We're all shocked at Shona's death." His tone was bland, giving nothing away.

"Larissa says people in the lab are nervous around her, afraid she's the killer. I'm pleased you're treating her normally."

He opened and closed his mouth several times before managing to speak. "Why does she think that? No one blames her. Shona didn't die here. The murder is sensational, sure, but it has nothing to do with this lab."

I'd surprised him, and now he shocked me. His words contradicted Larissa's opinion. I needed to proceed with care; rumors, ugly ones, could start based on conversations like this one. Had I already said too much?

I backtracked. "Larissa thought the world of Shona. She says everyone did."

Keith pulled a face and shook his head. "I knew Larissa had a bad case of hero worship, but let me tell you, most of us didn't share her opinion of our late colleague, Shiny Shona." His voice oozed sarcasm.

"I traveled all the way from Ontario in hopes of calming Larissa," I said. "She was very supportive when I was new in Toronto and having a tough time. I owe her a great deal."

Keith's eyes crinkled into a smile. "I don't blame you for being devoted to her. Larissa's a great gal. No one has a problem with *her*. She's nice to work with and always congenial. Besides, she's"—he licked his lips—"so attractive, she jazzes up the place." His grin spread across his face and became a leer.

Oh, Keith, enough already. After a few deep breaths, I said, "Then you won't mind if I ask some questions?"

His eyes seemed to glow. "Sure, fire away. I'd do anything for Larissa, actually. Anything."

Down boy.

So I was right—the guy was smitten. He didn't seem to realize Larissa hardly knew he existed. From what I'd seen, she was barely civil to him.

"Larissa's worried," I said, "about what the group thinks. After all, she's the only one who makes the tea for your lab every day. So I was wondering—"

"If this is going to take a while," he said, "let's go out in the hall."

We strolled down the hall in silence. I was feeling relaxed until Keith said, "Don't you feel awful in those wet clothes? I like the clinging effect of your blouse, though." He smirked. "Downright fetching."

I forced my face to register nothing. I needed Keith's help and merely shrugged. "What can I do? These are the only things I have to wear right now. The airline lost my luggage. Believe me, I'm embarrassed looking like this."

"Don't be." He flapped a hand in a dismissive gesture. "Most gals in this building don't dress any better than you look right now. "

He sounded so smug and judgmental that I wanted to smack him.

We reached a grouping of chairs and sat. I wrapped my arms across my chest, huddling to keep warm—and covered up. I'd show him who was smarter. He wouldn't even know he was being manipulated.

"What didn't you like about Shona?"

When Keith hesitated, I asked, "Was she hard to work with?"

He made a choking sound. "I can't stand argumentative babes. She was bright and knew it, had no time for anyone who couldn't keep up with her brilliance. But Americans are like that, compared to Canadians, eh? Sorry, no offense. Your accent gives you away." This time when his eyes crinkled, he looked insincere.

I struggled to keep my tone level with the jerk. "Don't worry. I asked for your honest opinion. I can take it."

"Okay then." He sat up straighter. "Shona was too sure of

herself. Sometimes abrasive, even, but never with Larissa. I could tell Shona liked Larissa, but then, all of us do. I was surprised they got along so well since their personalities were so very different."

"Did Shona ever mention her women's liberation group?"

Keith burst out laughing. "*Did she?* You should ask instead if she ever shut up about it. She was a real women's libber. She groused all the time about people not paying enough attention to her views because she was female."

"Maybe she had a good point?"

Keith twitched in my direction. "A chemistry department is no place for girls, no matter how smart they are. She must have known what she was getting into. Look at all the greats in science—all of them men."

Honestly, if he kept on like this, I was going to haul off and smack him.

"So what about Madame Curie?" I said.

He snapped his fingers. "Easy—the exception that proves the rule. Look, Shona didn't know her place, and she expressed her views too freely."

"Views on what?"

"You name it. Everything. From our research results to politics to women's role in society. Everything." He sat back in his chair, looking pleased with himself.

I bet he thought he'd made his case against Shona. What he'd done instead was cement my opinion of him. Keith became the first name on my list of suspects. Such an honor, and all his. He deserved it.

And now we were getting somewhere. This was new territory, a different view of Shiny Shona from what Larissa had told me. What was the true Shona like—unbearably pushy and obnoxious or a beacon of light and goodness? Somewhere in between or a mixture of both?

"So are there other female grad students in the Adler lab?" I said.

"Sure, a few."

"Did any of them go to the women's meetings—as Shona convinced Larissa to do?"

His eyes rolled to the ceiling and down again. "Only two other girls are in the lab, thank goodness, aside from Shona. Far as I know, only one of them goes to those dumb meetings."

"What's her name?"

"Emma."

"Do you think she'll talk to me?"

"Don't know why not. But why would you want to do that?"

"Remember, my aim is to calm Larissa down, make her feel better. Maybe Emma can help. If Emma's here today, will you point her out to me please? Just for some *girl talk*."

"Oh, sure. I'll introduce you. She's pretty quiet, though. Clever enough for a girl, but not pushy like Shona. Emma never bothers anyone, although maybe you'll have a problem getting her to open up. Quiet and no backbone at all. But I'll tell her to talk to you."

So with Keith a woman couldn't win. She was either too pushy or a milquetoast. A pushover.

Unless she was a gorgeous knockout, like Larissa.

His mouth twisted into a scowl. "It pains me to think of Larissa upset about the murder investigation. I hope we can assure her on that score."

We? Oh dear, what had I done? Larissa wouldn't like my dragging Keith into this any more than I did. Still, it was for a good cause. Something niggled at the back of my mind, but the sound of footsteps pushed it away.

The hall had been quiet, but now someone was clomping toward us. Keith and I looked up as Frank approached. He studied his feet as he walked and puffed hard on a cigarette. When he did glance up, a frown creased his brow.

He stopped a short distance away and took a heavy drag on his cigarette, then threw it on the floor and smashed it with his shoe, nudging it toward the wall.

"What're you two whispering about?" he said, his tone gruff.

"Anybody could've had an accident. Don't look at me like that." His pace quickened as he passed our chairs.

I leaned toward Keith. "Touchy, isn't he?" I kept my voice low.

"Yeah, there are some odd ducks in our lab group. He's one of many."

Great. I had to clutch my hands hard to keep from rubbing them in glee. Maybe Shona's killer was one of the many odd ducks. Frank joined Keith on my list.

I wanted to run through them all—with my rapier-sharp mind, if you please. Maybe they'd find out soon enough I was pretty smart *for a girl*.

Chapter Fourteen

KEITH AND I returned to the Adler lab. While he searched for Emma, I surveyed the large space. A blackboard stretched across the end of the room, and in one corner hung a large placard of the periodic table. Several signs stressed the dangers inherent in the work space. I counted seven versions of the skull and crossbones symbol.

Yikes.

If I were a chemistry student, those ominous signs wouldn't bother me. I'd be used to them, would scarcely notice. As it was, they insisted I had undertaken something dangerous by simply standing in the laboratory. All I remembered from high school science was how to use a Bunsen burner. I never took chemistry in college, and so this environment rattled me. Maybe a new element should be added to the periodic table. I'd call it *anxiety*.

Keith returned to my side and thrust a white lab coat at me. "Here. Not sure if this'll fit or not. You're big for a girl. Anyway, it's worth a try to cover up those clothes." He pointed at my skirt and grimaced.

What a mixed message—offering help and a slur at the same time. I stared at the lab coat. It was dry and clean. And maybe he was trying to be nice. I'd try to appreciate the offer.

"Thanks." I put on the coat. It wouldn't button all the way down; my hips were too wide. I let the coat hang loose. At least it took the chill off.

Keith looked over the top of his glasses and assessed my new garb. "Yep, now you look like all the other girls in this place—dowdy. That's why seeing Larissa is downright invigorating."

What a creep. Women were good to look at, so that should be our chief function in life?

A girl—*woman*, I kept forgetting to say that—with brown hair chopped short inched up to us, stopping in front of Keith. "You want to talk to me?" Her voice was whispery soft, and she didn't look him in the eye. No one would accuse *her* of being pushy. She must be Emma.

Keith thrust a thumb in my direction. "This is Austin Starr. She's a pal of Larissa's and wants to talk to you about Shona. I told her you would."

More rudeness. Shona hadn't tolerated treatment like this, perhaps challenging him at every turn instead, and he hadn't liked that. Motive enough for murder?

Emma hunched her shoulders and shrank deeper into her lab coat. She didn't meet my eyes either and barely managed to stammer out, "I'm, uh, Emma. Guess we can talk, but I'm timing an experiment, so I don't have long. I'm sorry."

"Don't let me interrupt anything important," I said. "Would you rather wait until lunch and talk then?"

"No, no. Now's fine. I must keep an eye on the clock, that's all."

Her timidity made my heart go out to her. I became more concerned to put her at ease than to pump her for information. Still, I must. I'd slide into it. Together we left the lab and went back to the chairs Keith and I had occupied.

I began by describing how I knew Larissa and why I was visiting her, emphasizing the importance of friendship. As I talked, Emma's shoulders relaxed and her eyes were able to meet mine. After a few minutes, I asked her opinion of Shona.

Emma's eyes brimmed with tears. "Shona was the most wonderful person I ever met in my whole life. I'm heartbroken she's dead. We all are." Her gaze lowered, and she fingered her lab coat.

"What did you mean—*we all* are heartbroken at her death?"

Her head came up. "Everybody liked her. *Everybody.*" Her eyes now bored into me and seemed to blaze.

I tried for my most soothing tone. "I don't want to sully her memory, but I'm curious if your male colleagues would agree with you. I know one who wouldn't. Sorry to push, but I'm trying to figure out who might've had a reason for wishing Shona dead."

"I understand," she said softly. "This is just so hard. She was very kind to me when no one else was."

"Larissa says that happened to her too." When Emma didn't say anything, I pressed on. "How did the guys in the lab feel about her?"

"Oh, them." Her voice dripped with scorn. "They hate having to conduct research beside women. If we *must* go out to work—not staying where we belong, barefoot and pregnant in the kitchen—they want us typing up a storm and making tea and coffee for them—the great, important male scientists."

"Have you always felt this way, or did the women's meetings you attended with Shona point you in that direction?"

Emma flinched. Her hands fluttered to her face. "Well, I guess I, uh, I always sort of knew things were unequal but never realized anyone felt the way I did. No one ever talked about it."

She folded and unfolded her hands, then put them in her lap. "There's strength in numbers, you know. Those meetings showed I'm not the only one who thinks girls—I mean *women*, excuse me—don't get a fair shake."

She stopped to check her watch. "Sorry, I don't mean to be rude, but I can't forget my experiment. I'll have to leave in about ten minutes."

"I appreciate you talking to me, I really do. But before you go, is there anything else you can add about Shona?"

She shut her eyes as she considered my question. "Come to think of it, yes, there is. Several guys in the lab gave Shona a super hard time." She settled back into her chair and looked prepared to talk more, despite her claims she needed to leave.

"A hard time how?"

"They doubted her research results and grilled her about them all the time."

"Was Keith one of them?"

"Yes." The word exploded from her mouth. "He always made fun of her, ran down her opinions. Sometimes she'd speak up, and no one would agree with her. Then after time had passed, Keith would pronounce the same ideas and everyone would agree. With him. Not with her." She scowled. "What he said counted— as long as it came from his mouth or from another guy's. This happened a lot. Shona never mentioned it, but I know she felt it. That always happens when women speak up or try to change people's minds. Once I saw the pattern, it made me angry."

Emma leaned closer. "Sometimes Shona's control slipped a bit. When their bragging and putdowns grew too much for her, she knew how to get under the guys' skin. Did it on purpose, as payback."

"Can you give me an example?" I asked.

Emma's eyes narrowed. "Shona was elected to Phi Beta Kappa in her junior year at the University of Washington. That may be a very big deal in the States, but the organization doesn't exist here in Canada. Still, any serious student here knows about it." She paused to clear her throat, and then began again.

"A few months ago Shona showed up at the lab wearing a necklace. She took it off and put it in her locker when she put on her lab coat. We can't wear jewelry in the lab, you see. Anyway, someone saw the necklace and asked if the key hanging from the chain had any significance. When Shona explained it was her Phi Beta Kappa key, several people gasped. I was there, I witnessed it all. Before that, people here could ignore how intelligent she really was."

Emma stood and walked to the window. When she turned to face me, she was smiling. "Shona asked the few other Americans in the lab if anyone else belonged to Phi Beta Kappa. None did. They were all males, those others from the States. After that day, whenever the guys gave her a really hard time, she'd wear that necklace the next day. It worked like a charm to make them back off for a while, and then she'd have to do it all over again."

Emma sat again. Her forehead wrinkled, and her eyes filled with tears. "Of course, that wasn't a perfect ploy. The guys resented her more, grew even more jealous. They didn't hassle her quite as much as before, but other stuff started to happen."

"Like what?"

"Two times someone painted bad words on her locker. Very bad. One was *bitch*. The other I will not say."

This was news. Real news.

"Who gave Shona the most grief?"

"Keith and Frank. Those two were the ringleaders. If it weren't for them, I don't think she'd have had any trouble. The other guys aren't so ego-driven. Mind you, this is just my analysis."

She checked her watch. "Okay, I've got a bit more time. I should tell you that the Mounties came in a few days back and asked each of us lots of questions."

"They talked to you?"

"Yes, me and a handful of the grad students. I know they talked to Mrs. Carson and I think also to Larissa."

I made a mental note to dig more details out of Larissa.

"What kind of questions were you asked?"

"Mostly about how Shona was treated in the lab. I confess I glossed over what I thought about the boys and how they treated her. The Mounties didn't push, just seemed satisfied when I said everyone liked her and that Shona was highly intelligent. The best I could tell, no one spent more than ten or fifteen minutes being questioned. I heard the Mounties spent more time over at SUB, where Shona died."

"Were you asked anything about Larissa?"

Emma blinked rapidly. "No. Why do you ask?"

I had to go carefully now. "Because Larissa makes the tea, right?"

She waved her hand in the air, as if dismissing my words. "Oh, sure, but no one thinks Larissa killed Shona. They were great pals. Hmm, come to think of it, the Mountie did ask if Shona had any special friends here, or enemies, and I replied that she really liked Larissa. The man made a note of that and changed the subject."

Maybe Larissa wasn't the prime suspect she thought she was.

Or maybe the Mounties were keeping their evidence quiet.

Emma took a tissue from the pocket of her lab coat and blew her nose.

Watching her dainty movements, I realized I had no idea what Shona had looked like. Was she small like Emma and Larissa or big and tall like me? Or somewhere in the middle?

I waited until Emma pocketed her tissue before asking her.

Emma's forehead wrinkled. "Why is that important?"

"It would help me to have a mental image of her."

"That's a funny thing, really. Lots about Shona looked average. Average height, weight, ordinary brown hair. But somehow the whole package came out as extraordinary. She wore her thick hair in a French braid down her back, and her brown eyes were lively and curious. She gave off such positive energy that people wanted to be around her. Most reasonable people that is, those who understood it was okay to be a brilliant woman."

I remembered that Larissa had also described how energetic Shona had been. I was beginning to regret I'd never met her. The picture of her was filling in, and it was a nice one.

Emma's shoulders sagged. "You're the only one other than Shona I've discussed some of these things with—how hard it is for a woman working in a chemistry lab."

Her face brightened. "Say, have you ever been to a women's liberation meeting?"

"No, not yet, but I may go tonight with Larissa."

Emma's grin warmed up her face. "You'll understand a lot

better why Shona fought back and what we're all up against once you've heard women share their real feelings. Tonight's meeting will be a revelation for you. Not to be clichéd about it, but your consciousness *will* be raised. Perhaps one meeting isn't enough to work this change, but it could be. Sounds to me as if you're halfway there already."

"Really?" I said. "That's surprising. I doubt if Larissa would agree with you."

"Oh? Why?"

"She's made me read a book so I'll understand things better."

"Which one?"

"*The Edible Woman* by—"

"Isn't Margaret Atwood wonderful? Her novel is a real eye-opener. I've never read anything like it before."

Emma looked at her watch again, then moved forward in her chair. "Darn it. I'm so sorry, but I must scoot. I must be there when my timer goes off. If you're a female in science, you have no margin for error. None. You have to be better than the boys, or die trying.

"Oh my gosh." She clapped her hands over her mouth, and her eyes bugged out. "What have I said?"

Chapter Fifteen

EMMA'S OUTBURST SEEMED to traumatize her. She jumped from her seat and flew down the hall. I ran to follow. By the time she reached the door that led into the lab, I had managed to catch up.

"Wait, please. Just one more question." I tugged on her arm, begging. "I've got to know." I lowered my voice. "Do you think it's possible someone from the lab killed Shona?"

Her hand lifted from the doorknob. She eyed me, her mouth twisted down. "Someone killed her, and it wasn't me." Her voice was a whispered hiss. "And it certainly wasn't Larissa. If the killer works in this lab, then the, uh, messenger of death is male. But I've no idea who he could be. That's a giant leap, from sexism to murder."

Emma clasped her hands in front of her face and turned toward the door. I rushed to get my next question out before she returned to the lab.

"That's it—motive. Who would have a reason to want Shona dead?"

"I don't know. But I'll give it some thought." She placed both hands on her cheeks, staring at me a moment before she continued. "I'll keep tabs on what people say, even better than I have before. I realize you're playing at detective, Austin, and I want to help you." Even though she reached out again to the door with a hand that trembled, Emma's smile reached her eyes. They crinkled up at the edges and looked at me with real warmth.

"Thanks, Emma." On an impulse, I reached out and hugged her. To my surprise, Emma not only hugged me back but clung for a moment.

Maybe it would be a good thing, this women's solidarity movement.

Emma disappeared into the lab, and I returned to the office.

Larissa was standing in front of a tall metal filing cabinet when I entered. "Where've you been?" She glanced around. "Mrs. Carson went off for an early lunch, and so we can, um, see if there's anything in the *kitchen*." She gave me a sly wink. "We need to check it out before the grad students flood in to get their lunch fixings out of the fridge. Let's hurry."

She walked to her desk and took her purse from a drawer, then got my bag. "Here." She handed it to me. "Better take this with you. We've had a few incidents of theft, and it's not safe to leave things lying around that you don't want filched."

"Interesting." I put a finger beside my mouth and grinned. "There must be a bad guy skulking around, maybe a *very bad one* indeed."

Once in the kitchen, Larissa showed me where snacks were kept. Just as she'd said, all the mugs were labeled with names. Twenty or more stood on shelves, waiting to be called to duty at afternoon break time.

"Who makes the snacks these days? Surely not you," I said.

"My lawyer advised me to refuse to continue my kitchen duties. Mrs. Carson lays out the goodies now. She detests it, feels it's beneath her to serve students, but someone has to do it."

"Why can't the students get their own snacks?" I asked.

"Remember I told you Dr. Adler is following Dr. Watson's pattern at his lab at Harvard? I guess having us non-scientists do the menial tasks frees up the great minds for doing great things. I don't mind, but Mrs. Carson does."

"I'm surprised she works."

"She has to. She says she's penniless after her husband left her two years ago for a younger—much younger—woman. She talks about their divorce constantly. I guess everybody has limits."

I grinned. "Are you talking about Mrs. Carson or the husband who fled?"

Larissa laughed and shrugged. "I don't know enough to have an opinion, but I do think that—well, you met her—Mrs. C. would be tough to live with."

I looked around the room. "So where's the infamous Earl Grey tea kept now, pray tell?"

"Mrs. Carson locks it in her desk. The tea box got moved when I quit playing kitchen helper."

I rolled my eyes. I couldn't help myself, even though I knew Larissa hated it when I did that. "I've never heard such a fuss made over tea before. As if it were flakes of gold, not leaves of a plant. Ridiculous."

Larissa heaved a sigh. "Believe me, I agree. But Dr. Adler adores that tea and refuses to drink anything else. He'd prefer we all drink it too, whether we like it or not. When it got pilfered a few times, that's when we began locking it up."

"What? The thief—whoever he or she was—could have used the pilfered tea to poison Shona's cup or thermos. I wonder if the Mounties know that? Damn, I wish I could talk to one of them. I'm beginning to appreciate what a godsend McKinnon was when David was in jail."

Larissa patted my shoulder. "Whoa, Austin. Easy, girl."

I sniffed, quashing an urge to do another eye roll. "Aside from being the bearer of poison, I still think it's ridiculous, all this fuss over Earl Grey, but never mind." I looked around the kitchen. "So, hmm, do people keep their own lunch things here— like Shona's thermos, for example?"

"Sometimes they do." Larissa opened the fridge. "See, there are several lunches in here, all labeled." She shut the fridge. "But Shona rarely left anything here. I don't recall about that particular day last week, but I doubt if she did. I never saw her thermos here and don't know where she stored it."

"Would anyone else know where she kept it? Maybe the poison was put straight into the thermos."

"Right, I thought of that too. She loved Earl Grey. I'm thinking she carried her full thermos over to SUB—the Student Union Building, that is—where she ate her last supper." She shuddered. "I didn't mean to say that. It sounds so flippant."

Now I patted her shoulder. "Come on. Let's get out of here. I've seen enough."

When we returned to the office, two students were waiting. Larissa wrote down their orders for new chemicals for the lab. After they left, I asked if she handled the ordering.

"If Mrs. Carson had been here," Larissa said, "she'd have written down the students' requests. Like I told you, I handle the most basic tasks. Ordering precise quantities of chemicals is deemed too difficult for my tiny brain." Her smile undercut the bite in her words.

"All right, I think you've given me a good idea of the setup here." I switched to what I hoped sounded like an ultra-offhand, casual tone. "So what kinds of questions did the Mounties ask you about Shona?"

Larissa twitched, and she faced me with startled eyes. "Thought we'd been over that before."

"Not really, not in detail." I waited.

"Well, umm, my memory is pretty sketchy about all that. I was tense, you know."

She scratched a red patch on her neck. She must have been digging at it for some time.

"What *do* you remember then?" I wasn't about to let her off easily.

"The first time I talked to them, I was here at work. The session lasted less than thirty minutes and was mundane. The Mounties talked to lots of us from the lab, Mrs. Carson included. The next time I had to go down to RCMP headquarters. I was there for a few hours, and my dad flew out to be with me. In the meantime we'd gotten a lawyer, and he came along too. We went over all the old territory, but that time they also asked about my relationship with Shona, little bitty things about how long we'd known each other, if we ever fought, and so on. Also they wanted to know about the tea. None of the questions were unusual, nothing stood out, that is. They were treating me like a suspect. Anyone who's ever read a Perry Mason story could dream up the same questions. Yesterday's interview was different. That's when they said a witness had implicated me."

Her fingers still scratched at her neck. The red spot was brighter, and I thought I detected a thin line of red. Blood.

"Doesn't your neck hurt?" I patted my own neck, giving her a gentle hint. "Look at your fingers."

She pulled her hand away from her neck, looked at her fingers, and yelped. "Good grief. I didn't know I was doing that." She stumbled to her desk, opened a drawer, and took a tissue from it. Dabbing at her neck, she said, "Does it look awful?"

"No, I figured you weren't aware of what you were doing. Come on, let's go grab some lunch. You've given me plenty to mull over."

"Figured I had." Larissa threw away the tissue and placed letters in a folder. "Listen, Austin, if we skip lunch and I work straight through, then we can leave early and shop for your new clothes. How does that sound?"

"Terrific. Just thinking about it makes me feel better already. Now I'll just curl up with that old blanket and dream about clean, dry clothes."

"And you can read the Atwood book."

But no book could've held my concentration, no matter how enticing. Thoughts of poison and possible killers filled my brain. They circled round and round like flies at a picnic and wouldn't be shooed away. I was worried about Larissa. She was more anxious than she admitted. The sooner the killer was caught, the sooner she could return to her usual happy self.

I wasn't equipped to figure out the crime details of means and opportunity, so I dismissed those out of hand. I thought instead about the piece of the murder puzzle that I could handle.

Motive.

Although Shona irritated her male coworkers, I couldn't understand how her existence was a serious threat. What would another student stand to gain from her death? I'd talked to Keith briefly and judged he wasn't destroyed, merely bruised, by her assertive attitude. Emma said I needn't suspect anyone around the lab who was female. I still figured attending the women's meeting would open new avenues for investigation. Perhaps the guilty party even lurked there.

A small piece of something poked at the edges of my consciousness. Something about poisons—I closed my eyes and focused. In a moment the information burst through. According to many mystery writers, poison was most often used by *women* killers. It was not the choice of men.

Hmm, maybe the women's group would prove fruitful after all.

My promise to David nudged me hard.

He'd be upset—even furious—to learn I was playing detective. But danger didn't seem to be prowling around, and what David didn't know wouldn't hurt him. I would call as scheduled tomorrow night and be able to talk to him with a clean conscience.

Good gosh, he wasn't the only one I needed to talk to.

I'd forgotten to check on Wyatt.

I needed to find out how he was doing with his new babysitter. Talk about guilt. This was the real deal—getting so engrossed and nosy that I'd forgotten my own son. What a dreadful mother I was.

I jumped up from the armchair. "Hey, Larissa, may I borrow the phone? I want to check on Wyatt."

"Do you need Mrs. Mirnaya's phone number?"

"Nope. I've got it here somewhere." I fished in the pockets of my skirt and found a damp slip of paper. When I unfolded it, I saw a blurry mess. "On second thought, could you please write it out for me?" I waved the soggy paper.

When I talked to Mrs. Mirnaya, she assured me that Wyatt was adjusting well. Satisfied with her description of his activities, I thanked her warmly, hung up, and returned to the armchair. Soon the troubled world of *The Edible Woman* engulfed me again.

Atwood's distraught heroine had developed a kinship with all foods. They were devoured, and she felt devoured too. As a consequence, she was unable to eat anything. How would she get out of this pickle?

I sat and read, Larissa worked, Mrs. Carson returned from lunch.

No one else stopped by the office. Everything was quiet. When three o'clock came, Larissa announced she had put in her hours for the day and could leave. By then I was galloping toward the book's conclusion and hated putting it aside.

When I tore my eyes away from the novel, I watched Mrs. Carson unlock a desk drawer. She drew out a large tin marked *Murchie's*. It looked so innocent. Not a likely cause of death. But the Mounties had declared tea the delivery system for poison.

This was obviously a new batch; surely the Mounties carried off the old stuff. Still, looking at the nefarious tea tin made my stomach lurch.

For my own peace of mind, I needed to clarify the facts.

"That's not the same tea used last week when Shona, um, was murdered, is it?" I contemplated Larissa as her head flopped down to her chest at my words.

Mrs. Carson said, "Of course not. This is a brand new tin and everything. The Mounties took away a whole pound of new tea. Dr. Adler was apoplectic, even though he understood why it had to be done. Why do you ask?"

"Seems I have a morbid fascination with police investigations."

She grimaced. "Read lots of the Nancy Drew mysteries as a child?"

"Of course."

"My daughters did too. Neither is as curious as you appear to be, though, thank heavens." She twisted around to Larissa. "Why don't you take the day off tomorrow? Then you two can spend it however you like. I'll tell Dr. Adler—he probably won't mind. You could use a break."

After accepting Larissa's grateful thanks, Mrs. Carson wished us well on our clothes hunt, after taking a few jabs at the state of my attire. She suggested a shop on Tenth, and then Larissa and I tromped back to the car through a mist too fine to even be called a sprinkle. Despite the weather, students lounged and chatted outside.

When I drew this to Larissa's attention, she laughed. "You'll see plenty of outdoor activity here when it's not raining hard. If people waited until the rain stopped long enough for the ground to dry, then they'd never play golf or work in their gardens."

"The clouds make everything look so dismal, so gray. Doesn't help that the university buildings are gray—either stone or poured concrete."

"The first two weeks I spent in Vancouver, it rained twelve days. I learned my lesson and quit counting." She gave a wry smile. "The natives say so much rain is worth it because when a day of full sunshine finally arrives, everything sparkles, making you forget the bad weather."

"Yeah, right," I said.

We reached her car. I saw a handbill tucked under the windshield wipers on the passenger side. I picked it up and crumpled it, then realized it was handwritten.

When I got in the car, I smoothed the paper on my lap. Even though the black printing was badly smeared from the damp, I could make out the words.

YOU ARE FOOLISH TO ASK QUESTIONS. DANGER!

I thrust the paper at Larissa. "Look at this."

She read the message, then banged her fist on the steering wheel. "No. No. No. I can't take anymore. I just can't."

Chapter Sixteen

I RETRIEVED THE paper from Larissa. "We have to keep this for the Mounties."

"They'll think I wrote it."

"Maybe so, but you still need to give it to them."

"They won't believe me when I say we found it, that I didn't plant it myself."

"I can vouch for you. I've been with you all day."

"That's the dumbest thing you ever said to me." She gasped. "Oh blast, I'm sorry. I shouldn't take my nerves out on you."

"Take it easy. As a matter of fact, stop and take several deep breaths. Do it."

We sat and breathed. When Larissa started to speak, I thumped her arm. "Just breathe."

Soon the car fogged up. I began rubbing off the damp and uttered a small laugh. "Okay, here's what I think. Maybe someone is worried about you. This could be a kindly warning. It wasn't necessarily written by a murderer. I don't think we should leap to conclusions. It's as likely to be a mean joke as a real threat. We just don't know."

Larissa wiped her eyes. I hadn't realized she was crying.

"Whatever it is," she said, "and whoever left it here—I don't care. I am seriously spooked."

"I don't blame you for that. But we're going to stay calm." We exchanged glances. "Well, as calm as possible. Right?"

She nodded.

"Do you want me to drive?"

She nodded again. We switched places, and I drove out of the parking lot. "Now focus, please, and give me directions to the store."

Maybe thinking about something mundane would help her calm down.

I pulled into a parking space on Tenth, and we went into a dress shop. The best I could find were two blouses with sleeves a little too short and a skirt a bit snug. Those pieces were on sale, so I could almost afford them. Not too many travelers' checks were in my billfold; I never dreamed I'd have to shell out money for clothes.

The blouses and skirt lay on the counter, and I appraised them critically. Dang it all. My sartorial standards had hit an all-time, rock-bottom low. Nevertheless I was relieved at being able to ditch the clothes I'd worn for three days.

Next we stopped at Mrs. Mirnaya's house. I was overjoyed when I saw Wyatt kicking his fat little legs happily in a play pen. I rushed over to pick him up and give him a cuddle.

"You are wonderful, Mrs. Mirnaya. Wy seems very happy with you. I can't thank you enough."

The lady was all smiles. "Look what baby can do." She took Wyatt from me and put him in the Jolly Jumper that hung from a door frame.

"Isn't he too small for that contraption?" I tried not to shriek.

"Is fine," she said. "Baby doctor say three months okay. He hold up head, is fine. Now watch."

She gently jostled him up and down. The coils squeaked, and Wyatt gurgled in delight. Sure enough, his head didn't droop as he bounced.

All tension emptied from my body. I envisioned it swirling out the bottoms of my feet, like water draining from a bathtub. Wyatt's wellbeing lessened my guilt at leaving him all day with a stranger. Even if she was an adoring grandmotherly type, this little Russian babushka was no substitute for me. A baby needed to be with his own mother. At least that's what *my* mother had drilled into me for years. No wonder I wore guilt like a familiar hair shirt.

I packed up Wyatt and his gear and headed for the door.

Mrs. Mirnaya said, "Will you bring baby tomorrow?"

"I don't know." I glanced at Larissa. "Do we have plans?"

She shrugged. "If I had any before, I've forgotten about them now."

I asked Mrs. Mirnaya if I could let her know the following day, and she agreed. She kissed Wyatt on his nose and waved goodbye from her porch.

We bundled ourselves quickly into the car. I returned to the passenger seat so I could hold Wy, and Larissa drove down the block to Raisa's house. As she pulled into the driveway, a dark sedan caught my eye. Inside it a man was reading a newspaper.

The minute we stepped inside Raisa's house, a blanket of warm, tangy air enveloped us. I fancied I could smell borscht simmering on the stove. This time, entering the house was warm and inviting. I figured I was getting used to the claustrophobic look; the place had begun to feel downright homey. And the smell was enticing. That woman sure knew how to cook. I began salivating.

Larissa ran up the stairs, and I stayed behind to talk to her aunt.

Raisa hurried into the living room, wiping her hands on her apron. "A man called for you an hour ago," she said to me. "His name was Jones, calling from Washington, D.C."

My heart took a nosedive. "Did he say why he wanted to talk to me?"

She shrugged. "Nyet. Only you phone him back." She dug a paper out of her pocket and handed it to me.

Larissa had come back downstairs. "Who's this Jones? Do I know him?"

I raised a finger to my lips and made a silent shushing

gesture. "I've mentioned him, but I'm sure this is nothing major."

She took the hint—that we'd talk about Jones later—and turned to her aunt. "We're in a hurry and have to get back out to UBC for my meeting," she said. "Any chance we can eat and run?"

I couldn't believe she was still intent on going to that blasted meeting. I thought she should call the RCMP.

"Konechno," Raisa said. "Will dish up your bowls now."

I was halfway to the phone to call Jones, but wheeled around to face Larissa. *Mind your manners, Austin,* Mother's voice whispered in my mind. "May I have a minute to call Jones? It won't take long"

Larissa's face registered surprise. "Good grief. We hardly have time to eat and rush to get to the meeting on time. You can call him later."

She rarely got huffy, but her nerves were making her into someone I didn't recognize. I almost snapped back, but then realized she was probably just as disgusted with her attitude as I was.

"If I don't call now," I said, hiding my annoyance, "I'll have to wait until tomorrow. Remember the time difference between here and D.C."

Larissa put her hands on her hips and pouted. "Just wait, will you? You know how important this meeting is to me."

I put my hands on my own hips and stared back. It felt like high noon at the O.K. Corral.

She stood firm. I wilted.

"All right, you win. But just so you know, I'm not happy about this." I flounced up the stairs, carrying Wyatt. I sulked while I changed into my new clothes, but then I lay on the bed with Wy, and almost immediately his giggles soothed me.

Right before we left Toronto, he'd rolled over for the first time, and now he practiced his tummy roll again and again. Our delight was mutual. His coos and laughs tickled me. Bringing him with me on this trip had turned out to be a wonderful mood enhancement.

By the time I went back downstairs for supper, buoyed by baby laughter and kisses and the scent of baby powder, I was back to my normal self.

In the next half hour I ate dinner, fed Wyatt, played with him again, and got him ready for bed. I was disturbed—well, *guilty*, really—at leaving him for the second time that day.

He looked so cute, kicking his chubby legs, lying in his little makeshift crib, but Larissa called from the living room.

"Hey, we're going to be late. Come on."

I whispered to Wyatt, "Wish she'd get off my back." He seemed to agree. He stopped wiggling and stared at me, all sober.

But then he yawned. Vancouver was acting like a sleeping powder on him. Wy'd had no trouble getting to sleep ever since we left Toronto. If he went to sleep right now, then he wouldn't realize his mother had left him again. Nancy Drew never had to juggle child care and sleuthing. Come to think of it, she'd never felt guilty about anything ever.

I gave Wy one last caress, kissed his forehead, and rushed down the stairs. Well, I didn't exactly rush, but I went fast for me. Stairs are one of my bêtes noires.

Larissa and I raced out to the car and jumped inside to get out of the rain. The very moment we were settled, with the door shut, she pounced on me.

Her words tumbled out, so rapidly that they swooshed together.

"I know what's going on. Jones is your old CIA contact, isn't he? Why would he call you? How'd he know you were here? That's freaky."

"I can't answer your questions. I simply don't know." I leaned closer and looked her straight in the eye. "Still, you got one thing right. His call is freaking me out too."

Chapter Seventeen

A SUDDEN LOUD thumping sounded behind me. I jumped and banged my head against the car door.

Raisa stood in the rain, hammering on my window. My heart had moved up to my throat and was pounding away there.

I rolled the window down an inch. "Is everything okay?"

"Hurry. Your husband on phone."

I threw an apologetic glance at Larissa and rushed from the car and back into the house.

"What's wrong, David?" I yelled into the phone.

"I've got a message for you from some stranger." David's voice sounded formal, bordering on unfriendly. A shiver ran through me, deeper than the chill and damp I'd experienced all day.

"What stranger?" I'd gotten so tense so fast that I squeaked.

"He called twice. He wouldn't give his name at first. The second time he called—when he demanded to know when he'd be able to speak to you—I told him you were visiting friends in British Columbia. Then he asked for the phone number. But when I hesitated, he said it was urgent, that his name was Jones, Mr. Jones, and—"

I swallowed, hard. "Jones? You're sure he said Jones?"

"Of course I'm sure, Austin. I'm not amused at any of this, if you must know."

"I'm sorry, David. It's just that—"

"Let me finish," he snapped. "Jones said he was your former employer and that he had news about a mutual friend. Because he sounded polite and seemed kind of old, he was able to convince me to give him Larissa's number in Vancouver. And then about two hours later, he called back. This time he sounded really agitated and all bent out of shape. Said he was worried he wouldn't catch up with you in time to warn you and insisted I take his message. So you'll be able to hear it, one way or the other."

"I'm listening." My blood pressure must have been sky high; I felt as if I'd combust from the inside. I gripped the receiver and realized I was holding my breath. I made myself breathe slowly, in and out.

"You got something to write with?" David asked. "I know you're not good with names."

Why didn't he just get on with it? I wanted to yell at him. Instead, I remained patient and dutiful, searching frantically around the room. Seeing nothing suitable for note taking, I called to Raisa to get me a pen and paper. I sounded rude but was so disturbed that I didn't stop to apologize. When she brought them, I merely nodded at her.

"Okay, I'm ready," I told David.

"Here's the bad part." His tone became snide. "Our erstwhile old *pals* Senator Simpson and Darrel will be in Vancouver at an international trade meeting. They arrive tomorrow, and they're staying four nights at the Bayshore Hotel." David paused. "Did you get all that?"

"Got it," I said grimly.

"There's more. Jones thinks Simpson may try to get in touch with you. He says by all means not to talk to him and—"

"Why did—"

"Jones didn't explain. Just kept stressing you have to avoid them. He mumbled something about how they might complicate things for you now." He cleared his throat. "What's this all about, Austin? Why is some man I don't know warning us about two people we tangled with last year? How does Jones connect to my old murder charge, for heaven's sake? If Jones was once your employer, how does he know anything about Simpson? I keep going round and round on this. It makes no sense, and it's very disturbing."

My mind raced into overdrive. How could I explain about Jones to David—while I was on the phone and in a dreadful hurry?

David never knew I'd undergone training by the CIA before we were married. He had no idea that Jones was my contact's cover name. And now wasn't the time to stop and explain. The truth was too thorny. David would be furious when he learned the whole story. In his view the Vietcong and the CIA were almost equally bad news. I never had to confess because in the middle of my training David and I got married and rushed off to Canada. Thus had ended my incipient career with the CIA.

Sometimes I still grew dreamy and fantasized about being a spy. *That* I would never tell my spouse.

Larissa was out in the car, no doubt seething because I'd make her late to her precious meeting. I had to think fast. Lying was my best alternative. If this were only a temporary lie—if I promised myself I'd explain everything at a later date—surely I could be forgiven.

I adopted a nonchalant tone. "Dr. Jones was someone back in Texas I worked with during a summer job, so insignificant that I must not have mentioned it before. When you were in jail last year, I talked to Jones on the phone, so he knows about your arrest. I guess he's trying to keep me from being embarrassed if I run into the senator."

"But why did—"

"Listen, honey, I've got to go. I'll call you back later tonight or tomorrow and explain everything, but—trust me—it's really not interesting. I've got to get Wy ready for bed, and—"

"How's Wyatt doing? Is he handling the trip okay?"

Curses. Would he just let me off the danged phone?

"Wy's doing great." I tapped my foot, tangled the phone

cord around my hand, and suppressed an urge to hang up on him and leap out the front door. "Larissa's in the car already, anxious to get to a meeting at, uh, the Russian Community Center." I stopped to take a deep breath. "That sound okay to you, honey?"

In other words, did I just lie like a trooper?

"I suppose so." David drew out his words, sounding doubtful.

"Great. Talk to you again soon. Thanks so much for delivering the message, David. I love you. Bye." I hung up the phone.

I slumped against the table, rage coursing through me. Why had Jones involved my husband? Now I'd have to confess my dabbling with the CIA. Damn, damn, damn.

I glanced up to see Raisa eying me curiously.

"Khorosho?" Her brow was creased.

"Da, khorosho." I tried to smile and look relaxed. I probably failed miserably. My heart still felt as if it were thudding in my neck. My feelings were *not* khorosho—not by a long shot.

"*Spacibo*, Raisa, *spacibo bolshoya* ." When I thanked her, she gave me a big smile that transformed her face. On impulse, I hugged her.

She returned my hug. "*Poshlii*," she said. I followed her advice and rushed off.

When I was back in the car, I scarcely had time to draw in my legs and shut the door before Larissa revved the motor. I expected she'd hurtle out of the driveway, but she couldn't. The dark sedan had moved directly across from the end of Raisa's driveway. Larissa backed out slowly, careful not to hit the other car. I tried to see the man inside, but dusk had fallen.

Once our vehicle pointed straight down the street, she gunned the engine. We tore down the road and rounded the corner onto Blenheim on two wheels. An exaggeration, but that was how it felt.

Larissa didn't speak until we'd turned west. Then, glancing over at me, she said, "If we arrive late, it's no big deal. But I feel kind of unglued. My emotions are out of control, and I do realize that I'm snappish. Really, I'm sorry, Austin. You don't deserve this treatment."

I didn't speak immediately. Finally, I offered my support.

"I was never a murder suspect, so I can't claim to know how you feel. Still, I'm sure I'd feel *unglued* too, as you put it. The situation isn't the same, but I felt wretched when David was in jail. I doubt if either of us—you or me—expected to be touched by murders any time in our lives, let alone when we're so young."

Larissa gave one of her characteristic snorts, gladdening my heart. She had relaxed.

"I know it sounds trite," I said, "but you'll get through this, and we'll do it together, one step at a time." I patted her shoulder. She gave me a warm smile and exhaled loudly.

She drove a full block before speaking again. "When we get back to Raisa's tonight, I'll ask Papa what to do about the warning I got. I hate to tell him, but I must."

I hadn't considered that. Poor Professor Klimenko. However, he would know how to tell the RCMP. Larissa's dad never got rattled.

"Shall I tell you what the group is like?" Larissa asked.

"Uh, sure." My head changed gears as fast as it could to keep up. "I expect it'll be like any club meeting I ever attended." I affected a yawn. "First someone will read the minutes, then someone else gives the treasurer's statement, and then—"

"Heck, nothing like that. You've no idea what women's liberation is all about, do you?"

"Maybe not, but I'm about to see for myself. However"—I lingered over my words for emphasis—"it'll help if you point out the girls who were Shona's closest friends."

"Sure, but don't call them girls. That's not done."

"I know I'm not supposed to, but I just don't get that. Why not?" Emma had corrected herself too when she'd said *girls*.

"It's demeaning, belittling. Would you walk into a room full of males—all over the age of twenty—and call them boys?"

114

"Guess not." I rubbed my temples. "That's hard for me to understand. Mother always talks about playing bridge with the girls. I heard that all my life, calling grown women girls."

"Exactly." Larissa flashed a big grin. Her voice grew louder and more confident. "You'll hear plenty that'll surprise you. You'll come away with lots more to think about besides finding a killer. You'll see."

"Who are the girls—women—you know well, besides Shona?"

"Let me think." Larissa pulled to a stop at a light, rolled her shoulders, and stared into the distance. She began to count on her fingers. "There's Mia, Delilah, and Janet for starters."

"Who're they?"

"I met them all through Shona. Janet is another who stands out in the group. You could say she was a leader, but we don't believe in that."

A group without leaders? Impractical as well as odd.

"Okay, how about the other two?"

"Mia's an old friend of Shona's—kind of quiet but snippy when she deigns to say anything. And Delilah is a new pal of Shona's, probably the most radical in the group. Delilah is—I mean, *was*—Shona's last roommate."

"Are both Mia and Delilah from Seattle too?"

"Only Mia. She came here for grad school at the same time Shona did."

"I'd better take notes. Names aren't my strength." I took a tiny notebook and pencil from my purse and jotted down the three names. "Anyone else I should know about?"

"There's Becky, and she's—"

A horn blared behind us. I turned and saw the driver behind us at the stoplight mouthing what looked like *move it, lady*.

We rode in companionable silence for several minutes. When the car reached the end of the parkland and entered the campus proper, buildings popped up on both sides of the boulevard. Larissa turned into a large parking lot.

"The meetings are held over there, in SUB." She pointed at a sprawling modern structure. "That's the Student Union Building. Everyone just says SUB."

"Reminds me of a concrete bunker." I tried to suppress my low opinion of the architecture, with little success. "More gray buildings—pretty gloomy, given all the cloudy days."

Larissa made a choking sound. "You made your opinion clear already."

I rolled down my window and watched the students amble past. "Wow, I've never seen so many hippies in one place. Look at those bellbottoms and beads. Backpacks, sandals, beards. Wow."

"They're not real hippies. That's just West Coast style." Larissa twisted around to look at me. "You don't sound very groovy. I look at it like this: if British Columbia is the Canadian version of California, then this has to be Berkeley."

She shook her head hard. "No, I forgot about Simon Fraser, the new university on a mountain top east of here. That place is *really* radical." She scratched the red spot on her neck.

I put my hand over hers. "Stop that."

She pursed her lips and removed her hand. "Vancouver fits its nickname. It's my own version of Lotus Land—relaxing and even liberating. You might like it eventually."

"If you say so." I heard the doubt tiptoe into my voice.

Out of the corner of my eye, I noticed a young woman with an enormous bosom flop past, obviously not wearing a bra. "The whole scene makes me feel like an old fuddy-duddy."

I considered my new prim skirt and blouse, trying to remember if I'd even packed jeans—not that it mattered at this point since if I had, they were in my lost luggage. At least I carried a macramé purse decked out with long fringe. That was about as groovy as I got.

I picked up the purse now—dried out since its morning swim in the puddle—and tucked my notebook back inside. "Okay, lead on. Let's see about getting me liberated. Whatever that means."

116

"I wish you'd stop being so dismissive. This is important to me," Larissa said.

I hung my head. "I'm sorry. I guess I'm intimidated, and it's easy to make fun of something you don't understand."

Feeling contrite, I got out of the car. We walked together to SUB, past clusters of students lounging on the steps, still damp from recent rain showers. I assumed the students were enjoying a respite from the interminable rain and wondered how soon the next downpour would start.

Inside the building throngs of students milled about. Some sat talking in groups. Others handed out pamphlets about student activities. I stopped to gaze at the crowd, fascinated by the noise and chaos. I caught popular phrases yelled from the ever-shifting groups.

"America at war is so ugly."

"Help end the war before it ends you."

"Flower power, right here at UBC."

Larissa grabbed my arm and dragged me forward. "Will you quit gawking? You can catch the scene another time. We're almost late."

I pulled back and stood my ground. "No, just give me a sec. I need a ladies room."

I hurried away from Larissa's clutches and pushed into a bathroom I'd noticed a few moments earlier. I entered an empty stall and enjoyed a quiet moment to myself.

That didn't last long, however. Women with excited, high-pitched voices entered the room. They stood near the sinks in front of my stall.

"You hear about the big fight Mia and Shona had last week?"

"No kidding? How'd it go down?"

"It was a doozy."

"For real? Get with the words."

I leaned forward, glued to my seat. My habit of eavesdropping on strangers might finally prove useful.

The voice continued, hushed, sounding confidential and

confiding. "Me, I overheard the whole danged thing from the next room. Mia accused Shona of keeping some of their stuff after they quit rooming together. Shona denied it, and they blew up into a shouting match."

"Outta sight. Kind of surprising, though. Doesn't sound like either one of them. They used to be tight. And Mia's so quiet most of the time, and Shona was—"

The outer door screeched open. A new voice called out, "Better hurry up. We're about to start."

I slapped my knee in frustration. I'd expected to overhear lurid and valuable details, but I didn't get the main course, just an appetizer. Now I'd have to find out for myself why Mia had been so mad at Shona—other than feeling jealous of that other roommate, Delilah, whose friendship was new.

Maybe that was all there was to it. Or maybe, just maybe, it was a motive for murder.

Chapter Eighteen

PEEKING THROUGH THE slit in the stall door, I tried to identify the talkers. I made it by a mere whisker, almost too late. The back of one red-haired girl followed someone else out of the ladies room. I noted the bright pink top the redhead wore.

I exited the stall and surveyed the tiled room. I was alone, no one to eavesdrop upon. I washed my hands but skipped combing my hair, even though it looked ratty. I didn't want Larissa to get steamed waiting for me, so I scurried out as fast as I could.

Outside, halfway down the hall, Larissa stood in front of a half-open door, tapping her foot. "Are you ready? This is the place."

"All set."

I wanted to get this meeting out of the way and then concentrate on talking to the group's members. Even if there were no obvious suspects in attendance, at least these people had information about Shona that could prove crucial.

We opened the door and entered a ballroom-sized space. A large circle of chairs was set up in the center. A quick count showed nearly one hundred chairs, all occupied by women. Going by their clothes—jeans, sandals, beaded Indian jewelry—I guessed half the attendees were my age—in their twenties. Their unlined, makeup-free faces glowed with enthusiasm.

I'd make a lousy member of women's lib. I'd never but never give up eye makeup. Mother said I had no face without it, and for once, she and I agreed.

Then there was a large group of older women I classified as almost *normal*—at least in my mother's sense of the word. Before coming to the meeting, these ladies had set and curled their hair, put on makeup and nice dresses or blouses and skirts. Mostly middle-aged matrons, plus one woman apparently in her seventies with curly gray hair. However, each had something about her that looked a little bit off. Some wore jewelry with peace symbols, and others wore Birkenstocks with their neat dresses. *That* was a look I could do without. Birkenstocks were the ugliest shoes on Earth. One woman wore white socks with hers. *Ugh.*

In another era this group would've been called bohemian.

I was trying to spot the redhead in a bright pink shirt when a dark-haired girl—*woman*—in a long tie-dyed dress and Birkenstocks called out, "Hey, Larissa. Glad you're here."

The brunette retrieved two metal chairs from a stack in the corner and brought them over. "I worried you wouldn't come after what happened to Shona." She enveloped Larissa in a big hug, then, disengaging, said, "How're you doing? Bet it's been tough for you working at the lab, eh?"

"Right, pretty tough." Larissa pushed me forward. "I want you to meet my friend Austin. She flew in from Ontario to give me moral support." Larissa looked at me pointedly. "Austin, this is *Janet.*"

Janet peered at me over the top of orange-colored granny glasses with pink lenses. "Happy you could join us, but gosh, you're here at an awkward time. We've lost an essential member of our group—not that each of us isn't significant in her own way, but Shona was special."

Janet turned to Larissa. "Delilah's not coming tonight. She called me an hour ago, almost incoherent, she was crying so hard. Hell, it's been a whole week. You'd think she'd have calmed down by now, but evidently not. However, Mia's here." She gestured to a petite blonde seated to their left.

Janet swung back around to me. "Delilah is—I mean, was—

Shona's roommate. The last one."

I bobbed my head in agreement. My heart was racing, and I was having a difficult time paying attention to Janet. I was too busy wondering what strategy to use in order to ask Mia about that fight with Shona. I needed to gather my thoughts.

I said to Janet and Larissa, "Let's sit down so the meeting can start."

Janet straightened, and a pained expression flitted across her face. I think she felt rebuked. "Right you are." Her tone was curt. "We do need to get down to business." She turned and strode to the middle of the circle.

I leaned close to Larissa's ear. "Who's that redhead over there?"

"That's Fayette," Larissa whispered back. "I don't know her, but I hear she's the biggest gossip in this whole group."

"Does she pass along the truth or fabricate stories?"

"From what I hear, she's fairly accurate. She loves to gather news and broadcast it. She cannot keep a secret. I learned that the hard way myself."

"I overheard her talking in the ladies room. She described a fight Shona had with Mia, as if it happened right before Shona got killed. Could be significant, don't you think?"

"No kidding." Larissa's voice rose. Several people looked our way.

"Who can we ask about the fight?" I asked in a whisper.

"Why not Mia herself? She's right over there." Larissa cast a sidelong glance in Mia's direction.

While I sat and absorbed this information, Larissa made a face, and then she continued. "However, Mia won't be reasonable if she guesses we see her as a possible suspect. You've seen how that affects someone."

A shudder racked me when I recalled David's incarceration for a murder he didn't commit. That wouldn't happen to Larissa, not if I could help it. "Who else can we ask about the fight besides her?"

"Eventually we'll need to ask Delilah. Shona may have told her about it, and Delilah can't stay in seclusion forever."

Larissa looked up, and I followed her gaze. A few women were watching us. Larissa stopped talking.

The room went quiet, and Janet called for attention. I moved away from Larissa and settled onto a folding chair, preparing to be bored, regardless of what Larissa promised.

"Thanks, everyone, for coming out tonight," Janet began. Her voice was loud. She oozed confidence. "I know many of you are working on the memorial service for our friend and sister, Shona. We all mourn her passing and will never forget her vibrant commitment to our cause. We know she would want us to keep on waging our struggle with all our collective might."

Murmurs of agreement arose around the room. Janet waited for them to subside. "So let's get down to the nitty-gritty. Who wants to begin? Who's got something to share?"

A middle-aged man in a brown blazer and tan slacks stood up. "I'll start." His voice was deep and resonant.

Wasn't this meeting for women only? I raised a hand to my mouth to stifle my surprise and sat with attention glued on the only man in the room. But as I listened and watched, I grew confused.

Short hair, male attire, deep voice, square hands. But still, despite the visual signs, could this be a woman? My brain grew dizzy trying to analyze the clues. I gave up and tuned in to his words.

"We've all been shaken by what happened to Shona. But she wouldn't want us to stop our struggle for freedom just because we've lost her. Rather, she would want us to forge ahead with renewed vigor. She would urge you to free your minds. Remember how she used to say we may not all want to be like Betty Crocker or our mothers or like Twiggy? But even when we don't want any of those things, we feel we *should want* to be like them."

He—she?—paused for a deep breath, then pressed on.

"Now I urge you in the strongest terms to keep up the struggle. To *fight* the stereotypes imprisoning us. Fight the gender roles forced on us by society, by our parents and boyfriends and husbands. Fight the images advertising pushes at us. Really, don't you just want to be your own wonderful self? Shona would want us to continue our struggle for equality. Let's move forward in her name."

Oh my God. My mouth flapped open. I felt as if a tank had run over me. The speaker was a woman.

A quavering voice came from my left. "I've been to many meetings, but this is the first time I've had courage enough to speak. I want to share something overpowering that happened last week." One of the *normal* women leaned forward in her chair and tossed her hair out of her eyes. She looked nervous but determined to carry on.

"Who's that?" I whispered to Larissa.

"Her name's Becky. I wanted to tell you about her," Larissa said.

I tuned back into what Becky was saying.

"I was driving down Granville Street, feeling bored and as vacant as the desert. I switched on the radio and heard the Stones sing 'Under My Thumb.' And *boom*. I felt like Saul on the road to Damascus. I got it. I understood what you all were trying to tell me. That song did it."

A chorus of shouts rippled around the circle of women, hitting me like a tidal wave.

"Right on."

"Yes, sister."

"Dig it."

More and more women piped up—a veritable Greek chorus lamenting Shona's murder, expressing fear about a killer on the loose, yet still wanting to fight oppression and desiring more freedom. One woman stood and sang a few lines from the sexist song by the Rolling Stones.

After years studying the French and Russian Revolutions in

college and grad school, I realized I was seeing women at the starting line of their own rebellion. This large group showed there were many, many women who felt the same way about women's rights.

While confusing thoughts swamped my head, one fact alone was certain: Larissa had known what she was talking about when she promised that my consciousness would be raised. I might need to join her on the barricades.

A blur of bright pink caught my eye.

Fayette tugged at her shirt as she stood and began speaking. "The first time I read a flyer about women's liberation, I was alone in the laundry room of my apartment building, crying my eyes out."

Larissa elbowed me in the ribs. "That's Fayette, the one you eavesdropped on."

"I know that," I hissed. "Now be quiet and listen."

Fayette was still talking.

"My husband and I moved here from Calgary, and I didn't know anyone. Dirty laundry is bad company, and I wasn't daffy enough to hold conversations with my striped sheets."

Becky giggled and raised her hand. "I have three kids, so I know all about laundry." Raising her hand to talk, Becky was the most timid of those who had spoken up so far.

Maybe I'd thought my own life was good enough already—or perhaps not deserving of improvement. The women gathered in this room were saying something very different, though. I needed to ponder this, but before I could go off into my own head, someone else raised her hand to talk—and I *had* to listen.

"*That* is Mia." Larissa shot me a meaningful look.

Chapter Nineteen

MIA SHOT FROM her chair like a tiny intercontinental missile and paced inside the circle, swaying a little as she walked. At first she didn't utter a word, only prowled like a caged circus animal. Her hands clawed through her pixie haircut, and her eyes shifted from person to person until finally, in front of Fayette's chair, Mia came to a stop.

She shook her finger in Fayette's face. "You said you knew nobody when you moved here from Calgary? Well, how about me? I came up from Seattle with Shona. I wouldn't be in Canada if it weren't for her. Hell, I might not even be alive, and now she's gone—gone, gone, gone." Mia's back arched, her eyes shut, and she let out a loud moan.

This was the girl Larissa described as quiet? Amazement zinged through me like an electric current.

Fayette reached out to Mia, but she jerked away and ran across the circle, where she continued to rant. "How can you sit there, so nice and complacent, acting like nothing's wrong?" She whirled around with her arm outstretched, pointing at everyone in the circle. "None of you would be in this room right now if it weren't for Shona. She was the leader who showed us the way, who pushed us along the path to liberation."

Janet jumped out of her chair, strode over to Mia, and grabbed her arm. I stiffened, expecting an angry eruption. Maybe they'd come to blows?

Mia stood statue-still and stared at Janet for what felt like hours. No one in the room seemed to breathe until Mia wrenched her arm away.

"You, Janet," she shouted. "You think you'll take Shona's place. Well, you can't. Nobody can. Nobody."

Mia's voice broke. Her hands flew to cover her face, and sobs escaped between her fingers. Her eyes peered out like black holes, looking around the room, searching for something, not finding it. Then she ran out, slamming the door so hard that its echo reverberated in my ears.

The silence Mia left in her wake was thunderous. Women sat as if imprisoned in their folding chairs. Their faces registered shock. Nerves prickled up and down my arms. I didn't know these people and was caught up in their drama. I'd never witnessed such an outpouring of emotion before.

Janet remained 'standing in the middle of the circle. Gradually, heads swiveled from the door and around to her.

Her mouth opened and shut several times before she was able to utter a sound. "I guess it was, it was, uh, too soon for Mia to do normal things." The words came out in spasms, not smoothly. Janet sounded dazed but regained strength as she talked. "Okay, then." She threw her shoulders back. "Shall we re-group, see where we go from here?"

A chair creaked. Beside me, Larissa stood.

"Listen here. Mia made a good point." Larissa clutched her hands in front of her. "The only reason I'm here is because Shona urged me to come. Sure, I didn't know Shona as long as some of you did, but she still made a huge difference in my life. Because of that, my world is rocked upside down. And I'll tell you what—right now my feelings are too raw to share with all of you, this many people, at once. My hunch is the more intimate setting of our small groups will work better as we try to come to terms with our grief and figure out how to move forward."

Smoke from a cigarette wafted into Larissa's face. She coughed and waved away the smoke. "Now, excuse me, but I'm leaving. I'm going to find Mia." Bending down to my ear, she whispered, "You better stay here. I'll find you later."

She rushed from the room, crashing into a table in her haste.

I stared after her. My mouth fell open again during Larissa's exit, but I quickly shut it, afraid to look as stupefied as I felt. I must have looked like a fish gasping for air.

Glancing around, however, I realized no one was looking at me. Everyone had watched Larissa's dramatic departure, and all eyes stayed fixed on the door.

How many minutes did we spend, collectively, staring at that stupid door?

For a few moments, no one made a sound.

The masculine-looking woman wearing brown stepped into the void. "Larissa's suggestion is excellent. Since our small groups meet in the next few days, I suggest we all share our feelings then. Perhaps we'll feel better able to cope with the new situation by next week's consciousness-raising session. And in the meantime, be careful. Somewhere out there"—she pointed to a window—"a killer is prowling around. We don't want another casualty. We don't know what his motives are."

Gasps swept around the room. Then murmurs of agreement swelled up. I heard no dissent.

Again, Janet tried to assume command. "All right, be quiet, everyone." She clapped her hands.

After a short pause during which I swore I could hear hearts beating, Fayette pushed her chair back with a screech and stood. "Don't know about the rest of you, but I'm going home now." Fayette flung back her red hair dramatically and marched toward the door.

After another brief pause, two other women followed. Then several more exited. Fayette's leave-taking had summoned a parade.

These women were revolting against Janet's purported leadership. *They voted with their feet* was Trotsky's description of overwhelmed Russian soldiers fleeing the carnage of World War

I, leading to Russia's defeat and then revolution. Trotsky's assessment—or Lenin's, as sources differ—flashed through my mind. This was real democracy in action.

Immersion in Russian history during graduate school led to thoughts like this. Maybe thinking this way wasn't normal, but my brain made comparisons anyway. I'd call it comparative thinking in action.

Janet's eyes grew wide as she watched women leave the room. Her lips pursed, but she managed to cling to civility. "Okay then. Let's do what Dr. Shirley suggests and meet again next week. Same time, same place." Her expression passed from grim to artificially cheery. Placing her hand on her heart, she said, "Until then, peace, sisters."

What a phony. The only useful part of her pathetic little speech was the name of the masculine-looking woman—Dr. Shirley. Otherwise, Janet's attempt at good spirits and optimism sounded false, a jarring end to a meeting meant to heal. I made a snap judgment, deciding Janet wasn't a good—let alone adequate—replacement for the abruptly departed, prematurely dead Shiny Shona.

Ducking my head, not wanting to meet anyone's eyes, I grabbed my purse and hurried out of the room, desperate to locate Larissa.

We needed to put our heads together. We needed to analyze this chaotic meeting.

Shona's leadership qualities were amazing—everyone agreed—yet they'd also caused disruption—jealousy and anguish, certainly—and perhaps even rage of the murderous variety. Maybe I'd witnessed the same high emotions that had given rise to murder.

Yet if I'd sensed possible motives, what about means and opportunity?

Could any of the women have slipped poison into her thermos at SUB when she wasn't watching?

I joined the tail end of the parade, and once I was in the

hallway, I mingled with the others. Some talked with their neighbors in hushed voices. Because no one knew me, I slipped easily through the crowd, on the lookout for Larissa. When I didn't see her, I tried the ladies room.

Larissa and Mia leaned against the sink, two short girls with their heads bent close—Larissa's long brown tresses covered most of Mia's short blond hair. Both were so intent on their conversation that neither looked up when I entered. I waited to see if they would notice me. When they didn't, I chose not to interrupt them. If they were so engrossed, it must be about something important. Better I just let them be.

I took out my comb and fixed my hair. Next I reapplied eyeliner.

Did Gloria Steinem wear makeup? She was so gorgeous, she might not need it.

Still Mia and Larissa whispered on, and I fought against my rising impatience. I was unsuccessful.

I cleared my throat. "Excuse me. Larissa, do you know when you'll be ready to leave?"

Larissa raised her head and eventually looked in my direction, blinking as if she didn't recognize me. She shook her head and passed a hand over her face. "What? Leave?" Again she blinked. "Uh, give me a moment."

She turned back to Mia, who held onto the counter with one hand and used the other to wipe her eyes with a paper towel.

"Will you be okay if I leave?" Larissa's voice was solicitous. "I'll call you tomorrow to see how you're doing."

In a tone made husky from tears, Mia said, "Sure. Go. Thanks for talking to me." She grabbed Larissa in a fierce hug. "You had nothing to do with Shona's death. I know it. Please, please, push that right out of your mind." Then Mia fled into a stall and banged the door shut.

"Let's get out of here." Larissa pushed me toward the door.

Out in the hall, she collapsed against the wall, and her legs wobbled. She pinched the bridge of her nose and rubbed her eyes.

"Whew. That was intense."

"Is Mia going to be okay?" I asked. "Back there in the meeting, she had quite a meltdown. But I swear you told me she was meek and mild."

Larissa cocked her head and raised her eyebrows. "Yeah, I know that's what I said, but she appears to have changed. From what she told me in there, she had some kind of breakdown and then came out the other side—like I said—changed. Her grief is one thing, totally understandable, but something else is going on too. She wouldn't tell me, but she's outraged about something—or somebody. Maybe it's Janet, but I doubt that's it."

"Maybe Delilah? Isn't she Shona's new roommate, the one who replaced Mia?"

"Right. But..." Larissa shook her head. "That's not it. Mia just told me..." Larissa looked at the students milling around beside us and mashed her lips together.

"What's wrong?" I asked.

"We can't talk here. Wait until we get back in the car."

"Okay, let's go." I was glad to get moving. My nerves felt frayed to the snapping point.

We weaved through the clogged hall and were about to break into the clear when someone stepped into our path.

"How about a copy of *The Georgia Straight*? It's always free." A fellow with a scraggly beard shoved a newspaper in my face.

Startled, I managed to hang on to my cool. "No thanks. I don't live here." I moved to push past the guy but then, realizing Larissa wasn't close behind, I turned and called to her. "Aren't you coming?"

She caught up with me and took hold of my elbow, bent close to my car. "That's Stan Persky. He used to hang out with Jack Kerouac and Allen Ginsberg in San Francisco. Now he's a UBC grad student and a founder of that activist rag he wants you to read."

"Is he a draft resister too?" Wasn't every young American male living in Canada these days?

"Oh no. He served in the U.S. Navy and was honorably discharged, but he's against the war anyway. Shona and he were great pals." Suddenly Larissa punched me on the arm. "Hey, maybe Stan knows if she made any bad enemies." She twisted to look back at Stan.

"You don't want to talk to him *now,* do you?"

"Guess not." Larissa hesitated, sounding crestfallen. "Yeah, you're right. We can catch him later. I need to digest what went down tonight—plus all that stuff Mia told me."

"So come on then." This time I grabbed her arm and dragged her forward, before she could dither and change her mind. "I want to hear Mia's news while it's still fresh in your mind. I crave the tiniest details, every last one of them."

We walked perhaps another ten feet before a loud male voice abruptly bellowed after us. "Stop. Wait for Mia."

I whirled and saw Stan Persky.

Following him was the small figure of Mia, running our way.

Now what was going on?

Chapter Twenty

TINY WAIF-LIKE MIA hurtled toward us—short legs pumping fast, arms flailing. Larissa reached out to catch her before she collided with us.

What was up? She was out of control.

She panted slightly, and her eyes darted back and forth. Short strands of her hair stood straight up, adding to her agitated appearance.

Larissa kept hold of her arm and peered closely into her face. "Mia, are you okay?"

Mia's panting slowed. Her head drooped, her eyes shut, and then she began to take great gulps of breath. When she raked a hand through her hair, I understood why it stood on end. She looked back and forth between Larissa and me. When Mia pointed an index finger at me in what I took as an accusatory gesture, I prepared for a verbal onslaught.

I couldn't have been more wrong.

She said, "I'm driving down to Seattle tomorrow to see Shona's folks, and I'll need company on the trip. Hell, I may even need someone to spell my driving." When she laughed, the sound was bitter and harsh. "Just look at me. I'm in no condition to drive, but I must go see the Spektors. Can you come with me? Please, oh please say you will."

Larissa looked at me, question marks leaping from her eyes.

I was, for once, speechless.

Mia plowed on. "Austin, we haven't met, but Larissa says you're hunting for a suspect in Shona's murder. Well, I want to know who killed her too. I know Shona thought the world of Larissa, and Larissa vouched for you, and that's good enough for me. If you want to come along, I'd be grateful. Maybe you can share your suspicions on the drive and then get background info from Shona's parents. I'll tell you anything I can." She swayed against Larissa, wilting into her body. Her energy was visibly draining out of her.

Larissa stroked Mia's head and murmured "there, there" and "it'll be okay" while I tried to come up with a response.

I couldn't have guessed she'd make such an offer. Wouldn't have guessed that anyone would.

Over the top of Mia's head, Larissa and I studied each other. When I smiled and nodded yes, Larissa gently moved Mia away. Larissa said to Mia, "If you think Shona's parents wouldn't mind our coming along, then we'll be glad to make the trip."

I added, "Thank you, Mia. I appreciate your trust." I sought the right words to reassure her. "I wanted to talk to Shona's parents but hadn't figured out a way to do that yet. This will be perfect."

Mia's expression brightened—her face beatific, like a Botticelli angel. "What a relief. I'm so grateful to you both."

With our agreement confirmed, Mia achieved a degree of control and strength that I hadn't seen in her before. We discussed our travel plans for the next day, and I was explaining that I needed to bring Wyatt, when Larissa yelped.

"Damn it, how could I forget?" She stamped her foot. "I can't go with you. The RCMP told me not to leave town. Damn, damn, damn."

Larissa rarely swore, even this mildly. However, since my arrival in BC, she'd already cursed more than she had over the course of our entire friendship. That in itself was a clue to the tension that gripped her. I silently congratulated myself for traveling across the continent to support her. I hoped my support would lessen her anxiety, even if I didn't discover the killer.

I bent my head toward Mia. "If Larissa can't come, do you still want me along?"

"Would you mind?" Mia asked Larissa.

One look at Larissa's face made the answer obvious. "Actually," she said, "if Austin is my stand-in, then I'll feel better. I'd planned to take the day off work tomorrow anyway, but now I won't. I'll skip work on Monday instead. Then we can have a free day to check any ideas you pick up from the Spektors." Larissa glanced at each of us in turn. "Sound good to you two?"

Mia and I nodded.

I was musing how easily Mia had accepted our role as sleuths when she spun around. "What is it, Stan?"

None of us had noticed that Stan Persky had stuck close by after he delivered Mia. Now, rubbing his hands together, he bowed slightly.

"I cared a lot for Shona," he said, "and admired her activism. If I can do something to help find her killer, anything at all, just tell me. I wrote a piece for the next issue of *The Georgia Strait* about her work for justice and equality. With her death we lost a great champion for freedom and fairness. She was a radical through and through." He hung his head for a few moments, and then heaved a mighty sigh. "Now I'd better get back to work."

Larissa thanked him, said she'd keep in touch, and Stan slipped back into the crowd—and returned to shilling his newspapers, I presumed.

Mia mumbled something—I couldn't hear her words, but she looked calmer than she had when she'd joined us. Maybe she just needed consolation. And maybe we could help her, but maybe not. Her despair seemed bottomless, but it was also laced with explosive anger.

"You all right now, Mia?" Larissa asked.

"Better, thanks," she said.

Larissa said, "Let's go somewhere and talk. You two can make your arrangements and get acquainted." She started to walk, then stopped so fast that I ran into her. "How about the pub on Tenth? I need some serious unwinding after tonight's meeting. A beer would work great."

"Hoping to see the nice waiter again?" I winked at her.

"Who's that?" Mia asked.

Larissa's cheeks flamed a becoming pink. "Never mind, Austin's joking."

Mia went off to get her car, and Larissa and I arranged to meet her at the pub after we swung by Raisa's house to check on Wyatt.

By the time we trudged our way to the car, we were soaked to the skin. Again. This was becoming a constant feature of my stay in Vancouver. Now my new clothes matched my old ones. What a climate.

I examined the windshield. Empty, thank heavens.

The car windows steamed up as soon as we got inside. Larissa found a towel in the back seat. She used it to pat her hair, then passed it to me.

"I'm glad we're going to the pub." I dabbed without much success at my wet clothes and hair and scowled at the ineffective towel. "Spending time with Mia tonight will make the drive tomorrow less awkward. She seems so mercurial, and I want to know how to get along with her. I don't want to set her off. I've seen how she can be, and it's scary."

"I don't know her all that well myself," Larissa said, "but like I said before, ordinarily she's quiet. I even thought she was shy, so her outburst tonight surprised me too."

"When you talked in the ladies room, did Mia share any thoughts about Shona's killer? Quick, tell me *everything,* and maybe there will be leads to follow up on." I gave up trying to dry my hair and threw the towel into the back seat. "I hope the meeting with Shona's parents goes well."

"You fret too much, Austin."

"Yeah, and what else is new?"

We cackled. This was one of our comfortable routines.

I cleared my throat and used the edge of my skirt to dry my legs. "By the way, you hadn't mentioned Shona's last name before. *Spektor* sounds Russian. Was her family Russian?"

"They're Russian Jews who arrived in Seattle after World War Two," Larissa said.

That sobered me up fast. "Were they Holocaust survivors?"

"I don't know. Better ask Mia."

Larissa swung the car out of the parking lot and headed toward University Boulevard. The campus wasn't difficult to learn. You could tell the direction you were going because the mountains rising above Vancouver were across the bay and always to the north. They never moved, and that was strange comfort. So far, the most comforting thing about being in Vancouver was not getting turned around, not getting lost. Growing up in the flat coastal plains of south Texas, I had never learned mountains could work like my compass. Even the Texas Hill Country didn't provide enough of a skyline to get oriented.

"Now, about Mia," I said. "You get any new tidbits from her?"

"Absolutely." The word flew out of Larissa's mouth. "She said Shona received threatening calls when they roomed together. Shona brushed them off, but the calls unnerved Mia."

"When did Shona move out and start rooming with Delilah? Did the calls continue after the move? And why did Shona move in with Delilah anyway, if she and Mia were such great pals?"

"Hold up, partner." Larissa chuckled as she swung out onto the boulevard. "You piled on too many questions for me to keep straight. Don't you realize conditions are hazardous in the rain?"

"Sorry," I hung my head. "I won't do it again."

"Oh, sure. That's a good one."

That caused another round of cackling.

"Okay, listen. I wasn't able to get Mia to tell me why Shona changed roommates. I *do* know it was six weeks ago."

She stopped at a light and waved a hand in my direction. "The main thing is, once Shona was gone, Mia says the threatening phone calls stopped. However, Mia doesn't know if the calls followed Shona over to Delilah's place. Shona refused to discuss the subject."

"So when the RCMP questioned Mia, she told them about the calls?"

"She did. Yet she also complained her interview with the Mounties was short and sketchy. She thinks they aren't concerned with how scared she and Shona were. Mia says the Mounties kept leaving to run down the hall to interview someone else about the other murder."

"The one at the nude beach?"

"Right."

"That has more sex appeal and will get more press." I leaned my head against the cool window. "All kidding aside, I wonder what makes that other murder more important than Shona's."

"Don't jump to conclusions just because of Mia's impression. She probably was a complete wreck when the Mounties talked to her. Her senses couldn't have been acute."

"You're calling the calls 'threatening.' What does that mean? What did the caller say?"

Larissa took a deep breath and let it out slowly. "The calls began with raspy breathing, no talk. They seemed like ordinary prank calls, according to Mia. Then, after a week, the pattern shifted. If Shona answered the phone, a male voice she couldn't identify made threats. The guy said stuff like this—*Be careful or you'll get hurt.* After several of those calls, he escalated the language."

"Escalated to what?" I asked.

"To death threats."

"Death threats? And the Mounties didn't take that seriously?"

A streetlight's beam illuminated a tear trickling down Larissa's cheek. "After that, Shona stopped answering the phone. And then she moved out."

Who was the anonymous caller? Certainly not Larissa. That should help get her off the Mounties' suspect list, assuming they believed Mia about the calls. But then, who had made those calls?

Mia and Delilah were still alive; could they identify the caller's deep voice if they heard it again? If so, were they also in danger? So many questions that needed answers, and so little time to find them. I needed to get cracking.

Chapter Twenty-One

TALK ABOUT DEATH threats sent my thoughts reeling back to last year—to Reg Simpson's corpse. It had been spread out on the floor in a church, floating in a lake of blood. Considering the subject of murder too deeply plunged me into memories of David's arrest for killing Reg. But just as I couldn't have stood helpless when David was under suspicion, I couldn't ignore Larissa's plight.

She bumped my arm. "Hey, pal, you're miles away. We're here."

I shook my head hard, both to knock sense into it and to snap out of my thoughts.

"Sorry. I'll dash in and check if all's well with Wyatt. I hope he's fast asleep, and if he is, I'll be right back. If not, I'll come tell you anyway, and you can go meet Mia by yourself."

The dark sedan was no longer parked across the street. I was mildly amused to feel my spirits lift. Maybe Larissa was right—I did fret too much. Here I was projecting imaginary bad guys onto a quiet street in safe Vancouver.

More good luck. Wyatt was asleep, looking like a peaceful cherub when I checked. As I walked past Raisa's door, she stepped out into the hallway.

"That strange man called again," she said, "asking to speak to you. Wait here. I will get phone number." She disappeared into her bedroom and returned in a moment with a slip of paper.

"Thank you." I eyed the area code for Washington, D.C. "It was Jones, right? Did he say anything else, Raisa?"

"Nyet. Jones wants to make sure you know he tried to reach you." She stepped away, back toward her bedroom, and then turned again to me. "Oh, also he asked if husband passed on message. I said not sure. Seemed to upset him."

I shut my eyes for a moment. "The time difference with the East Coast makes it hard to call Jones at a decent hour." I leaned back against the wall. "What should I do?"

"Is okay, Austin. I make clear you be back late. He said he calls again. Will catch you sometime." She peered over her reading glasses. "*Did* husband give you message?"

"Yes, he did."

"Khorosho. Next time I tell Jones." She tapped a finger beside her nose. "Oh yes," she said finally, "you had second call. Canadian Pacific found luggage. Is in Mexico City."

"What?" I couldn't help myself. I yelped loudly.

"Da, *pravda*. Will take days to come."

"Swell. My luggage will arrive after I'm back in Toronto." I clutched my newly acquired skirt, now rumpled and moist. "Guess I'll wear this again."

Raisa said, "I washed your old ones. Ironed too. You wear tomorrow."

Her dedication was touching. "Thank you so much, but you really shouldn't have. You are more than generous, putting me and my son up in your home."

She ducked her head. "Shall I make tea?" She pulled her robe tight around her neck and stepped toward the stairway.

"Larissa's waiting in the car, and we're meeting a friend at the pub." Even in the dim light of the hallway, I saw Raisa raise her eyebrows. Immediately I felt guilty.

"Wyatt's sound asleep now. I'll be back in time to give him his bottle around midnight. We need to talk to Shona's friend because we're trying to figure out who killed Shona."

Raisa jammed her hands into the pockets of her robe and

made a noncommittal noise that was not the *ochen khorosho* I hoped to hear. After she returned to her room, I fled outside.

If I got involved in the women's movement, would I have less guilt over wanting to accomplish something aside from being a wife and mother? Somehow I doubted it. My mother's repetitive admonitions provided the fully orchestrated soundtrack of my life, and I didn't know how to change the record.

When I rejoined Larissa, I told her about Jones's latest phone call.

"Just seeing the look on your face, I knew you were upset," she said. "However, you should listen to my aunt. She's right. There's no cause to be so tense. This situation—whatever it is—will work itself out. Besides, you know why he's calling."

"But I don't know any *details*." My voice sounded shrill in my ears. "Why is Jones warning me about the senator and his sidekick? Why do they care about me anymore? I never want to see either one again *ever*."

Five minutes later when we drew up in front of the pub, I was still moaning about Senator Simpson.

"Snap out of it," Larissa said. "Let's go inside for a cold one." The car's dome light turned on when she opened the door, in time for me to see the glint in her eyes. "Your overactive imagination will be engaged in there, watching to see if I flirt with the waiter."

The idea appealed to me, I confess.

"All right, let's go. That's more fun than worrying about the former senator." Larissa had met Simpson and his aide, and she wasn't concerned about them.

The pub was a blissful cocoon of good-hearted cheer. The rough voice of Bob Dylan sang "Lay Lady Lay." The sentimental ballad fit the atmosphere like Cinderella sliding into her glass slipper and reminded me of David saying "stay, lady, stay" only two nights ago.

Damn, but I missed him.

We walked past crowded booths to find Mia ensconced

already, nursing a beer and fidgeting with a coaster. She looked up when we approached.

"I didn't order for you. Didn't know what you'd want."

A tall waiter approached. Not Larissa's intended.

Larissa and I ordered Molsons, and I asked if Gary was on duty.

"Yep," the guy said.

"Would you ask him to come over when he's free? Please."

Somebody kicked my shin hard under the table. It wasn't Mia.

After the waiter left, Larissa glared at me. "Why'd you say that?"

"You already set me up for this"—I grinned—"so it's not my fault. Gary's the only male you've expressed the least bit of interest in. If you're *not* going to make a move, then I'll make one for you. I won't be here in Vancouver forever, you know. I don't have all month to get you two together."

Mia set her beer glass down. "I bet Larissa doesn't ever need to make the first move."

Larissa pursed her lips—as usual, an enchanting sight. No one else could make that expression look appealing. Yet she deserved a man who would appreciate her not just for her physical allure but for her kindness and intelligence. Maybe I could help her find one—Gary perhaps?

She said, "Guys can be so tiresome, but it's true. I don't need to flirt because—"

I jumped in. "All she does is enter a room, and wham, the boys fall down at her feet—or at least look as if they're restraining themselves from doing that."

"Gary didn't act like that when we were here the other night. Remember?" Larissa looked wistful, almost unsure of herself. This was new, her yearning for masculine attention.

"True enough," I said, "but he acted attentive and cared enough to pass on gossip he'd heard in the pub. If you still believe he showed little interest, then that's why he intrigues you. It's a new experience."

A bell rang in my head. Now I recalled what had been nudging at the back of my consciousness. "I need a good mental image of how Shona looked," I said, "Do either of you have her picture? How attractive was *she* to men? I was told her lab co-workers resented her, but I wonder about males in general."

Larissa and Mia exchanged glances.

Larissa said, "I don't have her photo. Do you, Mia?"

Mia's cheeks reddened. "Maybe. Let me check." She set her purse on the table. "She wasn't short, like Larissa and me, but not as tall as you either. Shona was about five six, I'd say, but she seemed even bigger. The force of her personality was that strong. But no, she wasn't what you'd call seductive."

Larissa and I sipped our beers while Mia rummaged through her purse and then her billfold. When she pulled out bits of paper and laid them on the table, Larissa's waiter walked up.

"Good evening, ladies. Did you want to see me?"

Hmm...I hadn't prepared anything to say.

But I shouldn't have been concerned. Larissa's feminine skills took charge.

She lowered her head slightly and looked up at him through the long fringe of her lashes. In a silken voice she said, "You were so kind when you told me the Mounties were here checking on me. Now I wonder, Garrett, if you've got any more tidbits of info to offer?"

He sucked on his lower lip and looked embarrassed. "How'd you know my name's Garrett? Everyone always calls me Gary."

Larissa's eyes grew wide. "Oh, good heavens. Now I remember you introduced yourself as Gary. I'm sorry. You just look more like a Garrett to me." She turned to me. "Didn't I tell you that, Austin?"

I bobbed my head, relieved not to speak.

"No need to apologize." His whole face reddened, poor guy. "I don't use my full name, but when you say it, I like it."

The two budding lovebirds gazed into each other's eyes long

enough that I got bored and wiggled around in my chair.

"So then," I said, "have you heard anything new, uh, Garrett?"

His answering smile was wide and showed his dimples, one on either cheek. Leaping way ahead, my overactive mind guessed that if he and Larissa ever made babies together, they'd be stunners too.

"Better if you all call me the same name—Garrett. But don't tell anyone else, eh?"

Bingo. Now I knew he was Canadian.

I crossed my heart with my right hand. "I solemnly swear."

Mia was still digging through her purse. "So, have you heard anything new or not?" Her tone was sharp. Larissa twitched a little, startled.

"Matter of fact, I have." Garrett bent low over the table and reached toward Larissa, but stopped short of touching her. Then he crouched down, putting him at her eye level.

He said, "Around noon, a fellow came in and hung around the bar a long time. He ranted like some do, about being unhappy at home, how his wife didn't understand him and so forth. Nothing new there. I wasn't paying attention until something he said snagged me. He'd switched to whining about women's lib. Said his wife had changed since she started going to meetings at UBC. Said he had to get a sitter tonight for their three kids because she wasn't home like she should be, tending to them, and he had to drive down to Seattle and back."

He paused to see if he'd caught our interest. He needn't have worried. We were staring in rapt attention, eyes glued on him. I wondered if Larissa and Mia felt as I did, with the hair on their arms at attention. Maybe this story wasn't about the killer, but it felt portentous. I crossed my fingers, hoping the information would lead somewhere interesting.

Or perhaps I was just desperate for a great big fat clue.

"Was there more? Did you get his name? " I couldn't stand the suspense.

"There's more." He rubbed the table top with the towel he kept at his waist and then leaned on the dry section. His eyes never left Larissa. "Another guy at the bar started challenging the first one. He suggested that if *he* were the woman's husband, he'd have no trouble reining her in. As you can imagine, that got the husband stirred up."

Larissa said, "Was the sexist pig a regular here?"

Garrett stood up to his full height, looking down on us. I didn't like how the deliberate maneuver made me feel.

"Now wait a minute," he said. "I don't take to name-calling. You don't want to get down in the gutter with the likes of that man, do you?"

Larissa's jaw jutted out, a sign of her anger, and one I knew well.

"If I have to, then I will. Most men don't have any idea what women have to put up with and—"

"Let's not fight the war of the sexes," Mia said. "We have other issues to focus on now. Like, for instance, did this man say anything else to Garrett?" She arched her eyebrows at him.

He didn't answer immediately. By the way his mouth tightened, I had the impression he was reining in his feelings, his temper.

"Okay, take it easy, girls," he said finally.

"Stop saying that. We are *women*, not girls." When Larissa said the word *girls*, she drew out the S for such a long time, she actually hissed.

Wow, if this was Larissa's idea of flirting, then it was a darned good thing she was so pretty. She was positively combative this evening.

"Let's keep to the subject at hand," I said. "Garrett, please finish your story. We can tell you're one of the good guys." Then the devil made me add, "Probably."

The grin that spread across his face and activated his dimples broke the tension. We all laughed, even if it did sound like a nervous titter.

"Okay, here's how the rest went down," he said. "The first guy—the sexist pig, if you will, or just plain husband—stood up and knocked over his bar stool. He sprang over to his challenger, grabbed him by the shirt, and demanded they take it outside. They'd see who was more of a man. I got a bartender to help separate them. Then the unhappy husband stomped out, hurling insults as he left."

"Has he been in here before? Did anyone recognize him?" I said, hoping for a lead.

Garrett said, "I asked around, but no one remembered him. I knew right away I wanted to tell you about him, Larissa, because of the murder investigation and all. I promised you I'd keep my eyes and ears open, and I have. Oh yes, now I remember. He said his name was Hank."

The bartender yelled at him from the bar. Garrett glanced over his shoulder, then back at our table. "Sorry, got to go. I'll stop by again later if I can."

Larissa reached out her hand and laid it lightly on his arm, where the contrast of its delicacy with his biceps was striking. "Please try to find out who that guy is. I'll write out my phone number so you can reach me if you have news."

His dimples reappeared. "Then I'll definitely see you again later." After giving a nod to Mia and me and a wink to Larissa, Garrett hurried off to the bar.

Larissa watched him leave, and her face took on a dreamy expression. I made a snap decision not to tease her about Garrett. I'd be pleased if she could snag something worthwhile out of the murder inquiry. A nice new boyfriend would count as such a trophy, so why kid her and get her defenses up?

Mia shoved her purse aside. "Sorry, Austin. I couldn't find a photo of Shona. I'd say she was cute enough, in her way. Had gobs of thick, wavy dark hair, but dressed like she worked outdoors." She looked down at her own clothes. "Kind of like me, as a matter of fact. However, men weren't drawn to her as a rule. She was too pushy. That's the word men used a lot, *pushy*, even some of her professors, and they should have known better." She gave a little sniff. "Does that answer your question well enough? I imagine you can see photos at her parents' apartment tomorrow, unless they're too distraught to show them."

"That's right," I said, starting to worry again about meeting the Spektors. Nosing around among the debris left behind by murder was not a frolicsome pursuit. What had I gotten myself into?

Mia said, "So let's settle our travel plans for tomorrow. What time can you leave, Austin? I want to do the roundtrip in one day, so the earlier we start, the better."

"My baby wakes up around six," I said, "so if you swing by around seven, will that work?"

"Sure," Mia said. "Driving down will take three hours, max, unless we get stuck going over the border. You never know. If we're lucky we can get to the Spektors' place in two and a half hours."

"Wyatt will probably sleep all the way in the car."

"I hope you have your driver's license with you," Mia said. "You'll need some kind of identification in case the border guards ask. We'll have a long day, but I'm up for it."

"Me too," I said. "At least we can show the Spektors support over Shona's loss."

"Plus gather background about potential suspects," Larissa chimed in. "Really, doing something, anything, is so much better than moping and whining and gnashing our teeth. Sure wish I could come with you. I always wanted to see where Shona grew up."

Mia giggled. "It's certainly different. But she didn't seem to mind."

I was puzzled. "What was so special about her place?"

Larissa took a swig of beer, placed the glass on the table top, and grinned at me. "The Spektors have an apartment a block from the University of Washington, so it's well situated."

Mia made a choking sound. "But that's not the key thing.

You're being too coy, Larissa. The Spektors' apartment is on top of a mortuary. Mr. Spektor is always on call, available to grieving family members whenever they want to stop by and visit with their deceased loved ones."

I smothered a gasp.

And I had signed on to visit this place tomorrow? Yikes.

A mortuary setting didn't bode well. I'd only been inside one once, for an elderly aunt's funeral, yet the experience had haunted my dreams for weeks after that. An older cousin had teased me without mercy, spooking me good. He told me what was behind walls, in locked drawers, and said he smelled human decay and nasty chemicals seeping out of cracks in the walls.

My imagination was too vivid for my own good.

And did I really want to take a baby into this mortuary apartment? Maybe my thinking was crazy. My cousin told me visiting a mortuary was like wallowing in death. The thought had stuck with me since I was eight years old, and I didn't know how to get rid of the memory.

And I most emphatically didn't want to wallow in death.

Chapter Twenty-Two

MY SLEEP WAS fitful, with images more macabre than usual playing through my dreams. My ordinary dreams were intricate and fanciful enough. A recent one had David show up as a polar bear, later become a butterfly, then turn into a wise and studious owl, all the while speaking German, a language he didn't know. I was used to that type of dream. But a skeletal version of David wearing the striped uniform of Nazi concentration camps was too much.

The dream grew worse as he hopped from one open casket into another and ended up dog paddling in a raging river of blood that formed a moat around Mad King Ludwig's Neuschwanstein Castle in Bavaria. My psyche had outdone itself. Signposts in the dream pointed out that Dachau was only one hundred kilometers away.

All this just because Larissa said the Spektors were Jewish immigrants who'd arrived after World War II?

In between flips and flops to one side and then the other, I had worried about getting up in time to call Jones first thing in the morning. I worried about returning from Seattle in the evening to call David on time. My worry lists were expanding and without end. Only this time they seemed more ominous than usual

Really, it was amazing I managed to get out of bed some mornings, I was such a worrywart.

Some people called that courage, keeping on in the face of

fear. I wasn't one of them, but hearing anyone make that point did serve to cheer me up.

As a result of all this, when the alarm sounded at six—dear little Wyatt, crying for his next bottle—I was less rested than when I'd gone to bed the night before.

The house was so silent, I assumed no one else was awake yet. I carried Wyatt downstairs to prepare his bottle. He was happily noshing away on it when Professor Klimenko entered the kitchen.

"*Dobroe utro.*" He went straight to the percolator and started coffee.

"Good morning to you too, sir."

"Larissa tells me your old CIA trainer called, *da?*"

"Da."

"What does he want?"

"*Ne znaiyu.* I do know he says Senator Simpson is in town with his usual sidekick, Darrel." I stopped to watch his face, to see how this news hit him. When Professor Klimenko winced but made no comment, I added. "I'll call Jones as soon as Wyatt finishes his breakfast."

"Let me help." He held his hands out to Wy. "I will hold him and you make your call to ease your mind. I remember how tense you can get." Smiling warmly, he took the bottle from me, and then gathered my son into his arms. He made clucking noises to Wy as I padded quietly out to the telephone stand.

I checked the clock. First I'd call David. Maybe he'd still be in our apartment, not yet on campus. Although I was a bit afraid of talking to him, I missed him. Hearing his voice would cheer me up. If he did harangue me to return to Toronto sooner than I wanted, that was a price I'd gladly pay.

But luck wasn't on my side. The phone rang and rang, no answer.

Damn it. Patience wasn't a virtue I possessed or, truth be told, one I wanted to learn.

What a pity we couldn't afford one of those answering

150

services some people used. That way I could at least leave a message, let David know I was thinking about him. He would have no idea I'd been longing to hear his voice.

I settled in beside the phone again and punched in the numbers for Jones. My call was answered after only one ring.

"What?"

Even from that one word, I recognized the growly voice of Mr. Jones.

"Austin here. You called me." Talking to him made me turn laconic. Always in a hurry, he appreciated terseness.

"Been watching your back for a year now, Austin. Ever since I dug up intel that says deposed Senator Reginald Simpson blames you for his political decline. So I keep tabs on your whereabouts and his. This week I tripped over something else. He hired a hit man. When I found out you flew to Vancouver and he and Darrel are there too, I figured you needed to be brought into the big picture. Have you seen him yet?"

Thud. Thud. Thud. My heart beat double time. I had trouble breathing.

"No, I haven't." I remembered the dark sedan from last night. "Unless he's shadowing the house where I'm staying. What can you tell me about this? Do you know what this guy looks like, who I should look out for? I'm here for—"

"Never mind that. I know all about it."

Damn, he was good. That was a comfort anyway. My relationship to Jones had developed like the one I had with DS McKinnon. Older men seemed to like me and want to teach me. I liked them if they were straight shooters and rational, like my father. Now I suspected that Jones was taking extra care of me once he'd tripped over the news that I could be in trouble.

I explained about the dark sedan.

"Dark sedan is my guy."

"That's a relief." And a surprise. "So what should I do? I have my son with me."

Mr. Jones whistled softly.

"That worries me," he said. "I'll warn my guys. And remember your training. Gotta run now."

He hung up before I got answers to my questions.

I sprang from the chair and stalked around the living room. If David learned about this, he'd flip out for sure. So I wasn't going to tell him.

What he didn't know wouldn't hurt him—my mantra since we'd gotten married.

After two circuits of the living room, I stopped to watch Larissa stumble downstairs in her pajamas, rubbing her eyes.

She hugged me. "I'm bummed I can't go with you. Don't worry about Mia. You two will be fine together."

"Piece of cake." I waved a hand in the air. "I've got bigger problems."

I plunked down on the sofa and spilled out the news from Jones. As I finished the story, Professor Klimenko joined us, carrying Wy. At the same time, Raisa came downstairs.

I sank back against the cushions and opened my arms to Wyatt. Once I held him, kissed his soft fluff of hair, I felt better. I retold the latest developments, knowing everyone in the house had to understand there was real danger afoot.

"In short," I concluded, "I'm really, really sorry for doubling your troubles. You don't need this additional hassle. Maybe I should move out."

Raisa stood, feet apart, hands on hips. "Nyet. We care for you." She moved over to Professor Klimenko, nudged his arm. "Pravda?"

"True," he said. "We are in this together."

Raisa walked to a cabinet, took a key from a drawer, used it to open another drawer at eye level, and pulled out a gun. "I know how to use. We both do."

Professor Klimenko nodded. "Let's finish our breakfast. You need to be ready when Mia arrives."

Their calmness reassured me, making my conversation with Jones like a bad dream. Still, I barely touched my breakfast. When

Mia swung by to pick Wy and me up, I asked her for the Spektors' phone number and gave it to Raisa. Events were piling up, making me too antsy to be out of touch, unreachable.

#

My mood was glum when our excursion to the States began. Yet by the time we hit the open road, my spirits recovered and actually started to soar. The day was bright and clear, no rain clouds in sight.

This was the weather Larissa had boasted about. I understood why natives said a day like this made other dreary ones bearable, even if there were far too many of them in a row to be reasonably endured.

Mia's VW minibus had big windows through which I watched the passing scenery—in all its over-blown gorgeousness. Wyatt lay snuggled in my arms, fast asleep, and Mia and I were buckled in for our one hundred forty-mile drive south into Washington and on into the heart of Seattle.

What a pity the purpose of our trip was so gloomy, to meet with grieving parents whose daughter had been brutally murdered, people who were possible Holocaust survivors who now lived in a funeral home. That seemed like tragedy on top of catastrophe to me. I studied Wy's sweet face, and the perfection of his peachy cheeks kept my thoughts from spiraling further. I'd do anything to keep him safe.

"Mind if I turn on the radio?" Mia trained her gaze on Wy, who lay on my lap. "Will the noise bother him? He looks so peaceful like that."

"Sure, go ahead. Car rides make him sleepy."

She turned on the radio and punched buttons until she hit a station with Dylan encouraging everyone to get stoned.

"This okay with you?" Mia said.

"Hearing that song and thinking about the words amuses me." My giggles disturbed Wyatt, who kicked and twisted in my arms but stayed asleep, thank goodness.

"A drug song—how perfect for a ride in your magic bus," I said, bopping my head to the music. "If Mother could see me now, she'd know her worst fears had come true."

Unlike my conservatively painted VW bus back in Texas—the old tired one that David and I had driven around our Texas college—Mia's version was decorated à la hippie fashion. Not one square inch of the exterior showed original paint. Instead, swirls and daisies and peace signs merged in a phantasmagoria of colors. Truthfully, I was a little embarrassed to be riding in this counterculture mobile, but nobody knew me, so why should I care?

"It's not a drug song," Mia said. " 'Rainy Day Women 12 and 35' refers to Bible passages about people getting stoned to death. Dylan's down on throwing stones, not up on getting high on marijuana."

"Good grief, are you sure? I love Dylan and read everything about him I can find. Where'd you pick that up?"

Mia shook her head and pursed her lips—signs I took to mean she was irritated I doubted her. "Some backup musician who'd played with him told me Dylan's interpretation. It makes sense to me."

I decided to be charitable. However, I really, really wanted to argue since I fancied myself an expert on Dylan.

Instead, I said, "Maybe you're right, but I bet you ninety-nine percent of the listeners think he's singing about getting high. And, hey, how about this? If I were visiting Vancouver as a musician, I'd call my trip the Rainy Day Women Tour. Pretty cool, huh? Like the Beatles and their Magical Mystery Tour, right? After all, with the exception of today, it's rained every day I've been out here, and the day hasn't ended yet. Naturally the *women* part comes in because Larissa is trying to make me into an adherent of women's liberation."

Mia took her eyes off the road long enough to scowl in my direction. "And you think that's a bad thing?"

"Of course not. I just don't like being pushed. If she'd quit proselytizing, she'd realize I'm moving in that direction without being harassed. Any woman who's not a feminist—anyone under thirty, that is—has to be nuts."

"Yeah, right on, baby." Her hand left the steering wheel long enough to wave a clenched fist.

We rode in companionable silence for a while, enjoying a succession of singers. First Marvin Gaye, then the 5th Dimension, and then The Guess Who singing one of my favorites, "These Eyes."

"You know that's a Canadian group, right?" I said.

"Yep. Heard 'em in concert once," Mia replied.

When we finally escaped Vancouver's sprawl, I felt jubilant at traveling. My mood crashed, however, when Glen Campbell started to croon about working as a Wichita lineman.

A tear trickled down my left cheek.

"Are you okay, Austin?" Mia's voice was gentle. "What's bringing you down? You seemed happy and spunky only minutes ago."

I found a tissue in my pocket and, hoping Wy wouldn't need it later, used it to wipe my eyes and blow my nose. I didn't know Mia well enough to show this much emotion with her. I was embarrassed and figured explaining would temper that embarrassment.

"My mother's parents live in Kansas, in a little town near Wichita. The song is sad anyway, but it reminds me I can't visit my grandparents much anymore, not like I used to. My good old days, as the saying goes, really were pretty danged good. I had a great childhood." I sniffled and mentally added a footnote about my difficult mother. Mia didn't need to hear me complain about her. Problems with parents were so tiresome, so common.

"Must be tough," Mia said, "your being up here in Canada, away from your friends and family. I know how important family is because I lost most of mine."

Mia's sad words made me feel bad for her. "I'm sorry. Funny

how we can take family for granted until they aren't around. Moving to Canada was not something I ever would've done, if it weren't for the war and my husband's refusal to fight in an unjust one. I support him, but it's a high price to pay, leaving your own country."

"A higher price would be fighting and dying for something you didn't believe in."

"Right, I know. David—that's my husband—said two years ago he'd either go to prison or move to Canada, but that he refused to fight. Way back when, when I thought we'd never have to worry about that, I told him if it came to that choice, then I'd leave Texas with him and move to Canada."

I sighed so deeply that Wyatt opened his eyes and looked up at me blearily. I only had to rock him a little, and he dozed off again. "I could blame my flip decision on being young and stupid, but I'm hardly older now than when I made that promise. Yet *now* I can see how frivolous I was back then, and I'm not exactly mature today—if that makes sense?"

"Yeah, I can dig it."

Since I had bared a bit of my soul to Mia, I decided to risk asking her a personal question.

"I've got a question about Shona. But, hey, if it's too close to the bone, then never mind."

"Shoot. If it upsets me, then I'll say so."

"Okay. So how come you were so distraught last night at the group meeting? Anyone can understand why you'd be mourning Shona. You were such great friends and all that. But still, there seemed to be an extra layer of emotion that I couldn't explain, but *felt*. Am I nuts, or is there something else?"

Mia made a sudden switch into another lane and then exited the highway at an off ramp. She pulled into a gas station and cut the motor. She never said a word.

When the car stopped, Wyatt stirred in my arms.

"Sorry. I forgot about him." She gestured with her chin at Wyatt. "I'm not used to having a baby around. I didn't realize he'd wake up if I stopped the car."

Wy started to fuss, and I knew he was building up to a full-blown cry. I felt bad about that and about upsetting Mia. Her behavior seemed to indicate she wasn't amused by my prying into her personal life.

"Let's take the opportunity to use the, uh, *washroom*, shall we?"

Her back was to me as she stared out the driver's side window. "You go ahead with your boy. I'll wait in the car."

"Right. I'll hurry."

"No need. Take your time."

Holding on tightly to Wy, I got out of the front seat, then dug his gear out of the back. We were in the ladies room no more than five minutes, but when we returned to the VW bus, Mia was nowhere to be seen.

The bus wasn't locked, but I wasn't going to leave Wyatt in it alone. I carried him into the filling station's office and looked around for Mia. I asked the attendant if he'd seen a young woman leave the VW. I put my hand out at shoulder height. "She's petite, with very short hair."

He rubbed his chin and looked thoughtful for a moment. "She walked up that hill and into the woods over there." He pointed outside in the direction of some tall pine trees.

"Okay, thanks. Guess I'll buy a Coke and wait for her out in the bus."

After about fifteen minutes, Mia appeared, holding a branch of a flowering plant, waving it the way I'd been taught at my Methodist church in Cuero, Texas, on Palm Sunday. When she drew closer, I saw she was beaming.

What on earth went on in her head? I couldn't possibly interpret her mood swings.

She climbed into the driver's seat. "Everything all right? Ready to go?"

I sneezed. "Hey, I want to apologize if I—" I sneezed again. I fished out another tissue and wiped my nose. I could've sworn I smelled—oh my lord, it was pot.

We were about to go over the border.

"Mia, you remember where we're going, don't you?"

Mia giggled. "Hush now. Let me get back on the highway and then I'll explain some things to you." She fumbled with her car key, had difficulty fitting it into the ignition.

Was she stoned?

I observed the expression on her face, noticed no tightness or frown, only a dreamy smile.

She looked up and caught my eye. "What're you looking at?"

"Are you—are you—high?"

"Sure. And what of it?"

"But we're about to cross an international border. There will be guards. Are you crazy? Where's the rest of your stash? Is it in here?"

"Nah, I'm not that stupid. I had a little weed left. Instead of throwing it out, I decided to smoke it, that's all. Besides, it's your fault."

"Mine? What did I do?" I was so surprised that I squeaked.

She put the bus in gear. "You, my friend," she tossed her head in my direction, "questioned the intensity of my feelings for Shona. My hunch was you wouldn't be satisfied until you knew the answer, and I decided to give you the truth. But I needed to mellow out just to talk about my shit, you know. But don't worry. Nothing's left in the bus. I smoked it all up and left the roaches in the woods." She giggled and raced out onto the highway.

Her words stunned me into silence. We passed a sign that indicated the border was only ten miles away. That's when she started to talk, laying out the saddest story I'd ever heard.

Chapter Twenty-Three

"MY FAMILY HAS lived in the Pacific Northwest a very long time, lumber barons from way back. I grew up in a Victorian mansion on Capitol Hill in Seattle that my grandfather built in 1904. His son was my father." Mia gripped the steering wheel so hard her knuckles turned white. Her foot pressed hard on the gas pedal too, and the bus sped up, leaping along the highway.

"Hey," I yelped. "Take it easy, okay? You don't have to talk if you don't want to."

"Oh yes, I do. I've begun my story, and I'll finish it. Otherwise you won't understand anything. Leastways"—she shot a look sideways at me—"unless you really do want me to stop?"

"Of course not. Let's just not go so fast." I pointed at the road ahead. "Please watch your speed. Sorry, but I'm a nervous passenger."

Besides, you fool, you're stoned. And my baby is in this blasted bus.

"Talking about my father is tough work for me," Mia said, "but I have to do this. I'll begin with the easy part." She took her foot off the gas pedal, and the bus slowed obediently.

Her mood swings unnerved me. If only she weren't the driver. My arms tightened around Wyatt, and I found myself gritting my teeth, worried about a crash.

"My father became a banker, and under him our family fortune grew and grew. My mother gave him four sons, but he still wanted a daughter desperately. Even though Mother was frail and wanted no more children, he begged, then demanded so often that she gave in and agreed to try for a girl." She flicked her eyes over at me.

Was she checking to see if she had my attention? If so, she sure as hell did.

"When I was ten," Mia continued, "my aunt told me everything, how I was the result of my mother's final pregnancy, how she died of complications a week after I was born. So you see, I was a marked child, the daughter my father had always wanted. I never had a chance."

What could I say? I murmured conventional condolences and was searching for more astute remarks, when Mia interrupted. She spoke rapidly and scarcely paused to take a breath.

"One by one my brothers went away—off to college in the East or to the military. I was left alone in the big house on the hill with, with—uh—Daddy. Gradually I became his—his, uh—his whole world. By the time I was in high school, I thought about killing myself every day and probably would have done it too, except that's when I met Shona. She saved me."

This story didn't add up. I was the center of my mother's world too. Mother made huge demands on me, but I never felt like committing suicide. What was I missing in Mia's narrative?

"I don't understand. How did Shona save you exactly?" I asked.

"She believed me when I knew no one else would. My father was too powerful and important. Shona only cared that I was sad and in trouble. She understood it was all my father's fault. Nothing else mattered to her. He could've been the king of Spain, and she wouldn't have cared. She would've acted the same, supporting me and taking my side."

"Look, Mia, I have to confess I don't get what you're talking about and—"

"He came into my bedroom every night. It was *my* fault he lost his wife. It was *my* duty to replace her. Now do you get it?"

Mia's rage erupted in a sharp voice so loud it filled the minivan. Wyatt woke and began to wail. Walls of sound pressed in on me. My claustrophobia was so thick, I couldn't have whacked through it with a scythe.

A glance at the odometer showed our speed hadn't increased. So that told me Mia hadn't lost her head entirely. I was both surprised and relieved.

She stopped yelling, and her face hardened into a grimacing mask, her jaw clenched. She leaned forward and stared intently at the road ahead.

Once I had soothed Wyatt, I tentatively reached out and touched her arm. "I'm so sorry. I didn't get it before, what you were trying to tell me. No wonder Shona was so important to you."

Gradually the look on Mia's face softened. Then, to my surprise, she patted my shoulder quickly before returning her hand to the steering wheel.

"You wanted to know," she said, her tone brusque, "so there you are. Nobody talks about this. Incest is so horrible that no one wants to admit it exists."

Her voice dropped to a whisper, and I leaned closer.

"I've told my story to very few people. Shona knew, of course. I've told you because empathy—not the cloying shit, but the cool kind—just oozes out of you. I didn't think you'd be judgmental. I felt I could trust you."

"Mia. I'm honored." Tears splashed down my face.

"I confided in my priest, but he said I made things up. I begged him not to tell my father. With no relief in sight, I ran away. That's when Shona saved me. The Spektors took me in, and Shona's dad defended me against my own father. Mr. Spektor was very brave. When I thanked him, he explained that after he survived the Holocaust, nothing held the power to scare him ever again."

I felt my wet eyes bulge out, and my eyebrows seemed to climb up to my hairline. I struggled to find words. "That's a lot for me to take in all at once. I've never heard a story like yours before."

"A story," she cried. "You don't believe me?"

Good lord. I'd started the trip afraid I'd say something to upset Mia, and now I'd gone and done it—not once but twice.

"No, no, no, that is *not* what I meant. I believe you absolutely, definitely. I'm just not used to hearing such, uh, raw experiences. My parents and grandparents never told me anything real and unvarnished. Mother insisted on shielding me from anything *ugly*. That was her term for real life. So I'm simply astounded at what happened to you. My world was colored by Disney. Yours was—" I paused, afraid to fill in the blank. I couldn't upset her more.

"Okay, that's enough. I see you do believe me. I'm just very sensitive, that's all."

"Of course you are. You're also very strong, Mia. I'm awed by your courage."

"I got a lot of help from the Spektors. Both of Shona's parents survived the Holocaust—not just her father—and they both lost most of their family members. I decided if they could keep on truckin' the way they did, then so could I."

She shot an unfathomable look at me. "Perspective, you see. It's all about perspective."

Exactly. I lacked the perspective and knowledge of the world and its ways to comprehend the horror of her confidences.

"What about your brothers?" I said. "Surely they keep in touch, don't they?"

She raised her eyes to the ceiling. "Don't be silly. Father controls everyone in our family with his wealth. I'm not in the will anymore, and my trust fund is kaput too. I imagine that my brothers have been threatened with that treatment if they have anything to do with me. Actually, having nothing to do with any of them is easier for me."

"So that's why you told me you'd lost your family. When you said that before, I assumed everyone had died."

162

"That's what I let people think. It's much simpler that way. The Spektors became my family—pretty weird for a good Catholic girl to be taken in by Jews who live over a mortuary."

She cackled for a moment or two. As her laughs escalated, I worried she'd tip into hysteria. But she didn't. Considering the enormous psychological pain she must have carried for years, her emotional control was better than one could expect.

She settled down and drove in silence. For once, I kept my questions to myself. Instead, I brooded about her background. I knew nothing about incest, only what I'd gleaned from novels, and they gave only the merest of hints. I remembered my psych professor saying that Freud's early clinical research showed women were often abused by relatives—even fathers like Mia's. However, when Freud presented his original conclusions on incest to his male colleagues in Vienna, they were outraged. They all agreed upstanding male members of society would never do *that*. Freud altered his theory after he was hit with an enormous backlash from his medical peers.

How a father could abuse his own daughter was beyond my comprehension. That horror belonged in fiction. I snuck a glance at Mia, who was achingly real.

Suddenly Diana Ross and The Supremes ripped into "I'm Gonna Make You Love Me." Mia had switched the radio on in time to catch the ending chorus. I shut my eyes tight and grimaced. Under the circumstances, it was an apt refrain. How many love songs could turn ugly if I imagined them taking place under gruesome conditions?

Ugly? There was that maternal watchword again. My mother had a solid grip on my worldview. I wished I could weed her out of my thoughts and form my own views of the world and how it really was or should be.

Watching Wyatt's sweet face helped me force alarming thoughts from my mind. I had asked for this information from Mia's life. Only now I didn't know what to do with it.

And what did Mia's father's behavior have to do with her

fury at last night's meeting? I couldn't see any connection, so I'd just have to ask.

"So now I'm wondering," I said, sounding timid and hesitant on purpose, "why you told me about your father when I asked why you were upset at the meeting. Excuse me for being dense, but what's the connection?" I stared straight ahead, out through the windshield, not daring to look at Mia.

She cleared her throat, turned the radio down low, and hummed a little. Finally, she spoke.

"My feelings for Shona weren't ordinary, not how I imagine someone feels for a regular best friend." She shot me a quick look. "You can relate, right?"

"What do you mean?"

"You've got a strong tie to Larissa, one I can feel but don't understand. Am I right?"

Her powers of observation astonished me. I supposed she was right. Larissa and I had been through a lot together, and she had never wavered in her support for me. I owed her complete devotion and was happy to give it.

"Well, sort of."

Another time I'd tell Mia how Larissa had rushed to be my friend last year. She'd been my mainstay when there'd been no one else to help me.

"So then imagine what would happen," Mia continued, "if you had lived with the Klimenkos for more than two years, had moved to Canada to attend graduate school with her, been her roommate for a time, and then—*bam*—your friendship with Larissa hit a rough patch. Imagine you disagreed over something so fundamental that it damaged your relationship. Wouldn't you be upset if you felt like you were losing something as precious as her friendship?"

I clutched Wyatt more tightly to my chest and considered her question. It was a scary one. I didn't even want to consider it, yet in theory, I was sure she was correct. Again, I said as much.

"Larissa said she'd told you about the threats Shona

received," Mia said. "When those calls came in to our apartment, I wanted to call the police. Shona wouldn't hear of it. She said the calls would stop eventually—that they weren't serious, that they wouldn't scare her. As the weeks wore on, the calls escalated in frequency and their content exploded. When they didn't stop, Shona and I argued every day. I couldn't make her understand the danger, that perhaps she was even imperiling me too. But mostly I was worried for her. One day we had an enormous blowup, and she stormed out of our apartment. When she came back hours later, she announced she was moving out. She had decided to move in with Delilah, who had just lost her roommate."

Tears ran down Mia's face now. Her face flushed bright pink. She was biting her lip, trying to regain control.

"You want to pull off the highway? Mia, I hate to see you so upset. Besides, we're almost at the border. We need to be calm."

She chewed on her lip before answering. "I've never had trouble at a border crossing, and I'm in a hurry to get to Seattle." She scratched her head. "Maybe it's a good idea, but only for a minute." She turned off at the next exit, headed for a smaller road, and, once there, pulled over to the side. She cut the motor and rested her head on the steering wheel. Soon her shoulders began to shake and then sobs racked her.

What should I do now?

Wyatt provided the answer. He woke up and began to suck his fist. Time for a bottle—a welcome diversion.

I turned around in my seat and reached behind me for the bag that held baby supplies. I had prepared a bottle and wrapped it in a plastic bag. We hadn't been on the road more than an hour, so the bottle would be fine. I gave it to Wyatt, and he drank with gusto.

After several minutes, Mia's sobs quieted and eventually stopped altogether. She raised her head and shifted her eyes to me. Her face was a wet, pink mess. Good thing she didn't wear makeup, because it would have slid off her face.

"You realize what's wrong, don't you?" Her voice was filled

with pain and anguish. She rubbed her eyes and threw back her head.

Before I could suggest an answer, she carried on. "I blame myself for Shona's death. I should have insisted she call the police. And if she had still refused, I should have called them myself. If I'd done that, Shona would be alive now. I will never forgive myself, never. I don't know how I can face the Spektors, but I have to."

"You can't blame yourself." My response burst from me so loud that Wy stopped sucking on his bottle and looked up with startled blue eyes. "Her death is not *your* doing. That's plain crazy."

Mia folded her arms across her chest and leaned her forehead against the steering wheel again. I strained to hear her muffled words.

"I want to agree with you, but I just can't. I failed my friend, the dearest person left to me. I failed her."

Her voice rose to a high pitch, hurting my ears. I covered Wyatt's so he wouldn't cry too.

"If you and your little boy weren't my passengers, then I'd rev up this old motor and run straight into that tree over there."

My eyes bugged out and I pulled Wyatt to my heart. And now I wanted to cry too.

Chapter Twenty-Four

I WAS WONDERING what to say about Mia's hint of suicidal thoughts when she downshifted and for the first time clashed the gears.

"Pay attention," I yelped. "We're about to cross an international border."

"I'm a competent driver, and besides, what's the big deal about the border?" Mia scoffed.

"Every time I cross between the States and Canada, I get a hassle."

"What? You're the straightest-looking chick on the planet."

I had to laugh. "Yeah, go figure. Last time I was quizzed for fifteen minutes. David says our names must be on some kind of watch list at the border."

Two minutes later we arrived at the checkpoint.

"What brings you to the States, ma'am?" The guard leaned out of his hut and peered into our VW bus. His voice sounded friendly, but his face was stern.

He looked the type to detest hippie-looking vehicles on sight. That prejudice was common among those who wore any kind of uniform these days. The man appeared to be in his fifties, meaning the chances were high he'd served in World War II.

Oh, great. Guilt blossomed in my heart and zoomed through every cell in my body.

Mia handed him her driver's license from Washington State.

"I'm a grad student in British Columbia, going back home to Seattle because a friend died."

The guard studied her license for a moment, then returned it without a word. He stroked his chin, stared past Mia, and focused on me. "How about you, miss? Where were you born?"

"In Texas." I made my voice sound spritely, proud, upbeat.

"Is that a fact? How about showing me some ID?"

"Sure thing. Just a minute, sir." I looked at Mia. "Can you hold Wy please?"

He was wide awake now and whimpering, not pleased at leaving my lap. When I moved his squirmy self to Mia, his pacifier fell out of his mouth and landed on the floor mat. Which was none too clean.

I bent to pick it up, but Mia and the guard said in unison, "Leave it."

He added, "Other cars are waiting behind you."

I suddenly realized that I needed to chill. If I stayed uptight, then I'd only make the situation worse. Really, this wasn't such a big deal, crossing over a friendly border between Canada and the U.S. Mia and I were not engaged in anything illegal, not right now anyway. The smell of dope shouldn't be strong enough to reach to his guard post. Furthermore, the man didn't even know my husband was a draft resister.

Or did he have my name on an official list? Ugh.

I decided to behave like Larissa and turned on the charm.

"I'm sorry, sir." I flapped my left hand at him, made the gesture look awkward—on purpose. "My hand has gone to sleep from holding my baby boy for so long." Big smile—a winning one, I hoped. "I know I'm being slow and clumsy, but I'll try to hurry. What do you want to see? Will my Texas driver's license do?" Another big smile, some eyelash fluttering, just for good measure.

Gosh, role-playing was kind of fun.

I looked up from my purse to see Mia's questioning stare. Was she shocked at my attempt to play the coquette? Perhaps she'd never seen Larissa in action then. My version was only a pale imitation, since I lacked Larissa's looks or skills.

I found my license and handed it to Mia, who gave it to the guard.

He glanced at it and passed it back to me. "What's your status in Canada, young lady?"

Young lady? Oh, that was rich.

"I'm a landed immigrant in Canada." My stomach churned, making like a washing machine on spin cycle. I hadn't felt so queasy since I was pregnant with Wyatt.

"You got papers to prove it?" he asked.

"You bet. Here's my card." Whew, I had that one covered.

He read my Canadian card, then made notes on a pad. "You live in British Columbia?"

"No, sir." I knew the generations older than mine adored good manners. Being called "sir" over and over usually seemed to work magic, proving I wasn't an arrogant young pup. "I'm a grad student at the University of Toronto. This week I'm visiting a friend who's working at UBC. She and Mia"—I pointed toward her—"are friends. I wanted to see Seattle so I decided to drive down with her."

Shut up. How could I forget what Professor Klimenko had taught me based on the many interrogations he'd endured in Soviet Russia before his escape to Canada? He drilled into me to offer no more detail than necessary to any authority figure.

The guard left his post, stepped over to the bus, and leaned closer to the window. His eyes never left mine. "So where is she? Why isn't your mutual friend with you?"

Why was he grilling me? Did he smell Mia's marijuana? I couldn't let my rising panic show despite the way my neck muscles tightened and my jaw tightened.

"She couldn't get off work. Mia wanted company on the drive down and, like I told you, I've never seen Seattle. I hear it's a nice place." I tilted my head, trying to look winsome. "Sir, have you been up the Space Needle?"

Mia made choking sounds. I couldn't tell if she was smothering a laugh or swallowing her aversion to my improvisation.

The guard stepped back. He crossed his arms and gave a huge grin. "Yeah, I finally got up to the top. Terrific view. Wanted to go since way back in '62, when my cousin watched President Kennedy open the World's Fair and bragged on how great the Space Needle was. Hope you have time to go up while you're in Seattle. And don't forget the monorail. It's good too."

He returned my landed immigrant card and slapped the driver's side door. "You girls have a safe trip." He looked at Mia. "And I'm sorry to hear about the death of your friend."

Mia flinched. "Thank you, officer." Her voice sounded tight.

She handed Wyatt back to me, put the car in gear, and drove off at a sedate pace. She kept her eyes pointed straight ahead as we passed the building that housed other guards in regular offices and the parking bays where drivers pulled in to await further questioning.

Once we cleared the official area, Mia and I both burst out laughing.

"Good lord, what was that all about?" Mia said. "As a good feminist I shouldn't approve of your flirting with a guard, but it did seem to work. I go back and forth over that border crossing all the time, but I have *never* been interrogated like that."

"Were you driving this same bus?"

"Absolutely. The only difference is having you and the baby along as passengers."

I laughed harder. "Guess Wyatt and I can't help being so dangerous it shows."

"Right on. I spotted your baby for a revolutionary the minute I laid eyes on him. Figured he'll try to bomb the Pentagon as soon as he can walk."

I played along, happy at her lightheartedness. "Don't blow our cover to smithereens. The authorities can't realize Wy organized the other babies. It'd be a shame if we had to go on the lam."

We riffed on radicalized babies, and Mia loosened up. When our patter ran down, we'd displaced our tension. Which was great because this innocent drive to Seattle was already more fraught than I'd expected.

Heck, we hadn't even hit the tough part yet—meeting the grieving Spektors.

The camaraderie between Mia and me was now friendly and relaxed enough that I decided to attempt a few more questions. I said, "Back there with the guard, were you worried—even the tiniest little bit—about the dope you'd smoked? Come on now, fess up."

She scratched her chin and appeared to give my question serious thought. "Nope. Went through my mind briefly, but that was about it."

How often did Mia smoke marijuana? She seemed awfully nonchalant about it.

"Are you uptight about talking to the Spektors?"

Mia squinted at the road. "I don't know. I already talked to them twice by phone—that is, since Shona, uh, died." She sniffled a little but didn't cry. "I hope our visit will do us all some good." She rubbed her forehead.

"Are you tired?" I asked. "Do you want me to drive?"

She shook her head.

"How much longer until we get there?"

"Girl, you ask more questions than anyone I've ever met. Yes, I'm a little tired, but I'll keep driving. In less than two hours we'll be there. Then we can eat. I should've bought a snack back at the filling station." She patted her growling stomach.

"So you've got an attack of the munchies, huh?" I couldn't shut up. It was true.

She nodded.

"In that case, let's just chill, listen to music. I don't know about you, but our encounter with the border guard drained me. Besides, I didn't sleep well last night."

"Okay by me." Mia began to hum and switched on the radio. This time she chose a classical music station. It lulled me to sleep and, when I awoke, we had exited the freeway and were driving through the heart of Seattle.

The landscape was hilly and green. While Seattle didn't appear as sparkly clean as Vancouver, at least the houses weren't decorated with pebble dash, thank goodness.

I regarded the dashboard clock. It was almost ten a.m.

"Made pretty good time, didn't we?"

Mia nodded. "We'll be there in a—"

She turned up the radio.

"...murder of a coed. The victim was discovered in the Husky Union Building early this morning. Her roommate called police when the young woman didn't return to her dorm after attending a women's liberation meeting. Police ask anyone who attended the meeting to contact them immediately. And in other news today—"

Mia gasped and switched off the radio. She steered onto a neighborhood street and took a curbside parking place.

Her voice shaky, she said, "I was in that group that meets in the Husky Union. That's at the University of Washington—did you hear the announcer say that?" She exhaled sharply. "Oh my God. Could this death be connected to Shona's?"

A tenet from my CIA training took center stage in my thoughts.

Never believe in coincidence.

Chapter Twenty-Five

WE STOPPED IN front of the Forkner Funeral Home. There were two entrances.

Mia pointed to the larger, fancier door. "*That* demands we dress in black and go to a funeral. I always use this one instead." She pointed at the entryway marked *office*.

"Makes sense to me. Let's go." I shifted Wyatt from one hip to another, trying to handle him and the diaper bag. I was such a slow learner. I should've been more adept at this by now.

We pushed through the small door and entered a reception area. Straight ahead a woman sat behind a desk. She looked up as we approached and pasted on a smile so fake she was worthy of a B-grade movie. Her hair was silver and tightly permed, her clothes all black and clean and crisp.

"Are you here to visit your dear departed?" Her voice dripped with a syrupy sweetness, too sticky to be enticing. "May I get you some refreshment? Coffee perhaps?"

Mia said, "We're here for Mr. and Mrs. Spektor. They're expecting us."

The receptionist's smile flipped into a scowl. "I see. Go up that way then." Her fingers tipped with scarlet polish waved toward a nearby staircase. "The Spektors are on the second floor. Apartment 2A." She gave a curt nod and returned to her typewriter.

I looked at Mia and shrugged.

"Stuck-up, isn't she?" Mia said.

"Be quiet. She'll hear you."

"What do I care?" In a lower voice Mia said, "She's new, only been here a few months, but the Spektors have been here for ages. It took him forever to find this position. They're such sweeties, the Spektors. You'll think they're in their seventies, but really they're twenty years younger. Trauma must've marked them." Mia scraped the heel of her work boots along the floorboards. "Look at this gorgeous place."

I turned my attention to the faded splendor of the mortuary's Jazz Age décor. Decades ago someone had spared no expense to build this classy repose for Seattle's wealthy deceased citizens. Heavy dark paneling and shiny wooden floors gave it an air of well-heeled stability—equally suitable for an elegant dining club. The interior decorations soothed me—until I peered down a hallway extending beyond the reception area. Two mahogany caskets lurked there, lids raised. I cringed and fled for the stairway.

I heard my cousin's voice in my head: "You should be so scared, Austin."

Even though I carried Wyatt, a bag heavy with baby gear, *and* my purse, I still beat Mia to the second floor landing. I stood there panting and waited for her.

"What spooked you?" she said as she joined us.

I chose to ignore the question. No need to tell her how much the funeral home creeped me out. Death was a part of life—but I didn't have to wallow in it before its time. I waved toward the door marked 2A. "Go ahead. You know these people. I don't."

Mia stepped up to the door, touched the *mezuzah* on the frame, and knocked. I had only a moment to register my surprise at a Catholic observing a Jewish tradition before the door opened.

There stood Mr. and Mrs. Spektor. Holocaust survivors.

Another first for me. The mere sight of them awed me— they were living history, with the emphasis on living.

At once Mrs. Spektor fell on Mia's neck, whimpering. Mr.

Spektor clutched a cardigan around his thin frame and peered over wire-framed spectacles, then zeroed in on Wyatt. The man raised a tiny smile and angled toward me.

"Welcome to our home. You must be the young Texan—is that your son?" His English was courtly, pronounced with a Slavic accent—not necessarily Russian, though. Bulgarian maybe.

"How good to see young life in this old place," he said. "Please do come in." He gently separated his wife from Mia. "Rachel, dear, step aside and let our visitors enter."

The Spektors led us into a dining room. It was surprisingly large, and centered in the room was an enormous table, able to accommodate sixteen chairs. If I blanked out my cousin's voice teasing about activities on the ground floor, I could appreciate the beauty of the place.

"Please sit," Mrs. Spektor said, a tic twitching her face. "You must be hungry from your journey. We have bagels, lox, cream cheese, freshly squeezed orange juice, and of course, coffee."

A huge smile spread across Mia's face. "You know what I like, and I'm famished." She leaned toward me and whispered in my ear. "Don't you dare mention *why* I'm starved—don't do it." Her glare was ferocious.

"Okay, okay." To Mrs. Spektor, I said, "My son must need a diaper change. Can you show me the best place for that please?"

She ushered me into a nearby bathroom. I took care of Wyatt's needs and played kissy-face with him as long as I dared. When we returned to the dining room, I caught sight of Mrs. Spektor in the kitchen, and we joined her there. I was admiring the carved oak cabinets when the phone rang.

Mrs. Spektor called, "*Motek*, can you answer that please."

Several minutes later he entered the kitchen. Seeing his anguished face was enough to tell me he hadn't heard good news. He hurried to his wife. "Darling Rachel, please come back to the table." He took her elbow, but she pulled away.

With a sweet smile, she said, "In a moment, motek. I must finish with the food."

"Rachel, please."

She shifted her gaze from the kitchen counter to his face. "Who was on the phone?"

Again he took her arm, and this time she let him steer her into the dining room, where she sat obediently.

He passed back and forth behind her, rubbing his hands. Finally he stopped and put his hands on her shoulders. "That was one of Shoshana's friends. She wanted to tell us the bad news herself, before we saw the newspaper."

He bent down and looked directly at his wife, speaking gently. "Bethany Furst was murdered last night. Her body was found about two this morning, in a janitor's closet on campus."

An instant wail ripped out of Mrs. Spektor. Mia and I exchanged glances, remembering the news item from the radio. A coed killed at the University of Washington was shocking. But the deceased was not just any coed, but one *who knew Shona.*

Mrs. Spektor excused herself and fled sobbing down a hall. Mr. Spektor sat down heavily and buried his face in his hands.

Mia said, "We caught the news on the car radio, but no name was mentioned. Bethany was a friend of mine too." She stared across the table at me with huge eyes. "I wonder what happened."

Mr. Spektor raised his head. "Strangled. The police say she was strangled." His eyes were dull, lifeless. His words came out in a monotone. "The Fursts are members of our synagogue. They helped us relocate to Seattle in 1947. They are family to us, the only family we have left. Bethany and Shoshana were in the women's movement together. Now Bethany is gone, like our daughter. Both before their time. After your visit, we will go over to their house."

He rose and walked to a window, pulled back a curtain, gazed out at the fir trees. His shoulders drooped, and his whole body seemed to sink into itself. When he spoke again, his voice was heavy with grief.

"What is the connection? Is it anti-Semitism? Is it anti-feminism? Or is it something else entirely? The police will have a lot of territory to cover."

His old head fell to his chest, and he let the curtain fall back into place. "Or perhaps there is no connection at all, although that doesn't seem plausible."

He returned to the table and collapsed into a chair.

"You must have given some thought to who killed your daughter." I paused, gathering courage to proceed. I felt guilty for barging into this new grief. "Before today, did you have any ideas? Does Bethany's death—this second murder—point to a possible suspect?"

He began shaking his head before I finished speaking. "No. Nothing. No one."

"That's not true, motek," Mrs. Spektor said. "You know that's not true. You might as well share our thoughts with Mia and her friend."

I hadn't noticed that she'd slipped back into the room. Now her eyes held no tears. Her face was dry, and its old, wrinkled skin looked like paper that would tear too easily.

Mr. Spektor took off his glasses and laid them on the table. He rubbed the bridge of his nose with two fingers before he followed his wife's advice. "Mia knows how strong-willed our daughter could be. Many at the university loved her for her passionate pursuit of causes, but she could also upset people. If she disagreed with you, she was merciless in attack."

"I begged her," Mrs. Spektor said, "to go about her work more smoothly, more judiciously, but she was so headstrong. Shoshana always said the rise of the Nazis to power proved that Jews in particular have to stand up and fight for what we want."

"Obviously we could not disagree with her," Mr. Spektor said. "Still, we worried. Even so, no special individual springs to mind as a murder suspect. No, I cannot see one."

Mia nodded vigorously. "Few openly opposed your daughter in debate. They would've been demolished. No one enjoys that."

"However, if she was championing you or your cause," he continued, "then Shoshana was your heroine. But Bethany was nothing like that at all. No, not at all."

"Dear little Bethany," Mrs. Spektor said, "such a plain child. Almost a mouse girl. She had strong convictions that tallied with our Shoshana's, but Bethany could never speak up. She let our daughter speak for her."

When Mrs. Spektor stopped to gulp air, Mr. Spektor took up the narrative.

"Bethany was always right by Shoshana's side," he said, "supporting her in everything she did. If Shoshana was set to give a big speech, then Bethany mimeographed the flyers and handed them out. Bethany often said if Shoshana succeeded, then she would glow in the reflection of Shoshana's success."

Each time one of the Spektors said "our Shoshana," their words pierced my heart. Their pride and loss hung in the air, so real I imagined I could reach out and touch them. And the more they talked about their daughter and her friend Bethany, the more I noticed that the two Spektors were weaving between them a complete tapestry, showing two young women viciously stopped just as their lives were about to take full flight. The Spektors had endured so much already, the unjustness of these new losses made my soul weep for them.

Mrs. Spektor rose from the table. "We must eat. Mia, darling, will you help me please?"

Mia sprang to her feet. "Of course."

Wyatt had been dozing off and on my lap ever since Mrs. Spektor had left the room in tears. Now he came to life and wanted to wiggle. I sat down on the polished wood floor and moved my macramé purse around in front of him. He loved to look at its bold colors.

Mr. Spektor was silent for a time, watching Wyatt and me at play. Then, in a thin, wistful voice, he said, "It's good not to give up hope at a better life. Even when things are darkest, you must resolve to go on. It isn't easy. I remember I used to say that to Jack when he would get so angry at——"

"Do you mean Shona's old boyfriend—that Jack?" I asked.

He looked startled when I broke in on his musing. He blinked, then continued. "Yes, that Jack. As a nice young American, he has not faced complex moral choices. He—"

"Excuse me, sir. What about the draft?" I asked. "Isn't that a complex moral choice? I don't mean to be rude, but I'd really like your opinion. This is something I struggle with."

Mr. Spektor peered over his spectacles. "Ah, yes. There is that." He pushed back in his chair and looked up at the ceiling, then back at me. "A childhood accident left Jack blind in one eye. He told me if had lost his *left* eye, it would have been a tragedy. Loss of his *right* eye was lucky. The Selective Service System disqualifies someone with total loss of sight in the *right* eye as unfit for military service. As luck would have it, Jack is still qualified to work as a lumberjack."

"That's the strangest draft story I've ever heard." I would have to tell David.

"Life is full of, hmm, vagaries." Mr. Spektor's voice fell. "Jack isn't Jewish, but our Shoshana was drawn to him anyway. This concerned me, but Rachel said not to worry, that they would never marry, so why raise a fuss. She was right, but for the wrong reason."

I had to get out of there. This sad, brave couple was breaking my heart.

"Here's the odd thing about Jack: he coped with Shoshana's boldness, but had no use for Bethany's meekness." He cast a tiny smile in his wife's direction as she entered the room carrying a full platter of food. Mia trailed behind with a coffee pot in one hand and a pitcher of orange juice in the other.

Mrs. Spektor set the platter of lox and bagels in front of her husband. "We never figured out why Jack didn't like Bethany. Isn't that right, motek?"

"Now you mention it, Jack did become ugly about Bethany," he said.

Ugly? Mr. Spektor had used my mother's word—such bad connotations. My mind whirred with horrid possibilities. Could

Jack be a suspect for two murders? Could he have snapped, grown enraged enough to kill? He knew both women rather well.

I tuned back in to the conversation. Mr. Spektor was still speaking.

"Of course, Jack was upset at Shoshana's leaving, and—"

"Very upset," Mrs. Spektor added.

Mr. Spektor patted his wife's arm. "Then Jack made plans to leave Seattle too. That's when he quit school and went off to work in the lumber camp."

Were Shona's parents suspicious of Jack? How could I find out without being rude? If they had no misgivings about him, then I might be shot down at once as crazy. *Mishuga*, I think that was the word in Yiddish. I determined to be circumspect. Like a crab, I would walk into the subject sideways.

I got up from the floor, picked up Wyatt, and seated us both at the table.

"Where is Jack these days? Out in the wilds of Washington, I suppose?" I tried to sound casual.

Mrs. Spektor passed the food platter to me. I took a bagel and declined the lox. She said, "Jack now works at a logging camp near Vancouver."

One hand flew to cover my mouth, forcing the words to stay inside.

If Jack had been nearby when Shona was killed, he could have killed her. And he had never liked Bethany.

Three suspects now. Two types of motives.

Maybe the Mounties knew none of this.

But they would soon. And just as quickly Larissa would be free from suspicion and out of trouble.

Chapter Twenty-Six

I STOLE A glance at Mia. Had she noted the significance of Jack's working nearby when his former girlfriend was murdered? Mia looked unruffled, to say the least, slathering cream cheese on her third bagel.

My qualms about Jack still wanted to burst forth. I devised a coughing fit to avoid giving away my feelings.

Mrs. Spektor started from her chair. "Shall I fetch you some water?"

I grabbed my glass of orange juice, gulped some, tried to calm down. "Thank you, no. I'll be fine in a minute." I slithered back to the subject of Jack's whereabouts. "Did Shona know Jack was working in British Columbia? Did they ever meet up?"

The Spektors looked at each other. She spoke first.

"We only know Jack wanted desperately to see Shoshana."

'Yes," Mr. Spektor said, "we believe he wanted to claim her again as his girlfriend."

"He got her address from us," Mrs. Spektor said, "but we don't know if he was able to contact her."

"Exactly." He put his fork down and frowned down at his plate. "Shoshana was out and about, all hours of the day and night. When we called, it was hard to catch her. Jack probably had that problem too."

Mia leaned forward. "Then you haven't talked to Jack since, uh, since Shona's passing?"

"He sent us a sympathy card," Mr. Spektor said.

"I'll get it." Mrs. Spektor left the room and only seconds later returned with the card. She handed it to Mia, who read Jack's handwritten message aloud.

"Without Shona in my life, I have nothing. You must feel wretched too. Please know that you are both constantly in my thoughts. Jack."

The Spektors clasped hands across the table, and I averted my eyes. Meanwhile, my mind whirred, processing Jack's brief condolence to them. It was ambiguous.

My determination to find out more about him solidified. "Does Jack's logging camp have a name?"

"An Indian-sounding name." Mr. Spektor glanced at his wife. "Something like *Cokitkit?*"

Her sad face crinkled with affection. "I believe it was Coquitlam."

I sat up straighter, now fully alert. "And that's near Vancouver?"

"Not far," she said. "The last time Jack called, he said he was boarding the bus to Vancouver and would get there in only ninety minutes." She swiveled toward her husband. "Right, motek?"

"I don't recall. I do know—*Coquitlam*, you say—is east of Vancouver, about twenty miles. I suspect Jack worked near Shoshana in case she changed her mind and agreed to take up again with him." He shook his head, tears filling his eyes.

Mia pointed at her wristwatch and stared at me, a determined glint to her eyes.

Everybody's eyes were speaking to me. But I took her hint. "Thank you for this wonderful feast, so nice after—"

"We shouldn't eat and run," Mia said, "but we must leave Seattle in time to get back to Vancouver before nightfall."

Mrs. Spektor's face puckered up. I hated adding to her sorrows, even by a little.

"Must you go so soon?" she said. "We hoped for a longer visit."

I gestured at Mia, then to myself. "We both have things we must do tomorrow. We would rather stay, but—"

Mia pushed back her chair and stood. The shriek of wood against wood startled Wyatt, and he let out a loud cry.

"Poor little boy, he got scared. May I hold him?" Mrs. Spektor asked. "I haven't held a baby in a long time."

Mia looked at her watch again, but now I was in no mood to rush. The plea of our hostess touched me. "Here you go." I gently passed Wy to her. "Wyatt, this is Mrs. Spektor."

Silently I prayed, Please, please cheer her up a little if you can.

A sense of wonder suffused Mrs. Spektor's lined face. She gazed at Wyatt with such an expression that the only word to describe it was adoration. And Wyatt, to my joy, looked back at her tired old eyes and stopped crying. He gurgled a tiny bubble and then yawned.

"Look at this, motek." Mrs. Spektor turned so her husband could see Wyatt's face. "He smiled at me."

This tender scene held no charm for Mia, who still was in a hurry.

"I know you want to go visit the Fursts. We just have time to walk on campus and—"

"Is it far to the Husky Union?" I had to ensure that that was on our agenda. "Shouldn't we see where Bethany was killed?"

Mr. Spektor said, "The police may not let you near the crime scene."

"We're in Seattle now and won't be back again soon." Mia began to pace. "I agree with you, Austin. We should at least try to see where Bethany was killed."

Mr. Spektor held his hands up in resignation, then turned to look out the window.

Mrs. Spektor said, "So, even if you must go so soon, at least please leave the baby with us. He looks like he needs a nap. We have a rocking chair in our bedroom. I could lull him to sleep."

No way could I resist her.

Mia was still unfazed, however. "We don't have time. If we take the baby with us, then we can leave immediately after we're done on campus."

I glared at her. "Let's do as Mrs. Spektor suggests. Coming back to get Wyatt will only add a few minutes. Besides, our jaunt will be quicker if it's just you and me."

"Okay, you win." Mia's tone was none too gracious.

Mrs. Spektor's face lit up. If this was all it took to bring a little relief into her somber life, then who were we to begrudge her?

In short order and a flurry of activity, Mia engineered our successful escape. Wyatt rested contentedly on Mrs. Spektor's shoulder as we promised to return in an hour. I kissed him on the top of his head, gave Mrs. Spektor's hand a squeeze, and raced out the door to join Mia, who was tapping her foot impatiently in the hallway.

When we hurried down the stairs, the receptionist looked up to note our passing but said nothing. Likewise, we passed her without saying goodbye.

Once we reached the street, I stopped and leaned forward, hands on my knees.

"What's up with you?" Mia said, bending over to look in my face. "Are you sick?"

I pointed to the second floor of the mortuary. "Didn't you feel their pain? I've never met anyone who's endured so much. What a miracle the Spektors can still function."

"I suppose I've gotten used to them over time, living with them, how stoic they are. The crap they've endured is unfathomable. So many of their family members swallowed up by the Holocaust, and now they've lost their own child."

"Oh shoot." I stamped my foot. "I forgot to ask for a picture of Shona. The phone call about Bethany's death tore it right out of my mind. Help me remember when we go back to pick up Wyatt."

Mia began to walk. I caught up.

"So I take it Shona is a nickname for Shoshana?" I said.

"Shoshana was her Hebrew name."

"It was so touching when they kept saying *our Shoshana*."

We trudged along the sidewalk. When we crossed an alleyway, I looked ahead and saw the campus. I chirped a happy sound, and then sighed, recalling scenes at the mortuary. The thought brought me down to the ground with a thud.

Mia slowed and glanced my way. "Why the big sigh?"

"Just thinking about the Spektors. Their woes make mine feel small in comparison. I've had an easy life. Anything I've suffered personally isn't even worth the word *suffer*. However, *you've* suffered." I cast a glance at her. "Compared to you and the Spektors, my problems are trivial."

Mia snickered. "So you think you have problems too?"

"What're you laughing at?" My feelings felt stepped on, like the sidewalk beneath our feet. "Are you making fun of me?"

Mia was beginning to get on my nerves. I tried not to disturb her volatile emotions, not wanting her to flare up at me over and over again, but I wasn't having much success.

She put her hands on her hips. "You struck me as naïve, but now I see maybe you just haven't lived enough yet. That would explain a lot."

I straightened to my full height, hoping to take command of the situation. "I make no bones about it. My mother said she wanted a 'nice childhood' for me because maturity would bring tougher issues to deal with. The only chore expected of me was making my bed every morning. I learned how to wash dishes at a friend's house when I was in sixth grade. That's how easy my life has been."

Mia scowled. "Well, lucky you." Her tone dripped acid.

"Look, I'm not bragging, and I won't raise Wyatt the same way. If I'd grown up with more responsibilities, then I wouldn't be so shocked when they land on me now. I've had a hard time even learning to take care of a small apartment—it feels like such a burden. So you don't need to tell me I was spoiled. I wasn't prepared for the real world, for all the hard knocks and ugliness, but I'm catching up now." Referencing Mother's word, *ugly*, made me flinch. "So don't tell me what the Spektors went through is unfathomable to you; I know you feel the depth of their pain. My life has been so sheltered that to run up against someone like them knocks me sideways."

At a main intersection we stopped for a traffic light. Mia hopped up and down, jiggled her leg. "Don't you realize I'm jealous of you? My family is stinking rich. I should be loaded with creature comforts and spoiled by servants, but no family money ever helped me. It only made Father more powerful and impossible to fight against. Most of the time I wish I were dead." She clasped her arms across her chest.

The enormity of the abuse she'd withstood from her father hit me anew. No wonder she was so touchy to deal with. I reached out to comfort her, touching her shoulder, but she stiffened. When her arms fell to her sides, I took that as a sign and gave her a hug. Eventually she relaxed into it.

When I noticed students stepping around us to pass on the sidewalk, I disengaged. Then I chose my words with care. "My grandmother always says you need to walk a mile in someone else's moccasins before you understand that person. At the very least, it's good to share experiences. When I learn about someone's life, I feel more human."

Mia drew back and gave me a startled look.

"What's the matter?" I asked.

"When I met you yesterday, I didn't like you very much, but you're okay." She punched my shoulder lightly. "Now let's quit being so dramatic and go find the Husky Union."

She scrutinized the intersection for traffic and was about to step off the curb, but I stopped her, seizing her arm and pulling her back. "Wait. What about Jack? What do you think of him?"

"You can't walk and talk at the same time?"

"I'm busting to know what you think of him. Tell me."

Two passersby slowed and circled us.

Mia rolled her eyes. "More questions." She exhaled sharply. "Jack seemed to like me better than he did poor dead Bethany, but not by much. He always said I was ballsy. I took that as a compliment. He doesn't like wimps, and that's why Bethany irked him. The problem with Jack and me, however, was that we were competitors."

"At what?" I said.

"We competed for Shona's time, attention, and affection. Jack and I never talked about it, but my sense is we both knew what was going on. He worked at getting under my skin, and he succeeded. Jack belittled everything I did, called me 'poor little rich girl.' He was jealous of my rich family, but I wouldn't let Shona tell him how I'd been abused."

"Sounds tricky for you to put up with. So what happened when he did succeed in getting under your skin? How'd you react?"

She ran her hands through her short hair and stared off down the street. I let her drown in her own thoughts, hoping she'd come out with something useful in solving the puzzle of two deaths. Or at the least Shona's.

Finally she turned to me and took off her sunglasses. "Once Jack and I came to blows at a party, and I ended up throwing the first punch. He was a drinker, and I did dope. In my experience, our two types don't mix well. That night he ragged on me about being rich, and I reached my limit. I drew back my arm, aiming for his arrogant mug, but Shona jumped between us. I pulled the punch and hit her shoulder instead, but not a hard blow. Jack cackled in triumph and started pushing my buttons again, making nasty taunts. With Shona there, I pulled my punches in general and just stomped off."

"Then I guess you won't have an unbiased answer to my next question."

"Go ahead," she said. "Lay it on me."

"Could Jack have murdered Shona and perhaps Bethany too?"

"My honest opinion?"

"Yes, please."

"Jack could be the murderer." Mia stopped and put her sunglasses back on. "Absolutely. No doubt in my mind."

Chapter Twenty-Seven

MIA LEAPT OFF the sidewalk and raced across the busy intersection of Forty-second Street and Fifteenth Avenue. Once she landed on the opposite curb, she waved at me.

I hurried to catch up.

"You're a tease, you know that? What makes you think Jack has it in him to be a killer?"

"I could be flip," she said, "and say everyone has the capacity for murder, but I won't. Jack has a mean temper. I saw him beat a guy to a pulp in a bar fight. It's not a big stretch to think he went berserk on Shona *if* she met him in Vancouver and turned him down again."

"So that leaves the question of Bethany. If the two murders are connected—which is debatable at this stage—why would Jack kill *her?*"

"Exactly," Mia said, nodding. "And was he even here in Seattle last night? As for a motive? Nope, can't see one."

"You know any of Jack's friends? Anyone who kept in touch with him?"

"Beats me. I'll think on that, but meantime, let's walk. Time's slipping by."

A few more steps and we entered the UW campus. Swinging along, unencumbered with an infant or his paraphernalia, I could imagine myself as a carefree underclassman again. That is, until I recalled the load I still carried. My sense of ease collapsed, a deflated balloon.

Point one—my husband was a fugitive from the Selective Service.

Point two—my dear friend Larissa was a murder suspect.

Point three—my husband's patience was running out. Must get a move on and figure out who killed Shona.

Point four—a crazed ex-senator was in Vancouver and had evil designs on me, at least according to the CIA.

Point five—*but never mind.* Even if I reached twenty things that bothered me about my current life, I knew my woes didn't stack up to what the Spektors had suffered. Or to Mia's anguish.

So I shoved my concerns aside to enjoy the walk. My problems, however, still thrummed away, idling to the side of my mind, casting shadows over my mood.

To my surprise the campus didn't turn out to be completely gorgeous. It was a work in progress. Once we ventured inside the circle of trees that ringed the university, we ran into mounds of torn-up grass plus piles of building material and equipment. The scene was far from tranquil.

I tripped over a brick lying in the middle of my path.

"Ouch, that hurt." I bent to touch my sore foot.

"You'll live," Mia said.

She was all heart, this chick. I shot her a dirty look and rubbed my pitiful toes, slowing her down, just for spite.

She didn't seem fazed, but launched into a travelogue.

"A parking garage will go under here. This green lawn will become red brick." Laughter erupted from her. "The campus newspaper already calls it Red Square. Student activists like connecting to the famous namesake in Moscow."

I cast a dubious eye on the ripped-up ground.

"But Red Square in the USSR is enormous. It envelops you in Soviet power."

She leaned over and spat on the sod.

"How do you know? Photos?"

"I've been there."

Mia's eyebrows rose.

"Thought you said your life was boring."

"No, I told you 'safe and sheltered.' There's a difference."

We began to argue. Not watching where we walked, we ran into a workman carrying a bucket of cement.

"Hey, girlies, watch where you're going," he yelled.

Mia jolted to a stop and shot him the finger. "Watch it yourself, asshole."

Jack was right. Ballsy was the *mot juste* for Mia. I could never behave like that, even if I wanted to. The mini version of my mother, who lived inside my head, wouldn't allow a response in kind to rude behavior. A young matron—that would be *me*, though Mother's term curdled my blood when I heard it—must be polite always. I bet a workman had never yelled at *her* though.

We walked in silence, taking care to sidestep other workers. When we passed a building covered with architectural flourishes, Mia pointed to it.

"My grandfather donated money for that, the Suzzallo Library. As a kid, I overheard my father talking to university planners when they came looking for handouts."

She edged over to a surviving area of grass and spat again.

Her forehead puckered.

"Fat lot of good my family money ever did me. Their self-importance appalls me."

Okay, I got it. She used to be stinking rich, but maybe she missed being part of that world? Mia was one complex person.

Mia pointed ahead.

"There's the Husky Union Building. Everyone just calls it the HUB."

Looking around at the buildings, I made a snap judgment.

"This campus appeals to me, more than UBC with its gray buildings blending into gray skies. This Collegiate Gothic is welcoming, and the red brick warm things up too. Whether it's revolutionary or not, I don't care."

"Well, la dee dah, and aren't you the wiseass?" Mia said.

What the hell? I decided to blow off her comment. After all, she had a point; I could be pedantic. But I just couldn't help myself.

"My grandfather was an architect." I kept walking. "Some of his knowledge rubbed off on me."

Behind the HUB I saw several police cruisers, unoccupied. We entered the building, which, even during the summer semester, buzzed with life. Students were everywhere—talking, laughing, smoking, lounging on chairs, and spilling off those onto the floor.

"Our meetings used to be held on the second level," Mia said. "Let's try there first."

She led the way up the stairs, and upon reaching the second floor, she gestured to the third room on the left. That was where we found a gaggle of policemen.

I rushed ahead of Mia, too excited to be circumspect. A mistake.

A cop stepped forward. "You can't go in there. It's an official crime scene."

"We know that." I waved Mia over. "The dead girl, Bethany, was her friend. She's devastated."

"I understand," the policeman said, "but you still can't go into that room."

"So what's going on over there?" I pointed to a small door marked 'janitorial.' "Does the crime tape mean that's where Bethany was found?"

"Can't talk about that, miss. Move along please." He made a scooting motion with his hands.

Mia and I walked to the end of the hall, then looked back at the policemen hovering around the marked areas. Behind us came the sound of feet, clattering up the stairs in a hurry. From our vantage point at the top, I watched a girl dressed in cut-offs, a T-shirt, and Birkenstock sandals approach. She jerked to a stop when she spotted Mia.

"What're you doing here?" she asked. "Thought you'd gone

up to UBC."

"That's right, Lydia," Mia replied, "but I'm here to see the Spektors. You know about Shona's murder, right? We heard about Bethany's death on the radio and—"

"We came over to see what was going on," I said.

Lydia's hands flew to her face. "We're all in shock. Is it a double murder or totally unrelated deaths? Our group's really frightened. What do you think?"

"We're not sure." Mia pointed at me. "This is Austin, and she's also interested in figuring out the two murders. The whole deal is devastating."

"Unbelievable," Lydia murmured.

"Say—" Mia said, her tone casual.

Now she'll ask about Jack.

"—have you seen Shona's old boyfriend, Jack, lately? Wonder how he feels about Shona's murder?" Mia shifted her eyes over to me for a second.

I hoped that look meant she'd try to be subtle. Time would tell.

Another girl joined us on the stair landing.

Lydia said, "Hey, Amy, you seen Shona's Jack lately? Mia wants to talk to him."

The girl named Amy adjusted her skimpy halter top and threw her cigarette into an ash tray. "Nope, but I was hanging out on Bainbridge Island this summer. Better ask someone else."

Hosts of questions swirled in my head. I chose one and dived in.

"Did either of you"—I looked from Lydia to Amy and back—"know if Bethany was into anything new?"

"What do you mean?" Lydia asked.

I wrinkled my nose in thought. "Say, for example, did Bethany do anything daring or unusual lately?

Amy made a choking sound. "Are you kidding? Not her style."

"If Bethany was so quiet," I said, "then why would anyone

bother to kill her?"

Lydia nodded. "Right on. I thought the same thing."

"Beats me," Amy said. "Bethany never made a scene, just disappeared into the crowd. Guess she was the wrong person in the wrong place at the wrong time."

Amy and Lydia shook their heads and scuffed their feet. They reminded me of Tweedledee and Tweedledum—but female and lots thinner.

This was getting us nowhere. How could I blast open the door to key information?

I said, "Had you talked to Bethany recently? Did she mention Shona's death?"

Lydia looked at Amy. "She knew about Shona's murder. That's right, isn't it, Amy?"

"Right," Amy said. "Bethany was overwhelmed with grief. Like we wonder why anyone would kill Bethany, she was stunned someone killed Shona."

"Hey, wait a sec." Lydia's voice was like a thunderclap. "Here's something that might be significant. Bethany said Shona called her a day or two before she got murdered. Shona told Bethany someone wrote her threatening notes."

Notes? "Where were they left?" My scalp prickled, as if my hair sensed a breakthrough.

Lydia said, "At the lab where she worked. That's all I can remember, although I know Bethany gave me more details, but hell, I've forgotten."

Forgot the details? Good lord, what bad luck. And Larissa hadn't mentioned anything about notes.

Tamping down my frustration, I kept my voice calm. "Did Bethany know if Shona told anyone else about the threats?"

Lydia shook her head so hard that her curls bounced. "Don't think so. Bethany thought she was the only one Shona confided in. Who knows if that's true, but Shona said not to tell anybody else."

"Have the police questioned you yet?" I looked at Lydia, then Amy.

They shook their heads.

"Then I suggest you tell them this possible connection between the two murders. Then I think—"

"God damn it." Mia stomped her foot. "Damn, damn, dammit to hell." The thump of her work boot made us all jump.

Mia's face burned scarlet. "I told Shona she should've told the cops about those threats. She wouldn't listen to me." Her hand curled into a fist, and she hit the wall.

Amy and Lydia rolled their eyes. They shifted back and forth on their feet while Mia pounded the wall several more times. Finally she stopped, but she kept muttering under her breath.

I knew Mia's anger was turned inward and covered up a deep despair at failing to save Shona. I cast a beseeching glance at Amy and Lydia, but they were already saying their goodbyes.

Lydia said, "Great seeing you, Mia. Gotta run."

"Yeah, me too," Amy said. She turned to walk down the stairs, and Lydia followed. At first they moved slowly and then they picked up speed.

"Don't forget to tell the police, Lydia," I called after them.

By this time Mia stood quietly. Only her huffing breath showed she hadn't returned to normal. That is, if she ever felt what I'd call *normal*.

Mia was more damaged than I'd guessed at first.

Could she have killed her friend Shona? Was I misreading her anger?

When the question pushed into my mind, I shoved it aside. Mia's anguish seemed real to me. The only way Shona's murderer could be this young woman standing in front of me would be if Mia had two personalities.

The thought brought me up short.

A distinct possibility, though I could hear the authorities and their doubts already. But dual personalities did exist. Joanne Woodward won an Academy Award for *The Three Faces of Eve,* based on a true story.

The sexual abuse Mia suffered at the hands of her father

could have triggered multiple personalities. Who was I to know? I was no shrink, sure, but I saw no signs of a second person peeking from her—only rage erupting from time to time, and it seemed consistent with my understanding of her.

I stared in pity at Mia. Would another hug help to calm her down now?

Inching toward her, I held out my hand, touched her arm. She didn't flinch, only peered at me with such sorrow in her eyes that her gaze overpowered me, making me step back a few feet.

Relentless, I pressed on. "How about a hug?"

Mia whimpered, and then ducked her head. She flung herself forward so hard I had to reach out and catch her in my arms. She hung on me, sniffling. Then I felt tears sliding down my neck. I bet we made quite the dramatic scene. Since I was taller than Mia by a good eight inches, I looked over her shoulder to see if anyone was staring at us. What luck. The cops were huddled in a confab, and no one else was nearby, thank goodness.

Was this the first time she'd let herself cry over Shona's death? I guessed she'd been holding her feelings in, unable to deal with the fullness of her grief. That is, until now.

Mia was no killer. I'd stake my life on it. And in a sense, I was. If I were wrong, she could turn on me, kill me.

Patting her shoulder, I whispered in her ear. "Shona's death was not your fault. You tried to save her. You tried very hard." Her short hair bristled against my arm.

Mia gulped. "But if I'd only done more, I could have kept her alive."

"Hush now, hush. You don't know that. Go ahead and grieve, feel it, then you can prick the boil, let the wretched feelings drain out. But don't beat yourself up. Put down your guilt. You don't deserve to carry it."

"I'll try." Her words were a soft murmur in my ear.

Behind me came the hard clatter of shoes on the stairway. I disengaged from Mia and looked up to see Lydia topping the landing. When she reached us, she bent over and hung her head, catching her breath.

When she looked up, excitement shone out of her eyes. Lydia's face was red, and she looked ready to burst with her news.

"I just ran into a pal of Jack's. He said something that could help you."

Chapter Twenty-Eight

GOOD GRIEF, HAD Lydia stumbled across a clue? If so, I'd have to figure out a way to get the news to the Mounties. No way was I going to approach them.

Mia stood up straight and dried her eyes, then blinked rapidly. "What did you say?"

When Lydia repeated herself, Mia began yelling. "What friend of Jack's? What were his exact words? Tell me."

Poor Lydia backed up in the face of this rapid-fire assault. Her lips flapped wordlessly.

Mia stamped her foot. "For God's sake, hurry up. You're killing me here."

"Shut up and let me talk, will you?" Lydia faced me. "Can't you stop her?"

"Mia, baby, calm down." I leaned toward Mia, two inches away. "You'll drive Lydia off, and then we won't learn anything. Easy does it."

Covering her face with both hands, Mia mumbled between her fingers. "Sorry, Lydia. Please, what did Jack's friend say?"

Lydia's shoulders sagged, and she mouthed a silent "thanks" in my direction. "You remember Casey Dunlap, don't you, Mia?" Lydia's tone was gentle. She looked my way and said, "Casey was Jack's last roommate here at UW. I ran into him as I left the HUB. When I asked about the last he'd heard from Jack, Casey said Jack called him, oh, maybe ten days ago. Jack was excited, saying he was off to Vancouver to meet Shona. Jack thought he could get her back because she'd sent him a letter saying how much she missed him."

Now at long last, maybe we were getting somewhere.

"When was this?" I asked.

"Casey *guessed* it was ten days ago," Lydia said. "Jack had taken the engagement ring he'd bought for Shona out of hock and planned to offer it again. Casey warned him not to rush her, but Jack was lost in the romantic la-la-land of his imagination."

Here was real news. Jack might have been in the city at the time of Shona's murder—just what I'd been wondering about. He'd stay put on my suspect list and at the top. My need to talk to him dialed up to urgent.

"Where's Casey now?" Mia spoke in a surprisingly soft voice.

How long would this calm phase last? Her mood swings were getting to me. They came closer together and seemed more extreme with each angry outburst. And I still had to drive back to Vancouver with her—me *and Wyatt*. Not a prospect to relish.

Lydia set down her backpack and slumped onto the tiled floor. I joined her, and Mia followed suit. I suppressed a giggle, thinking we might burst into a chorus of "Kumbaya" any minute.

A cop from down the hall called to another one. "Look at those hippie chicks." Guffaws and whistles followed from the uniformed policemen.

Mia didn't appear to notice, but Lydia and I rolled our eyes at each other. Men—or rather, boys, since that's what they acted like—would be boys, even if they did wear an official uniform. Good grief, we were just tired, tuckered out, spent from too many tempestuous emotions. What was the big deal anyway, sitting on the floor?

Lydia said, "I was lucky, running into Casey. He was in a rush to meet friends, hitching down the coast to Oregon, and he doesn't know when he'll be back."

Mia said, "Sorry I lost it a minute ago. Shona's death, well, it's kinda undone me."

A flicker of surprise ran across Lydia's face, yet she merely shrugged, saying smoothly, "Don't worry about it. Now, folks, I really do have to split."

She stood in a smooth, fluid motion. I wondered if she practiced yoga and envied her her lithe body.

"Hope Casey's gossip helped some," Lydia said. She made the two-fingered peace sign and loped back down the stairs.

Left in Lydia's wake, Mia and I stared at each other. I considered what to do next, with no earthly idea what Mia was thinking. Her face was drawn, and exhaustion enfolded her like an ugly sweater. While I felt jazzed up, looking ahead at all the lines of inquiry to pursue, she registered defeat in every sagging feature.

She spread her hands. "What now?"

"For starters," I said, "we hurry back to the Spektors and pick up Wyatt. We need to get back on the road pronto."

She looked at her watch and winced. "Look, Austin, I just can't think straight. Does Casey's story help us out? I can't tell. I feel shattered, depleted, so shaky I'm scared to drive. You're gonna have to do it. Will you be okay with that?"

I nodded. "Of course, but then you'll have to hold Wyatt. *Are you* up for that?"

"Guess so. Maybe I can snooze for an hour while I hold him, then I'll take the wheel."

"We'll figure it out. Let's get going."

My legs couldn't take me out of the HUB fast enough. Mia raced to keep up with me as I dodged piles of brick and workmen hauling their equipment around the burgeoning Red Square, Seattle style.

"Slow down, damn you." She pulled on my arm. "We're not in that big a hurry."

"Can't you see I've turned into a racehorse and the bit's between my teeth?" I gave a whinny and pawed the ground with a pretend hoof.

Mia laughed in my face. "You are so strange."

That was rich, coming from her.

"I was horse-crazy as a girl." I adjusted my purse on my shoulder and straightened my blouse. "I'm energized silly and can't wait until we turn up some good hard evidence of who killed Shona."

"Okay, okay." Her tone sounded grudging. "And maybe Bethany too."

Fifteen minutes passed while we walked back to the mortuary. Mia flapped along beside me, working hard to keep pace, breathing too hard to talk. The opportunity was perfect to mull over what we'd learned in the HUB.

Back there with Lydia and Amy, in the passion of the moment, I'd focused more on keeping Mia from totally flipping out, maybe even more than taking in what they had said. That was the only excuse I could come up with for letting the most important fact almost slide right by me.

Written threats to Shona had been left at the lab where she worked.

That detail pointed to a killer hanging about the science building. Of course, Larissa worked there also. My guess was she wasn't cleared from being a suspect, not yet anyway.

But this fact pointed suspicion away from other members of the women's group—also away from Jack as the killer. Still, he could have vital information Shona herself had told him. Maybe she'd even shared the name of someone she suspected of trying so hard to scare her.

I tramped on, ignoring the beautiful trees on campus, the complaints of Mia at my brisk pace, the glorious sunshine that was a relief from the constant rains. Yet I couldn't ignore the one thought that kept pounding in my head—I did not want to get on a plane back to Toronto if Larissa was still on the RCMP suspect list.

I needed to call David and tell him Professor Klimenko had made my return ticket ten days after my arrival. That suited me, but telling David wouldn't be a pleasant task.

Soon Mia and I were back knocking on the Spektors' door. Mrs. Spektor opened it with Wyatt in her arms.

Reaching out for him, I gushed, "Oh sweetheart, have you been a good boy?"

"He's a little angel." Mrs. Spektor's face glowed, a delight to see. "We had a little nap. I was about ready to change him."

As I settled him into my arms, the phone rang.

"I'll get it," Mr. Spektor called out.

I changed Wyatt's diaper, singing the itsy-bitsy spider song and tickling his toes. Mrs. Spektor gave us a bag of snacks to munch on during our return trip. We were chatting when Mr. Spektor wobbled back into the living room on legs so unsteady that he had to clutch a side table for stability.

The lines on his face seemed deeper than when he'd left the room. He spoke slowly in a solemn voice loaded with pain. He wasn't speaking English, so I couldn't tell what was wrong.

His wife dropped Wy's plastic baby bottle.

"What's he saying?" Mia demanded. "What's going on?"

Mr. Spektor sank onto a chair and stared at us with sad eyes—eyes numbed by all the evil he'd seen in his lifetime, I imagined. "That call was from Canada, from your friend Professor Klimenko. His daughter is in the hospital, and he wants you to return as quickly as you can."

"What's wrong with Larissa?" I started to shake.

He consulted a piece of paper, and then his desolate eyes sought mine. "I knew you'd want the details, so I made notes. His daughter was attacked at her workplace. A colleague found her lying on the floor in the ladies room. She was beaten badly." His eyes flicked down to the paper and back. "The police were called, and an ambulance took her to Vancouver General Hospital."

Oh my God.

My heart hammered hard in my chest. I hugged Wyatt so tightly that he cried out. "She'll live, won't she?"

Mr. Spektor's gentle smile reassured me. "The hospital lists her in critical but stable condition. However, she has several broken bones, and the complete extent of her injuries is not known yet."

"Didn't Professor Klimenko want to talk to me?"

"No, he was rushed and needed to return to his daughter's bedside. He asked me to convey his message and to urge you to drive back to his sister-in-law's house right away. He asked you please to hurry but to stay alert for anything that looks strange. He wants you to be careful and stay safe."

"Be safe? Why's he worried about me? Does he think the attacker will come at me next?" My heart raced even faster now. "Is that it, Mr. Spektor?"

He looked at me over the top of his spectacles. "No, my dear, he didn't say that, but I assume that's what he meant. Be cautious on your return to Vancouver. That only makes good sense, doesn't it?"

He rose from the chair and began to pace, still fingering the paper. After a full circle of the room, he stopped and jammed the paper into his shirt pocket. "And I am afraid there is more information about the attack. Professor Klimenko said someone wrote awful things across the ladies room mirror. Larissa's broken lipstick was in the sink, and the contents of her purse lay strewn across the floor. Evidently the brute used her lipstick to display his venom."

Wyatt gave a small cry. Mrs. Spektor winced and passed the baby bottle to me, and Wy lunged for it greedily. Then only the slurping sounds he made broke the tense silence in the room.

"What were the words, motek?" Mrs. Spektor crept up to her husband and placed a hand on his arm. "Do you know?"

"I do, but are you sure you want to know?"

Mia and I nodded, but Mrs. Spektor turned away and crossed the room to the sofa, where she sat and twisted her hands.

"Then I must tell you two." He took the paper from his pocket and smoothed it out on a table. "I cannot say these things aloud. You can read the thoughts of this demented man for yourselves."

Mia moved toward him with outstretched hand, and he passed the paper to her. She read his notes, and a deep growl began in her throat, turning quickly into a cry of pain.

Mrs. Spektor reached for the paper, but Mia snatched it back. "You don't want to see this." Mrs. Spektor backed away.

Mia thrust the paper at me. "Austin, you have no choice. Read it."

I read:

death to feminist bitches
God said men rule
leave my happy home alone

Chapter Twenty-Nine

MIA SETTLED INTO the passenger seat of the minivan with Wyatt, and I got into the driver's seat. All the while I was getting situated—adjusting the seat, the rear-view mirror, and so on—she chattered nervously beside me.

"Holy crap, Austin. What in hell is going on? The guy is sheer evil. He has to be, to hurt a tiny, lovely girl like Larissa."

Shut up, please shut up. My precious friend Larissa was hurt, and anxiety had me sick to my stomach. I didn't blame Mia for being agitated, but her rant didn't help me calm down.

Only a huge effort kept me from plunging the gas pedal to the floor and racing back to Vancouver. I had to get to Larissa. I had to.

By the time we hit Interstate 5, Mia's babbling slowed. She nestled into the seat and cradled Wyatt in her lap. She held him the way I had suggested, and I could only hope that she didn't drop him if she fell asleep.

Mia remained silent for more than an hour. I drove, she held Wyatt. I kept checking to see if she went to asleep, but her eyes never closed. We stewed in our own thoughts.

The toll of women felled by the madman was mounting. In Vancouver one was dead and following the death of another in Seattle, a third was badly beaten. Although I had no solid data that connected the attacks, my intuition said they were related. Someone just had to prove it.

McKinnon had told me how slow inter-departmental communication between police forces was. Who knew when the Seattle police and the Mounties would get together? If Mr. Spektor had told Professor Klimenko about Bethany's death, the latter would have told the RCMP. And if he hadn't done it, then I would make sure someone did. I couldn't. Both David and DS McKinnon had drummed into me that I should stay away from them, period.

I hoped McKinnon had called with information he'd gleaned from the Mounties.

You promised David you wouldn't mess in the inquiry—remember? The tiny voice whined from a corner of my mind.

I pushed it aside. I had to avenge Larissa. And if I could help save another girl from attack, then I would do that too. I had to solve the puzzle. I was into this mission too deep to back out now. Not willingly anyhow.

Why did he hate females so much? The written evidence slashed in blood-red across the mirror indicated the killer was a male who was furious at women trying to live more independent lives. Then again, perhaps that was only a clever ploy.

What about the warnings sent by my CIA mentor, Mr. Jones? Could the former senator and his aide be involved? That seemed a bit of a stretch, but still....

I was glad Jones had someone keeping tabs on me. I wondered if Jones knew about the attack on Larissa. Things were getting murky.

I pushed stray hairs away from my face and tried to see the clues more clearly. The idea of Simpson's involvement might be farfetched, but I didn't want to leap automatically to the obvious conclusion that a woman-hating male was rampaging around the Pacific Northwest. Even if I was convinced that were true, I had to stay open to other possibilities.

Three attacks on feminists had taken place at two universities. The murderer must have some connection to academic life. Possibly he was a student, but not necessarily. A guest lecturer?

Although I never for a minute believed Larissa was guilty of murdering Shona, part of this horror show did bring me some relief. Larissa could not have beaten herself up. She was now a victim too—surely that would take her off the RCMP's list of suspects. It was a tough way to achieve that goal, but still, it was the only silver lining I could see.

I squinted at Mia and Wyatt. Both now snoozed peacefully, and I accelerated the VW minibus to the maximum speed limit. While they slept, I had time to let my mind range freely. I fingered the photograph of Shona in my shirt pocket. Mrs. Spektor had offered it after I asked to see one.

In the picture, *her Shoshana* stood in front of a giant monkey puzzle tree in a playful pose. Her arms mimicked the form of the tree's odd limbs. Her hair was a springy mass of dark curls that refused to be ruled by her headband. Her smile was so broad and genuine that I regretted not having met her. I might also have ended up calling her Shiny Shona.

We passed Bellingham, Washington, and a sign that noted the Canadian border was seventeen miles away. Should I pull over and insist Mia take the wheel? After all, this was her vehicle.

Oh, what the hell. I didn't care. I wanted to race to the hospital and see Larissa as soon as possible. I could drive across the border myself just fine. Easy as pie.

High school geography taught me that the US-Canadian border was the world's longest undefended one. The Peace Arch marked the border on its western end, and now the top of its classical revival grandeur, in all its brilliant white glory, came into view. The scene looked so serene. I wished my mind felt the same. The thought of Larissa lying in a hospital bed with broken bones and who knew what other ailments made me ache.

When I slowed the van to a stop for the border guard, Mia woke and stretched. Wyatt began to cry. The guard looked in, did a speedy tally of our drivers' licenses, and waved us through quickly. Off to my left I spotted the American guard who had processed us into the States earlier. I waved at him, and he waved back with a huge grin stretching across his face. He gave me a thumbs-up sign, and we were on our way back to the Great White North.

Mia shifted in her seat, and Wyatt wiggled in her arms. When he reared back and hit her chin with his head, she yelped in surprise.

She rubbed her chin. "Why don't you let me drive now? I'm rested up, and your baby needs his mom."

"Don't you want more practice so you'll make a good mother some day?"

The scowl on Mia's face showed my attempt at teasing had backfired.

"I'm never having kids," she said. "No way am I cut out for that. I have enough trouble taking care of myself."

"So you're not a fan of the rule that says a woman's place is in the home?" Again I meant to tease, but also to gage her views on the women's movement.

"You're kidding, right?"

"Well, kind of. I would like to hear what you think women should be doing these days. What have you learned at all those meetings?"

"We should be free to do anything we damned well choose. And that's final."

She hadn't paused to think before she snapped her answer out.

I mused about that for a few seconds and then said, "So you never had anyone tell you what you should do with your life—no insistent female relative say you should be the best at everything yet also a perfect wife and mother?"

Her response was a glare.

I pulled off the highway so we could change places. When I cut the engine, I heard her growling to herself.

"Speak up," I said. "I can't hear you."

"My father told me—no, showed me—where my place was.

In his goddamn bed. I ran from that and I've been running ever since. To what, I'm not sure, but my future holds no children. I'd make a lousy mom. Besides, I don't like kids. Well, with the exception of your son, of course."

At least she had the good grace to add that for my benefit.

"When I was in junior high," she said, "my father made me babysit for a young cousin. In front of my brothers he always said—in his sugary, sickening-smooth way—that he wanted to make sure I had experience with infants so I would be a dutiful mom one day." She inhaled sharply before she continued. "No wonder I loathe everything involved with procreation, with that monster preaching about it."

This peek into the dark world of Mia's life made my nerves bunch up even tighter. "And who could blame you?"

We switched places, and before she could start the engine, I put a hand out to stop her. "Do you think you've been treated differently at school because you're female?"

"What a stupid question," she shot back. "Of course I have."

"Can you give me examples?"

"Sure thing." Putting the minivan in gear, she drove back on the highway, humming. A maniacal-looking grin spread across her face. I didn't like the feel of her mood. In no time at all she was exceeding the speed limit.

Admittedly, I saw why she wasn't high on men. But surely there were some in her life who had treated her well. Mr. Spektor, for one. I made a mental note to point that out.

"Before I begin my wretched litany," she said, "why're you asking these questions?"

"I'm trying to get into the mindset of a guy who'd beat up and kill women, who would write those awful things in the ladies room. That is totally outside my experience. Totally."

She hooted, and Wy twitched in my arms. "You *have* led a sheltered life. All my experience with men says they are the scum of the earth, and the exceptions are the nice ones."

"Like Mr. Spektor?"

"Exactly. The exception that proves the rule. Let me tell you what happened to me as an undergrad at UW. For starters, my looks and my sexuality were openly discussed by one of my professors and some of the male students."

"That's despicable."

"One time I entered a speech contest, one of the few females. I came in first and was justifiably proud. After the awards were announced and trophies awarded, I was drinking in the praise. One of the male competitors, the guy who'd placed second, sidled up to me. He got close enough so no one else could hear what he said. He whispered, 'Of course you won. You sexualized the whole event. No one heard a word you said. The old judges were drooling all over you.' "

She cleared her throat. "Great way to honor my achievements, right? Demeaning any skill I had. And Shona had it just as bad. One prof joked he allowed only pretty girls to work in his lab. Some creeps in her labs talked all the time about her breasts and questioned her sexual history. But I'll give this to Shona—that stuff made her more ferocious in demanding respect for her intellect. She was a fighter, that girl."

"Oh my God," I said.

"What?"

"You said *creep*. That made me think about Larissa's attacker. I wonder if she saw him. Does she know who he was and has she told the police yet? Can't you drive faster?"

Suddenly I didn't care how fast Mia drove. Speed was our new friend.

Chapter Thirty

MIA DROVE SO fast that I held onto the armrest in fright. The nervous Nelly inside me wanted to say "slow down," but the curious Nancy Drew who coexisted with Nelly won out. I could endure high speed for the sake of getting to Larissa sooner.

I gritted my teeth, held Wyatt tight, and prayed silently for safe travels.

After agonies of time we whizzed into Raisa's driveway. We clambered into the house with Wyatt screaming his little lungs out, frustrated at being awake. We found Raisa in the kitchen. Of course Professor Klimenko was at the hospital with Larissa.

"Visiting hours end soon," Raisa said. "Must hurry to see her. Then you must rush to UBC. Larissa's friend called about emergency meeting of women's group. They worry about danger after attack on Larissa. You want to go, da?"

I whirled around to look at Mia.

"Are you up for this?"

"Damn straight, I am, and I'll drive you."

My shoulders sagged. I couldn't take Wyatt with me. I'd have to stay put.

Raisa must have read my mind—or my body language.

"Let me take baby. You two go now."

I slapped aside my guilt at not spending every waking hour with Wy and accepted her offer. These long hours apart from him were an anomaly, not a regular practice.

"If you're quite sure?"

"Da. Wyatt, I can handle him."

I threw my arms around Raisa.

"Thanks so much. You're a brick."

"Brick? I am brick?"

"An expression."

"I do not know it."

"Never mind." I waved my hand—the one not holding onto Wyatt. "Tell us, did Larissa recognize her attacker? Maybe he's the same person who killed Shona."

"You think so?" Mia's voice was heavy with sarcasm. "Seems pretty damned obvious to me."

Raisa took Wyatt from my arms.

"Not sure what Larissa saw. Her father there with her all day. I talked to him, yet I do not know for certain. He says she doped up. The Mounties tried questions, but doctors gave few minutes. She has concussion."

Oh, my poor friend. I dreaded seeing her, damaged and pitiable in a hospital bed. I had to though, regardless of her medical condition.

Mia and I rushed to the minivan and raced across town to the hospital, arriving with only fifteen minutes left during visiting hours. They were strict at this hospital, Raisa had said. Mia waited in the car with the motor running, and I ran in to see Larisa.

I stopped short when I saw Garrett sitting in a chair outside her room.

"What are you doing here?" Oh damn, I sounded accusatory. "No offense. I'm just shocked to see you."

Garrett stood and stepped close to me. He twisted a copy of *Maclean's* weekly newsmagazine. His eyes were rimmed with red.

"The RCMP couldn't post a guard on Larissa's door—too few men on duty. I took off work so I could do it myself."

He rubbed his eyes with his free hand.

I gestured to the closed door to Larissa's room.

"How's she doing?"

Garrett shook his head. "Not very well. She's hardly ever conscious, but of course she's sedated to keep her from feeling pain. Nurses come and go looking grim. Her dad's in there with her. He'll know more about her prognosis than I do."

The seriousness of Larissa's condition unnerved me. I hadn't expected she'd still be knocked out, not like this. I gripped Garrett's arm. "Sounds bad. How long have you been standing guard?"

"I came as soon as I heard she'd been attacked. I'll stay as long as it takes."

"Can I go in?"

"Of course. I'll stay here though." He cast a wary glance up and down the hall. "Her attacker could be anywhere."

"Did she see him, recognize him?"

"Doesn't sound like it. Ask her dad. He'll know for sure."

"What you're doing is extraordinary. You are a hero, Garrett."

Color rushed into his cheeks, and he ducked his head.

I pushed open the door and entered the room. Larissa lay in the sole bed—a private room then. Professor Klimenko didn't look up.

"Hello," I said in a whisper.

His shaggy head twitched. When his eyes met mine, his face lit with a smile. He pushed off the chair and walked toward me with a stiff gait.

"At last. Is baby Wyatt all right? Are you?"

"We're fine. What about Larissa?" My eyes shifted toward her, lying prone and pale, oh so very pale. The room and its contents—the one exception being her dark hair spread across the pillow—were devoid of color. Without life, without blood.

I didn't like the look of this one bit.

Professor Klimenko outlined her condition briefly, repeating the facts that Garrett had shared, providing no new details. While he talked, I moved closer to Larissa and laid a hand on her arm. At least she looked peaceful and showed no evidence of pain.

"When she wakes up, does she know you?"

"She does. She smiles and drifts back to sleep. Her doctors don't say much. At first they were upbeat, but now…they are just waiting."

An armchair sat in a corner. I pulled it beside his chair so we could sit and talk quietly. "Did Larissa see her attacker?"

He shook his head sadly.

"Do the Mounties have any leads? What have they told you?"

"Not much. That the investigation continues. I'm sure they're doing their best." His expression belied his positive words.

"Are the Mounties still treating Larissa as a suspect in Shona's murder?" I asked.

Professor Klimenko's lips almost curled into a smile. "The officer I talked to did not mention it. Therefore, I asked, and he admitted she is no longer a suspect. A small consolation. Surely there was an easier way to prove she's no killer."

He pushed his chair back, stood, and wandered around the room. He stopped beside my chair. "The situation is more dangerous now. There's also Senator Simpson to worry about. You must stop now, Austin. Remember what you went through last time."

He couldn't scare me enough to make me quit.

"Even though Larissa's name is cleared, I have to do something." I choked back a sob. "Look at her—she's a victim now too. Who could do this to her? No ordinary fiend. I must help find him."

Immediately I regretted my words. Perhaps I'd said too much. Professor Klimenko didn't need to hear my anguish. I glanced sideways to see if I'd disturbed his composure.

His face twisted as if he were in pain. "Leave the case to the professionals. I beg you. You are another daughter to me." He stopped and swallowed. "I can't have you risking your own safety. I don't want that on my conscience too."

Any minute we were both going to break down and cry. Neither of us needed that.

Professor Klimenko's face changed. He leveled a stern gaze from under his bushy black eyebrows. "I want you to stop. Larissa would want that also."

When he spoke her name, Larissa's eyelids flickered and then closed again. As I watched intently, her eyes opened fully. Her unfocused gaze darted around the room and came to rest on me.

"Austin. You came." Her voice was no more than a feather floating on air.

"I'm here." I reached for her hand, but her eyes had shut again. "I'll get him, Larissa. I swear I will."

My whole body sagged, and I could no longer hold back my emotions. Tears dripped down my cheeks. I heard Professor Klimenko step closer to me. Without turning around, I said, "At least she knew me."

I turned and he moved as if to hug me. I shook my head and inched around him, dropping into my chair. Several minutes passed while I cried silently until, finally, I managed to compose myself.

I dug a tissue out of my purse and blew my nose. "Has Garrett had a break? I admire how he's kept watch for so long, but he looks so tired. And how did he end up here anyway?"

"He called to ask Larissa for a date, but got Raisa on the line, right after she learned about Larissa's attack. Raisa blurted out the news, including that Larissa was going by ambulance to Vancouver General. He rushed over here and just stayed. I encouraged him to go home and rest, but I cannot get him to leave. He refused."

"I'll see if I can have any luck. You must be exhausted too."

"I cannot leave—surely you understand. I will sleep in the waiting room."

"Of course."

A nurse appeared in the doorway. "Visiting hours are over. You must go now."

I stood, but my legs were shaky. I grabbed the back of the chair to steady myself.

Professor Klimenko held out his good left hand, and I took it in mine. He'd already suffered so much in his lifetime, and now this. I opened my mouth to say this, then shut it. Now wasn't the time.

Foolhardy or not, I had a killer to track down. I must focus on that.

Chapter Thirty-One

WHEN I REJOINED Mia in her minivan, I noticed right away, across the street, a pale-colored Ford. I thought it looked suspicious.

"See that car back there?" I said.

"Sure," Mia said.

"I don't like the look of it."

"Don't be silly. It's nothing."

"I'm not so certain. The man in the driver's seat is reading a newspaper *in the dark*. That seems awfully fishy. That Ford followed us onto this street earlier and stopped over there, where it has *stayed*."

"You're getting paranoid."

"Am not. I made some enemies last year and was warned they might be looking for me while I'm here in Vancouver."

Mia whistled. "Doesn't sound like a 'safe and easy' life to me."

"I know, I know. I could be dreaming up problems that don't exist, but don't look at the sedan when we pass, okay?"

"All right." Mia put the van in reverse and backed up several feet, then stopped. "Shall I ram him, just for kicks?"

I chuckled, Mia giggled. Then our laughter erupted, breaking the tension that had felt combustible.

Perhaps I was being paranoid. Even so, after we had gone two blocks, I turned to see if the Ford followed us. I thought it was a couple of cars back, but couldn't say for sure we were being tailed. The nerves in my neck tingled, revving up my fight-or-flight defenses, just in case.

Twenty minutes later we were on campus and dashing into the meeting room at SUB. Fewer women were present this time—about fifteen or so—and I knew only two by name. Janet, who fancied herself the natural successor to Shona as leader, was holding forth when we joined the group. Fayette of the flaming red hair was present too—the one who reported gossip accurately. One older woman, conservatively dressed in a shirtwaist dress with long sleeves, was introduced as a representative of the university administration.

One striking girl caught my attention. She looked like she belonged in a pre-Raphaelite painting. She had a cascade of black hair and wore a tunic of blue velvet, a long gauzy cotton skirt, sandals, and a daisy in her hair.

"Who's that?" I leaned toward Mia and nodded in the daisy-wearer's direction.

"*That* is Delilah." Mia's tone was bitter. "Now you see why she makes me jealous. Well, there are a host of reasons."

Whoa. Mia confessed to being jealous of Shona's last roommate? That was news. I knew she resented Shona's decision to move out, but this sounded different.

Still, there she stood, right in front of me—the elusive Delilah. I vowed to corral her after the meeting and get answers to questions I suspected only she could answer—like what was Shona's state of mind before she was killed and why she'd moved out on Mia and in with Delilah. Delilah's perspective on Shiny Shona should help me see her in a fuller light.

Janet stopped her speechifying when she saw Mia and me take seats near Fayette. Janet said, "Hello, Mia and, uh, Houston, is it?"

"Austin."

"Sorry. My mistake." She tugged on her shirt collar, smoothed it down with trembling fingers. "Well, so glad you made it tonight. Have you been to see Larissa yet?"

I waited for Mia to answer. When she didn't, I said, "We just returned from a whirlwind trip to Seattle, paying our respects to Shona's parents. When Larissa's dad called about the attack on her, we hurried back to see her in the hospital, then came straight here. She's in a bad way, with broken bones and a head injury. She knew me, though."

"I've got news of Larissa too." Beside me Fayette sat forward in her chair, zinging with excited energy. "There's gossip around saying she was beat up by someone who hates women."

A low murmur ran through the room.

"So you don't believe me? Well, that's what I heard. I confess I don't know if the rumor is credible or not."

Should I address this? If so, with how much detail?

Did the Mounties want to keep the anti-feminist graffiti quiet? I had no idea. Damn, I wished I'd tried for contacts within the RCMP, no matter what Detective Sergeant McKinnon had advised me. Before I could make a snap decision, someone else answered Fayette.

"Yes, you heard right, Fayette." To my left, Emma was speaking. "Before the police cordoned off the ladies room in the chemistry building, I saw the graffiti the guy left on the mirror. Whoever attacked Larissa was furious at women, especially women who want any kind of modern life." Emma hesitated, then looked my way, as if asking if she should go further.

"Fayette and Emma are right, but the police don't want key details to get out," I said, giving an account of the scrawls on the ladies room mirror but with only sketchy details—avoiding the actual words. But of course I remembered them. They were carved into my memory. Nothing like this had ever confronted me back home in Cuero, Texas, population seven thousand. I was learning more about the full range of human nature than I'd ever bargained for when I so eagerly left the protection of my parents' home and their sheltering attitudes.

All around the room, questions rang out.

"What are we going to do?"

"What on earth *can* we do?"

"We need an escort program to protect us as we walk around campus," Janet said.

"And our escorts would be who—*guys?*" Contempt spiked Mia's comment.

Janet looked daggers at Mia. "Then what's *your* big idea, missy?"

"Don't talk to me like that." Mia rose from her seat, but I thrust out an arm and pushed her back down.

"Be quiet. You'll make things worse," I said in a low voice.

"We need posters warning about the maniac on the loose who's hurting women." Fayette's tone was as bright and vivid as her red hair.

"We need mace, like the cops use on protestors." This suggestion came from an older woman with sunken cheeks.

"I carry a can of hairspray," another woman said. "Aim at an attacker's eyes, and then you disable him long enough for you to run away."

Murmurs of excitement ran around the room. The woman representing the university expressed the need for caution and safety.

"Let's get Stan Persky to put a story in *The Georgia Strait*," said a young women in bell-bottom jeans.

"Right on," several others shouted.

Rumblings that sounded like agreement rolled through the room.

Someone behind me spoke up. "Anyone see any RCMP officers on campus today?"

"I did," Fayette said. "I spied a Mountie sitting in his car near the chemistry building. If I hadn't been late for an appointment, I would've gone into the building and nosed around, just to see what I could find out."

This girl—excuse me, *woman*—was someone I could relate to. She thought like me. But I was no gossip. I just fancied myself an older version of Nancy Drew.

Thousands of miles east of me, my husband must have felt twinges of horror, thinking, *I knew I shouldn't have let her go to Vancouver.*

I cleared my throat. "Has anyone actually talked to the RCMP—been interviewed by them, I mean?" I glanced around the room. Delilah met my eyes and nodded.

"The Mounties interviewed me," she said.

"Do they know about the death of another student, another feminist, in Seattle?" I said.

The room immediately filled with gasps and bursts of "what" and "oh no" and numerous swear words. Mia and I took turns explaining what we'd learned about the death of Shona's Seattle friend, Bethany Furst.

"This is getting frigging scary."

The speaker was one I recognized from the previous meeting. Even though she was soft-spoken and diffident, she had confided her anger over Mick Jagger singing "Under My Thumb."

Her eyes were wide with alarm. "I had no idea the women's movement would make men so angry," she said. "And now I won't go inside the chemistry building. It's not safe for woman over there."

A lively discussion broke out between two sides—one expressing defiance and the other claiming fear. After five minutes of emotional venting, Janet jumped in and called a halt.

"Enough. Let's get down to making practical pl—"

"I moved out this morning."

All heads swiveled toward the speaker, Jagger's non-fan.

"That's Becky, right?" I whispered to Mia.

She nodded and then said, "Shh."

"My husband refuses to babysit when I come to meetings," Becky said, "and even accused me of seeing another man and using our meetings as a ruse." She stopped to brush away a tear that straggled down her cheek.

"Then what you're doing is very brave," Janet said. Others

mumbled their agreement.

"My husband is being ridiculous. This is 1969, not the Middle Ages. I may be just a housewife, but I will not be stopped."

"Don't put yourself down," someone called out.

Janet perched on the edge of a table. "Remember when the suffragettes demanded the vote in England right before World War One broke out? They were thrown in jail and force fed. It got downright ugly. It's all about power. Men don't want to share. They are fat and happy with things the way they are. Our potential for power scares them. Sisterhood is powerful."

Ugly. There was that word again.

Oh, Mother dear, why did you devote your life to protecting me from the ugliness of people? Didn't you realize I would meet up with it sooner or later? And be ignorantly unprepared?

Fayette leaned toward me. "Tonight's only the second time Becky has spoken up. I always figured she was repressed at home. Sounds like I nailed that one."

Becky was still talking. "Down through the ages women haven't gotten credit for successes and discoveries. For example, did you know an unsung woman helped discover DNA? Three men won the Nobel Prize, yet Rosalind Franklin showed them her discovery of DNA's structure and—"

I'd never heard a housewife discuss DNA before.

"—so I used to study chemistry but now only my husband does."

"Sorry I'm late." Dr. Shirley strode through the door with masculine-sized steps. "There's a big ruckus outside. Can't you hear the fire engines? A van is in flames outside in the parking lot."

Mia and two other women ran to the window. Only Mia let out a shriek. "Holy shit, Austin, let's go." She ran to grab her purse and then tugged on my arm.

"Okay, but give me a minute." I rushed over to Delilah. Leaving without talking to her would be a crime. She might think I was nuts, but desperation made me bolder than usual.

"You don't know me, but I've wanted to talk to you about Shona. I want to find the man who hurt my friend Larissa and killed Shona. Can we talk soon?"

Delilah fingered the daisy in her hair. "Yes, we must talk. I see your aura is mostly yellow, so I'll be able to relate to you easily. I know things about Shona and Mia that you need to hear. Let me give you my number."

Chapter Thirty-Two

DELILAH SNAGGED MY curiosity, although I didn't care what color my aura was. What on earth did she need to tell me? As I raced out of SUB and into the parking lot, I wondered why she hadn't tried to get in touch with me before.

A fire engine roared into the parking lot with sirens shrieking. Firemen jumped out and began to deploy their hoses near where Mia had parked her van. Where were the endless rains? Tonight they would've been useful.

And where was Mia? I couldn't see her anywhere. The crowd had grown large and boisterous. Students seemed to enjoy the blazing show. I couldn't tell if the fire was consuming Mia's van or not. If there had been colorful hippie designs, they were obscured by flames and water now.

I heard my name called and turned to find Mia waving frantically at me.

"Come here," she yelled.

I pushed through the crowd to join her. She cursed loudly, using every swear word I'd ever heard and then some.

I pointed to the van. "Yours, right?"

She spat on the pavement. "You think you're a Sherlock, but you're really just an idiot."

I could forgive her calling me an idiot since her car was destroyed, but I really wish she'd quit spitting; it was crass. I'd have to mention it sometime. She shook her fist at the smoldering van. Some other time.

"It's not my fault your van is on fire, so don't take your anger out on me."

She stamped her foot. "I'm not the one who has nameless bad guys combing the city for me. That's *you*."

Bile rose in my throat. Could she be right? Maybe this was the work of Simpson and not the berserk killer. My stomach did back flips. I moved away from Mia.

"Where are you going?" she yelled after me.

"Off to find a trash can. I'm going to be sick."

By the time I found one, I didn't need to throw up after all. I stumbled back to Mia's side, only to find a campus cop questioning her. Thank heavens she was more under control now.

I tried to hear their conversation, but the noise of the fire engines, the crowd, the roar of the flames—all that filled my ears and masked their words. Mia gesticulated wildly, and I hoped her swearing had abated.

After several minutes, the cop moved away and Mia turned to me.

"What's going on?" I asked. "How did the fire start?"

"That guy wasn't sure, but they're guessing it was started on purpose. There's a strong smell of gasoline leading up to my van, like someone poured it from a can." Mia grabbed my arm and thrust her face into mine. "I blame you for this. Probably that car you worried about tailed us here. He wasn't after me, though. He was after you."

I wrenched my arm free. "An hour ago you called me paranoid, and now you say the fire is my fault. Make up your mind, sweetie. You're being illogical."

"I wish I'd never met you and—"

"You two need any help?"

I looked up to see Delilah standing in front of us. Spangles on her velvet tunic shone in the fire's blaze. She looked like a gorgeous apparition backlit with the fires from where? Hades?

Mia stepped back two paces. Even in the shadows, her face

registered despair. Her mouth turned down, and she looked like she smelled something sour.

"Why would I ever want your help?" Mia said.

To her credit, Delilah remained calm, at least on the surface. Who knew how she really felt?

"You'll need a ride somewhere," she said. "Just figured I'd offer you two a lift." She glanced at me. "How about it?"

I eyeballed my watch. Almost time to call David—one more hour. "Sure, I'd love a ride. I'm not going far. Thanks."

"Suit yourself," Mia said. "I'll ask someone else for a ride. Or I'll hitch. I'm not riding with you, Delilah." With that, she stomped off and pushed her way through the milling throng, which consisted mostly of red-jacketed engineering students. Larissa had told me they were infamous for their high spirits and eagerness for trouble.

What should I say now? Delilah's beauty intimidated me. If anything, she was even more exquisite than Larissa. I had doubted that was possible, yet here was living proof.

"Gosh, uh, Delilah, you were, uh, kind to offer a ride." Why was I stammering like a teenage fool? *Get a grip, you dunce.*

My first meeting with Larissa flashed through my mind. Meeting hopelessly beautiful girls always made me feel inferior. Mother always wished I would be one of them, but I'd never attain such exquisite beauty.

I pushed my inferiority complex aside and said, "I'm staying just east of the university, so I hope it won't be much out of your way."

She took the daisy out of her hair and twirled it in her fingers. "No sweat. I'm not in a hurry and don't have anywhere special to go. Want to go back to SUB, have coffee, and I can try to answer your questions?"

For a heavenly vision, Delilah seemed surprisingly down to earth. My shoulders lowered, and my breathing slowed. Maybe she'd be easy to talk to after all. Compared to dealing with Mia all day, talking to Delilah might be a snap.

226

Double-checking my watch showed I needed to hurry if I wanted to call David on time. "Sounds good, but I can't stay long. I need to get back to my baby."

"We'll leave whenever you say."

We threaded our way through the crowd and walked back into SUB. Off in a corner, Janet had buttonholed Stan Persky. Even from a distance she looked agitated. Her hands were wind-milling and her mouth was moving rapidly. Stan lounged against a wall, his expression one of pained forbearance.

Delilah followed my gaze, saw the two talking, and smiled. "Stan's a good guy, but it'll take him at least half an hour to extricate himself from Janet. I'm sure he'll give us ink in *The Georgia Strait* about these murders. He's one guy who's not afraid of our cause. He supports it, even calls himself a feminist. That's rare."

She led the way to a table in a quiet area, still holding the daisy. She placed it in front of her and slowly plucked the petals off, one by one. In a quiet voice, she intoned, "He loves me not, he loves me." Her voice was so melodious that I stopped listening to the words, lulled into a sort of stupor. Suddenly I tuned back in.

"She loves me, she loves me not."

I cocked my head. "What're you doing? Are you trying to tell me something?"

Somehow I guessed what she was hinting at. Perhaps I had always known.

"Mia doesn't like men. She loathes them." Delilah laid aside the ravaged flower.

Confirmation.

"Yes, she told me what lies behind her loathing." I wrinkled my nose. "It's not a pretty story, so who could blame her? Not me." I wasn't going to shy away from this conversation. "Has she ever had a boyfriend that you know about?"

Delilah's lips twisted into a rueful grin. "I doubt it. The idea is almost laughable. She has wanted a girlfriend, however."

I nodded. "Shona?"

Delilah put both hands on the table, palms down. She looked directly at me. "Yes. And that's why Shona switched roommates and moved in with me. Mia's timing with Shona was awful. Shona was under so much stress, getting threatening phone calls that grew in intensity. Also, at her lab, the guys jealous of her brilliance bugged her all the time, and her old boyfriend was trying to get back together with her. Then—*bang*—Mia announces to Shona one evening that she's in love with her. Shona was a super strong gal, but even she crumpled with that much to handle. So she fled."

A waitress appeared at our table. "Two coffees please," Delilah said. She looked at me. "Okay with you?"

"Sure," I said, too distracted to give the drink order another thought.

I watched the people around us, happy, laughing, having a fine time. Carefree student days—had either Mia or Shona ever experienced those? Certainly didn't sound like it.

I cleared my throat. "So this news you've shared with me, has it got any bearing on Shona's murder?" I clutched a paper napkin in my hand and held my breath. Mia might be maddening, but I didn't want her to be a killer. Besides, she couldn't have attacked Larissa since I was with her in Seattle at the time. Thinking she could be a killer showed just how unhinged I thought Mia was.

"You'll have other questions to ask me, I'm sure," Delilah said slowly, "but I wanted to get this fact out on the table. Lately when I can't sleep, I worry Mia might've been able to keep Shona alive. That is, if Shona hadn't moved in with me. I feel guilty. I'm afraid her murder is my fault."

"That's silly. I understand why you feel guilt, but you couldn't have protected Shona in the lab or here at SUB when someone laced her thermos with poison."

"Here's the thing, though." Delilah leaned across the table, looking so earnest that it touched my heart. "Shona told me Mia

228

wanted her to contact the police and tell them about the escalating threats. Maybe if Mia had been able to talk her into that, then Shona would be here with us today."

The distress in Delilah's face raised a lump in my throat. I tried to talk around it.

"Theoretically," I said, "Mia might've been able to keep Shona from harm, but we'll never know. So let's drop that line of conjecture and try to figure out who had a motive to kill her. Got any ideas about that?"

Delilah lowered her head, holding that pose, evidently pondering hard. After a few moments passed, she sat straighter. "Okay, here are my thoughts, such as they are. I can't give you the name of the murderer, but ideas rumble around in my head. I haven't shared my hunches with anyone. Since you're here—all trustworthy and compassionate and not the killer—you get to hear them."

I beamed at her. "That's great, thanks. I traveled all the way from Toronto because Larissa is my best friend and she seemed high on the Mounties' list of suspects. That's primarily because she made the tea that got poisoned and ended up killing Shona."

"Your devotion to Larissa is admirable, and so is your aura, like I said before." She stroked a string of beads that hung around her neck, acting dreamy and pensive again. "However, about your aura, well, I now see blue in it also. You need to guard against taking on too much and neglecting your personal relationships."

Her words were an ice-cold dagger plunging into the core of my very being. Did my aura suggest neglect not only of David but also of Wyatt?

I choked back my conscience and tried to sound calm. "All you need to know about me, really, is that Larissa helped me out of a very serious jam once, so I owe her and her father. I'll be eternally devoted to them."

The waitress arrived with our coffee. I picked up my cup, struggling to control my guilt. My buttons labeled Bad Wife and Bad Mother had been pushed hard.

The coffee was too hot and burned my tongue.

I looked Delilah straight in the eye, wondering what color my aura was now. "So you and I both want to find Shona's killer, each of us for our own reasons."

"Right on. Are you ready to hear my thoughts then?"

"Shall I take notes?"

"Something tells me you have a pretty good memory. Still, it wouldn't hurt, eh?"

The Canadian *eh* was charming coming from her lips. I rummaged in my purse, pulled out paper and a pencil. "All set, fire away. I hope for some big juicy leads. Lord knows, this case needs them. Women are dying."

Chapter Thirty-Three

"LET ME MAKE one thing clear." Delilah held the plucked daisy tight in her fist and gestured with it. "I wasn't close to Shona. We weren't bosom buddies, nothing like that. She never revealed her innermost thoughts or secrets to me. I can tell you observations about her behavior from the outside only, so to speak."

"Doesn't matter." I shrugged. "I'll be grateful for whatever you can share."

"She did confide in two people. One was that dead girl in Seattle, Bethany Something—whatever you said her last name was."

"Furst."

"Right, Bethany Furst."

Delilah twitched her head, as if waking up her brain. "Anyway, I roomed with Shona only a month or so. For the first few weeks whenever I came back to our pad, Shona was burning up the wires, talking to that Bethany. When Shona heard me come in, she'd break pretty quick, so I never heard what they—"

"Maybe Shona felt guilty calling long distance when rates were high?" I said. "Just being devil's advocate."

"Don't think so. I told Shona to make calls whenever she wanted. No, I know Shona and Bethany talked deep stuff, close to the bone. If Shona was afraid of anyone, Bethany heard those fears."

"What rotten luck." I heaved a huge sigh. "Bethany can't divulge those secrets now. Did anyone else know about Shona's connection to Bethany? For their deaths to be connected, the killer had to know Shona confided in Bethany."

Delilah's nose wrinkled. "Check with the secretary at Shona's lab. Shona talked to her a lot."

"You're thinking maybe someone in the lab overheard Shona talking to Mrs. Carson?"

"Yeah, that's it. Maybe." Delilah sounded uncertain.

"Mrs. Carson is no fan of liberated women. Still, she could have said something about Bethany in innocence, but to the wrong person."

I wondered what she thought of Shona. I never thought to ask her. Had I skipped a possible suspect?

Mrs. Carson thought a woman's place was in the home.

Mrs. Carson worked at the lab with Shona and Larissa.

Mrs. Carson might have known something about Bethany.

Delilah was nodding. "Those are the only possibilities I can think of that got Bethany killed." She looked around the table. "Where's my—" Her eyes went down to the floor. "Did I drop the daisy?"

"Open your fist. You squashed it a minute ago, and I wondered why since it somehow seemed like an extension of you." I grinned at her. "Part of your persona. Or your aura, if you will."

A shot of wickedness ran through me. I wasn't used to being so bold with a new acquaintance, unless of course someone got right in my face. Like Mia had, come to think of it.

A vision of Mia rose in my mind. No wonder she hadn't confessed what caused the quarrel that made Shona move out. Mia was hurt and humiliated.

I tuned back in to hear Delilah's laughter.

"Oh well, guess I'll pick another from the garden tomorrow. Now, where was I?"

"You hinted a second person might know something. Who is

that?"

Delilah took several sips of coffee before she answered.

"The week before her death, Shona talked every day on the phone to Jack. She wasn't as secretive with him, but I still don't know what they rapped about. Since he's alive—that we know about, anyway—you need to contact him. He may know who she was scared of, especially at the lab.

"By the way, that's where I see the evil coming from, the infernal chemistry lab. When I threw the I Ching sticks last night, someone from the chemistry department came out as the culprit. I couldn't tell if there was only one of them or more. Maybe a professor in league with a student?"

Delilah folded her hands over her stomach and gave me an enigmatic Mona Lisa smile.

Strange beauty, this one. I wasn't sure what to make of her.

"I lean in that direction myself, the killer having a connection to the lab." Even if I didn't agree that the I Ching could provide answers. "Your information has given me lots to chew over, and I appreciate your candor." A glance at my wristwatch told me it was time to leave. "Sorry, but I need to dash."

"Sure, let's blow this pop stand."

On our way out, Delilah stopped to talk to several people. By the time we reached her car, I was in a tizzy of tension. Clusters of engineering students still watched firemen clearing the wreck of Mia's van. Seeing the burned-out hulk heightened my unease.

What if the bad guys had gotten to Wyatt? There seemed to be more than enough evil men to go around these days.

I guess my aura—or my white-knuckled fingers—gave Delilah a clue, because she said, "What's made you so uptight?"

"I feel guilty when I leave my son. Wyatt is three months old, and I'm sure my own mother never let me out of her sight at that age." I gave a short laugh, the sound harsh. "One reason I insist on doing my own thing is because my mother smothered me with her rules. I was hemmed in by the Shoulds. That's what I called them. *You should do this, you should do that.*" I stopped and stared at Delilah. "I can't believe I just told you that. I hardly know you."

"You're such a dear, innocent soul. I threw the I Ching for you too last night, and I'll check it again tonight. I do feel danger out here in the parking lot, though." She pushed me gently to her car. "Quick. Get in."

It was a miracle I didn't hyperventilate after her revelation.

She swung her car onto University Boulevard and tromped down on the accelerator.

"I've been up front with you because you felt so trustworthy, and you just responded in kind. Don't worry about it. When you return to Toronto, I suggest you join a women's liberation group. You'll get support in living the kind of life you need. Change is in the air, and it's a good thing."

When we drove up to Raisa's house, change seemed to have struck there too. Every window in the two-story house blazed with lights. No ominous car loitered on the street, but was that a good or a bad sign? On the one hand, ex-senator Simpson wasn't there to take me down. On the other, no appendage of Mr. Jones loitered, ready to keep Wyatt and me safe.

I opened the car door, then turned to tell Delilah goodbye. "I really appreciate the ride. I'll let you know if I figure anything out about the murders."

"Please do." She reached over and stroked my elbow. "Take good care of yourself now, you hear?"

"Of course." Muscles in my shoulders tensed. "By the way, what did the I Ching say about me last night? Does my aura really suggest I'm in danger?"

I willed her to smile warmly and say all was well. Unfortunately, she didn't.

"Like I told you, be careful. Dark shadows surround you. But you knew that already."

I sighed and hung my head.

"Don't look so glum. My hunch is you'll emerge from all the

murk and be just fine."

That was more like it. My shoulders, once up around my ears, now fell by a good three inches. I sent a shaky smile Delilah's way. "Thank you for being so nice to me."

She returned my smile. "Now go nail that murdering bastard who hates women."

I hopped out of the car and ran into the house with renewed vigor, eager to hold Wyatt and call David.

Raisa met me at the door. To my alarm, she was holding Wyatt. It was ten o'clock. At least he wasn't crying, but he did look bright-eyed and active.

I reached for him. "What's going on? Is everything okay?"

Wy snuggled on my shoulder, cooing like a morning dove.

Raisa said, "Phone rings and rings. I put baby down for night, but phone wakes him again. And again. Three men call for you."

I nuzzled the top of Wy's head, blissed out that he was okay. "Three men?"

"Da." She walked to a side table and picked up a piece of paper. "Here are names and numbers. I wrote for you."

David. Detective Sergeant McKinnon. Shona's old boyfriend, Jack.

Hell's bells.

Now why did Daddy's favorite almost-swear word pop up just then? Maybe because I needed some grownup-type help?

No, I had to be my own grownup now.

I planted a big kiss on Wyatt's cheek. He squirmed.

"Did you have any problems with him, Raisa?"

"Nyet. He good boy."

She pointed to herself. "Brick? Da?"

I nodded, smiling, and turned away.

"There is one more thing."

I whirled back. One thing? I didn't like her tone.

"What's that?" I tightened my grip on Wyatt, and he squawked.

"Man rang doorbell. He wanted to use phone. I shut door in

face. Not like his look."

Hell's bells rang again in my head. "Did he leave right away?"

"Da."

"Where did he go—maybe a neighbor's house to ask to use another phone?"

"Nyet. He got in car and drove off." Could it be Darrel, Simpson's minion, or was it someone sent by Jones? I'd better ask Jones and soon. Ice was forming in my toes and moving up my legs. My nerves were working overtime tonight. I wished they'd lay off.

Fear of Senator Simpson was the problem. This stranger could be connected to him rather than to Shona's murder. Then again, perhaps the man was an innocent who'd really needed help. It was difficult to know when to be on guard and when to feel safe. A full-blown case of paranoia wouldn't help my detecting skills. I willed myself to breathe and calm down.

I walked back and forth across the living room floor, jiggling Wyatt slightly, hoping to lull him into a sleepy state. My mind buzzed with questions.

Maybe the man hadn't been sent by Simpson but was just a student.

"Raisa," I said, "can you describe the man please? What color was his car?"

"He wore dark suit, white shirt. Had evil in his eyes"

"Was he a student?"

She pursed her lips. "Nyet. I said *man*, not student."

Damn. A connection to Simpson seemed likely.

Oh my God. Would they hurt my baby? I'd been so stupid, blithely expecting he'd be safe with Raisa just because she had a gun and knew how to use it.

"Did this man see Wyatt?"

"Nyet."

"What time was it?"

"Right after you left for university."

I remembered the blaze made by Mia's van in the parking lot

at UBC. Perhaps the visitation by this *good-looking man* and the fire were connected.

I realized that Mia's van wasn't the only thing that had heated up. My whole situation in Vancouver had too.

Chapter Thirty-Four

IN MY IMAGINATION, the three men I needed to phone stood in front of me. My long-suffering husband, my pal Detective Sergeant McKinnon, and the faceless Jack.

Who should I call first?

Although I was most eager to talk to Jack, duty demanded that I call David first. I just didn't want to, suspecting he'd hassle me about coming home. The prospect made my stomach curl with anxiety.

Holding Wyatt in one arm, I pulled a chair close to the telephone table with the other. I sat and dialed our home in Toronto. After two rings, David picked up. Within seconds we ran into the thicket of our disagreement.

"When will you be back home?" Those were his first words after *hello*. Our conversation slid downhill from there.

"Let me tell you the latest." I willed my breathing to stay steady. "Larissa was attacked yesterday, and she's in the hospital."

"I want you and Wyatt on the next plane out. I knew your idea was too dangerous."

I had never heard David so paternalistic.

"But, David, honey, I think——"

"Home, Austin. Come home. It's where you belong. I know you want to help your friend, but that's why this country has Mounties. Let them protect her. It's not your job. You've done enough already. Too damned much, if you ask me."

We went back and forth a few more times. Neither of us persuaded the other to yield. Finally I chose conciliation. Who knew? Perhaps he was right to worry about our safety, Wy's and mine. *I* was certainly worried for Wyatt. Maybe I should get the hell out of Vancouver and do it soon.

"Okay, how's this? It's Friday night. I've only been here two days. If you insist, I'll call a travel agent first thing tomorrow and see what can be done about changing my return. The return flight is a week from tomorrow, but ma—"

David's shout hurt my eardrum.

"What? You never told me that."

"Yes, I did. You just don't remember."

"I'd remember something like that. You actually planned to be gone ten days?"

Better to ignore this and plunge right on.

"Well, anyway, I'll try to get a flight back to Toronto for Monday."

I heard a loud bang and imagined David tossing stuff around—symptom of his infrequent fits of temper.

A long silence ensued. I waited.

"Monday morning would be good if you can arrange that." His voice was tight.

"Thank you, sweetheart." I put all the feeling into my response that I could muster. Besides, if I flew to Toronto on Monday, I'd have two more days to uncover clues. Surely I could make some headway before I had to leave Vancouver.

"Why can't you leave on Sunday?"

Damn, he was not giving up.

"I'll ask the travel agent if that's possible. There may not be a ticket on such short notice, or it could be terribly expensive. Dr. Klimenko is paying, and I don't want to abuse his generosity. Are travel agencies even open on Saturdays? I don't know."

"God damn it to hell, Austin. You're worried about everyone but your husband."

"If I've made you feel that way, then I'm sorry, honey. I'll be home soon. I promise."

We managed a few minutes of happier talk, then said our goodbyes. After I hung up, I looked down at Wyatt, now sleeping peacefully on my lap, and sighed. Why hadn't someone warned me it wasn't as much fun to be a grownup as I'd expected it to be? Perhaps they'd tried—and I'd chosen not to listen.

David's explosion had shown him more angry than hurt. But I guessed he used anger to cover up his hurt feelings.

Well, at twenty-three, I was no longer a kid and had adult responsibilities. Deciding what was a reasonable request made by my husband and what was an unreasonable one was hard. Mother had made many unending demands on me, and mostly I'd complied. Always doing what someone else told me to do exhausted and depleted me. I wanted to make up my own mind.

Was this why women were turning to the liberation movement in droves?

Pulling Raisa's list of callers from my pocket, I eyed the remaining names. I wanted to call Jack. He, however, lived in Vancouver's time zone, and McKinnon lived in the East. McKinnon's name seemed to pulsate on the paper, so I dialed his number. He answered immediately.

"Hi, this is Austin. Do you have news about the investigation of Shona's murder? Is that why you called earlier?"

His answer was a choking sound.

"You are so single-minded," he said. "No pleasantries? No *how-are-you's*? Just cutting straight to your current obsession?"

"You know me so well"

"I do indeed, young lady."

Oh brother. When he called me that, I knew I was in for a lecture.

Before he could begin, I hurried on.

"Have you picked up any gossip on your police pipeline that says the RCMP has made headway on Shona's case?"

"Well," he drew the word out slowly, giving me the sense he was reluctant to share information with me, yet wanting to despite himself.

"Please, Detective Sergeant. You understand how dear Larissa is to me. She's off the suspect list, but the killer beat her up. Or someone did. Likely the killer. She's in the hospital—broken bones, a concussion. I've got to know who did that. Throw me a lifeline here."

He spoke about his concern for Larissa and his respect for her father, then returned to the subject at hand—information. "That's why I called in the first place. You asked me to keep my ears open and to tell you if you heard anything about the Mounties' investigation. Well…I've heard something."

Hot damn. This was more like it. I got ready for the good stuff.

"I heard two things. The first doesn't sound relevant now that Larissa is no longer a suspect. The person who supposedly witnessed her poisoning the tea was a chemistry grad student."

"But that's great to know. Maybe that was the killer himself, throwing blame on Larissa."

"Good point. Here's the other thing I learned. The Mounties have been focusing on figuring out how the poison got into Shona's tea. They've interviewed lots of students who were at someplace called Sub, but they've not made much progress yet."

"Okay, got that." I thought for a moment. "Did you hear there was a second murder of a college student involved with the women's lib movement?"

"What?"

"In Seattle. And she was an old friend of Shona's."

Quickly I ran through what I knew about Bethany's murder, and then threw in, just for kicks, the other murder that happened the same day as Shona's, the one at the nude beach. I hadn't spent any time speculating if there was a connection between the two Vancouver murders, but suddenly I wondered. DS McKinnon listened while I informed him of the timing.

After I finished my information dump, he didn't speak for a long time. I drummed my fingers and waited. Finally he said, "I heard nothing about either of the other two murders. I must say that right now the RCMP detachment in Vancouver is spread pretty thin. Their manpower issue is slowing them down."

"That's interesting." I mulled this over. "Then perhaps I can be of real help. Should I try to contact a Mountie, although I don't really want to, but—"

"No, no, no. You promised your husband you wouldn't poke your nose into matters that belong with law enforcement. Clearly you're ignoring that promise."

"I proved before that I can take care of myself." My face felt hot with the indignation rising within me.

"You call taking a shot in the shoulder taking care of yourself?"

"I discovered the killer last time, didn't I?"

He didn't respond.

"Well, didn't I?"

"True enough," DS McKinnon said slowly, "but at what risk to yourself?"

"There's no point in arguing. I just talked to David and promised him Wyatt and I would fly back to Toronto on Monday."

"Excellent news." His voice brightened. "Glad to hear it."

"I'm not happy about it, but that gives me two more days to dig up leads."

"Don't do anything foolish, Austin. I won't be around to pick up the pieces this time."

"You won't have to."

"So you keep telling me. Well, keep your nose clean, young lady."

After I replaced the receiver, Raisa appeared. "I hear conversation. Are you khorosho?"

How should I answer that? Was I khorosho?

I nodded slowly. "Yes, I think so."

"Let me show you trick. Come." She walked into the kitchen, and I followed, carrying Wyatt.

Raisa opened a cupboard beneath the sink and pulled out a can of Lysol. "Take this."

"You want me to disinfect something?"

"This for protection when you leave house."

She pointed the can in the air, about the height of a tall man. She mimed spraying him in the face and grinned.

"Disable him. Works always. You have chance to run. Get help."

"At tonight's meeting one woman recommended using hairspray."

"This better. Much better."

I took the Lysol from her.

Raisa moved closer.

"You take care of yourself. I am sure of it."

"I can, yes."

"Da, your situation...*nichevo*."

Perhaps not really nichevo—nothing, as she said—but her faith in me boosted my faith in myself.

"Thanks for your support, Raisa. You've been wonderful. Someday I want to hear about your own adventures, but right now I need to make one more call."

Wyatt arched his back and wailed. How I wished I'd gotten Mother to stay with him in Toronto. I'd made a big mistake on that score.

I guess my feelings showed—or Raisa was clairvoyant.

"Okay, you call. I put baby to bed." She took Wyatt and went upstairs.

I returned to the chair beside the phone. Please, Jack, have something juicy to tell me.

I dialed his number. After twelve rings, someone old and gruff-sounding answered. I asked for Jack.

"Sure thing, sister. He be standing right here, waitin' for your call."

"Austin? That you?" This male voice sounded younger and tense.

"Jack? I've been eager to talk to you. I'm Larissa's friend and came to Vancouver to—"

"Mr. Spektor called me earlier. He explained what you're trying to do and urged me to call. So here I am. What do you need to know?"

Mr. Spektor had sanctified my questioning Jack. What a great relief.

"First, let me say how sorry I am for your loss." I searched for nice things to say about someone I'd never met. "All I've heard about Shona makes her sound extraordinary."

I heard him gulp, knew he must still be grieving, and doing it mighty hard too.

"Thanks. Her death devastated me. She was so full of life, and now this. You can't imagine. It's just, just—"

His voice broke. I let him regain his composure.

"All right, let's continue," he said. "How can I help you?"

"Have the RCMP been around to talk to you?"

"No. Should they have?" His voice registered surprise, maybe even shock.

If I'd been a Mountie, I would've interviewed Jack. Maybe they didn't even know he existed. Depended on the questions they asked the Spektors, probably.

"Just thought they might," I said, "since I hear you talked to Shona a lot right before her murder. How worried was she about the threatening calls and notes she'd received?"

"In our first phone calls, she described the threats but blew them off. Then they got more frequent and more serious. She finally admitted to being scared. That wasn't like Shona, so I got scared too."

"Did she have any idea who was threatening her and why? This is super important, Jack. Try to remember any tiny thing she said that relates."

His answer was an eternity in coming.

"Her hunch was someone in the chemistry department. One prof was rough on her and insulting. Several of the male grad students were crude around her. She loathed the people in her lab, for the most part, but said she wouldn't give the haters and sexist pigs—her words, not mine—the satisfaction of leaving. She would stand and fight, never give in, no matter how hard they tried to push her out."

"How about her women's group? Any suspects there?"

"Are you nuts?"

"I don't think so. I'm about to rule them out, but just want to be sure."

"Those girls all loved her. Excuse me, she encouraged me to say *women*. One even had"—his voice lowered—"a, uh, a big crush on her."

"Okay, now here's a question that I don't want to raise, but I must. Could Mia have, er, could she have been so overcome with jealousy that—"

"Stop right there. The answer is no. Mia is plenty messed up, but she could not have killed Shona. I don't like Mia very much, but she's no murderer."

"I'm relieved. She can be tough to put up with, but I do like her."

He hooted. "Then you're a saint."

"I'm not, but I always try to put myself in someone's shoes and see how they feel."

"Shona would have liked you. It's a shame you never got to meet."

"Thank you, Jack. I know that's a huge compliment. So now, let's see." I paused, pretending to consult a list, but really just trying to halt the slide into sadness our conversation was causing both of us. "On my notes I'll cross off all the members of the women's group, if you're certain I can."

"Definitely. Concentrate on the lab group."

"Good. That jibes with my inclinations. Anything specific you can tell me?"

Again Jack's silence stretched forever.

"Okay, here's something," he eventually said. "Shona told me she was suspicious about a connection between one of the guys in her lab and a shy woman in her group."

Like a hound dog's, my ears perked up. "Tell me more."

"Maybe this is important, maybe not. In one of our last phone conversations, Shona said one of the grad students was married to a woman in the group."

"Far out. That has real potential."

"Good. I want to help find Shona's killer."

"Any ideas who this married couple was?"

"I don't know." His voice fell. "I just don't know. She did say the guy had forgotten his lunch, and his wife brought it to the chemistry department office when she happened to be there." His voice became a low whisper. "Sorry, but that's all I've got. No names. Nothing."

"Don't apologize. This sounds—"

"Wait. I remember something else." His voice yelped through the wires. "Shona got angry when she saw how the guy treated his wife. Her opinion of the student, low already, got worse. When Shona ran into the wife later in a store, she told her about the women's lib meetings. To Shona's surprise, the wife showed up at the next one. The wife stayed quiet but kept attending."

"Great. This could be the link I've been looking for between Shona's lab and her group activities. You need to call the Mounties, tell them what you told me."

"If it helps bring down the thug who kills and brutalizes women, I'll feel I've helped avenge Shona's death."

"I understand, Jack. I hope your information is the big clue that's needed."

Jack had sounded so consistent and sincere that I had almost ruled him out as a suspect, but I needed to confirm my hunch.

I added, like it was an afterthought, "By the way, how did you like Shona's new place with Delilah?"

"I never saw it. Never actually saw her again after she left Seattle."

When he started to sob, I felt downright mean.

"I hope you can...can...*bag* the bastard."

I hung up with visions of Daddy and me going deer hunting in Texas in my mind. He bagged deer, but I never did. To tell the truth, I never tried that hard. This time was different. Even if I courted more danger than was good for me, I wanted to bag the killer—get him right in my crosshairs and pull the trigger.

Deep in thought, I tried to figure out if either Keith or Hank could be married to a member of the UBC women's liberation group. Mrs. Carson would probably know, but she wouldn't be at work on a Saturday. Still, if I turned up at the lab, someone there might have her phone number.

Keith? Hank? Another student?

I hadn't spent much time with Hank, but Keith had said enough to let me know how keen he was on Larissa. He didn't sound married to me.

So I needed to find out more about Hank.

I slapped my forehead. No, *Hank* was the name of the guy at the pub who'd caused a ruckus. The chemistry grad student was *Frank*. My mind was slipping.

Or was it? I tapped my forehead again, but softly.

Had Garrett made a mistake? Had I? Or had I perhaps hit on a connection? Maybe it was *Frank* at the pub who had given the wrong name on purpose.

For the first time since arriving in Vancouver, I was excited. I could taste a viable suspect.

Through the front window, I saw a dark car pull up across the street and stop. The headlights went off.

For five minutes I watched—never moving my eyes from the car. Nothing happened.

Plenty was happening inside me though. My excitement had turned to fear.

No, wait. I slapped my forehead again. Mr. Jones had probably sent that car.

Well, hell. Why not just go out and talk to the driver right now? Fear and anger were jostling in me, each trying to win. I tossed the victory to anger and strode outside.

Chapter Thirty-Five

TAKING CARE TO shut the door behind me without making a sound, I walked onto the front porch and glared across the street. All I could tell was that the person in the driver's seat appeared to be male.

I couldn't stand the suspense. Was this friend or foe?

What the hell, girl. You're being foolhardy for standing outside the house.

While a corner of my brain buzzed with that opinion, my feet moved me forward and down the steps, across the lawn and the street. I approached the car and stood beside the closed window. I stared in. The man stared back.

He rolled the window down.

"What are you doing? I'm supposed to be undercover. No one's supposed to look at me."

This guy wasn't scary at all. He was my age, for Pete's sake. How much backup would he provide if I got into trouble?

I stuck my hand through the open window. "I'm Austin Starr. Thanks for keeping watch."

He sputtered and coughed. "I know who you are. Get back in the house right now."

"Why don't I tell you where I'm going tomorrow so it'll be easier to follow me? And, by the way, what's your name?"

He thrust his head through the window and somehow managed to yell at me in a fierce whisper. "That's not how this works."

"I don't care. I don't want you to lose me tomorrow. I'll be taking my baby boy with me and don't want him to get hurt."

He blinked. "Why don't you get a babysitter? I've never covered an infant before." He rubbed his forehead. "I wish you'd get the fuck back inside."

Now it was my turn to blink. No one ever used that word around me. Well, Simpson's aide had that one time.

"So tell me, how many adults have you shadowed?"

He looked away. "A few. Enough."

"Tomorrow morning I'm going to visit a sick friend in Vancouver General Hospital. Later I'll go to the chemistry department at UBC. You got all that? You can pass it along to your replacement tomorrow."

"You don't get to give me orders."

I glowered at him. Even in the darkness I saw his mouth was set, his expression sour. "Just trying to be helpful."

"Are you keeping your baby with you all day tomorrow?"

His question set me back. "Yes, I plan to." Really, I had no idea.

"Go inside."

"Goodnight." Wheeling around, I walked with my head held high, in what I hoped was a stately fashion, back to Raisa's house. When I went through the front door, she stood inside, waiting for me.

Her hands were on her hips. Her feet were planted two feet apart. She looked like my idea of a matron of a Soviet prison. "Who is that?" She motioned toward the car with her chin. "He wanted my phone."

Relief and exhaustion rolled over me. "Let's sit and I'll fill you in."

Thirty minutes later Raisa knew the background story to Senator Simpson and his aide, Darrel. I even divulged the existence of Mr. Jones and how he had entered my life, back in the States, when I was sure I'd wanted to work with the CIA. Yes, by this time I trusted her, swearing her to secrecy. While my husband was doctrinaire and theoretical and would judge me harshly for my CIA connection, this Soviet woman was hard-nosed and practical. Besides, I had to confide in someone.

During my entire soliloquy she uttered not a word. Even when I talked about the CIA, her expression never changed. Once I concluded, she stood. "Lysol not enough. Come."

She marched into the dining room, and I followed. Raisa opened a china cabinet and moved heavy silver serving pieces aside. From the back of the shelf she drew out a cardboard box and carried it to the dining table.

"Sit," she commanded.

I sat.

She opened the box and took out a small gun.

That innocent-looking cabinet held *two* guns.

Raisa caressed this second gun. "I traded father's service revolver—Tokarev TT-33—for Makarov pistol. Belonged to émigré from Soviet Union. Was his service revolver, last decade in Red Army." Raisa hefted the Makarov in her hand. "Is good weapon for you. Small, good stopping power, easy to use. I show you."

She demonstrated how to use the pistol, giving details in Russian and then adding her own English translation. As the lesson wore on, I entered a trance-like state. Was this real or was I dreaming? Here I stood, far from my Texas birthplace, in a kitchen in Western Canada. A former resident of the Union of Soviet Social Republics was giving me gun lessons in preparation for an attack by a former Unite States Senator.

What a Cold War nightmare.

I swayed a little and felt my eyes stretch wide. I feared they were bugging out of my skull.

Raisa reached a hand out to steady me. "You okay? You use gun before, da?"

I shook my head. "Plenty of practice with a deer rifle, but only a little with a pistol."

"Khorosho. Dostatochno." It's enough.

When Raisa passed the gun to me, I almost dropped it. "Good heavens, it's heavier than it looks. But don't worry, I'll manage. Mr. Jones was training me with a Smith and Wesson J-frame when I left the program."

And now I wished I hadn't left so early.

Raisa and I looked at each other and smiled. And suddenly into my head burst the title of a book I'd seen at the group meeting—*Sisterhood Is Powerful.*

Wow. A Russian woman was preparing me for battle. Not to be overly dramatic about it, but she was helping me protect myself. I also had to protect Wyatt. What about him?

"Raisa, I must go to the hospital again tomorrow morning to see Larissa."

"Da, konechno. I drive you."

"And the baby."

She nodded. "We stay in waiting room. You see Larissa."

A sudden impulse to hug her surged through me. I followed through on the urge.

Raisa let out a small gasp. "You surprise me."

"Sometimes I surprise myself."

"Give me gun. I put back. We get tomorrow."

I handed it over, and Raisa carefully returned the gun to its special box and placed everything in the back of the cabinet.

Together we climbed the stairs to our bedrooms. Outside her door, Raisa stopped. "If baby not wake you, I knock on door at eight. Khorosho?"

I grinned and tiptoed down the hall. In my bedroom Wy was sleeping peacefully in his makeshift cot. I turned on a small light and undressed as silently as I could. Only once did he make a sound—when I accidentally dropped my shoe on the bare wooden floor. He whimpered in his sleep but didn't wake.

What a mercy. I bent to kiss him goodnight, turned out the light, and slipped into bed. We had a big, nerve-racking day ahead of us.

Although I needed all the sleep I could grab, it evaded me. Visions of Larissa—beaten and possibly near death—curdled in my mind. The specter of more female victims frightened me. I had to stop this madness.

Chapter Thirty-Six

THE HOSPITAL CORRIDOR stretched in front of me—interminable, bright and white, smelling of disinfectant. I waved at Raisa and Wyatt sitting in the waiting room.

We had run late and almost missed the morning visiting hour. I had wasted time trying to contact a travel agent to change my return flight to Toronto. Once I finally had an agent on the phone, another half hour passed before arrangements were finalized.

Garrett still sat outside Larissa's door. He was asleep but woke up when I approached.

He looked at his watch. "Is today Saturday?"

I nodded. "Have you gone home yet?"

"I'm here for as long as it takes."

Larissa was asleep. When I told Professor Klimenko about Jack's theory that a husband of someone caught up in the women's movement could be the bad guy, his gloved right hand slammed his leg.

"The coward," he muttered. "Attacking young women."

"I'm going to the chemistry building after I leave here. Got a hunch who this fellow is and want to check it out."

"If the killer works there, you should not go."

He couldn't scare me enough to make me quit.

"Even though Larissa's no longer a suspect, I must do something." I choked back a sob. "Look at her—she's a victim now. Only an evil person could do this. I must find him, and I'm running out of time. David insists we return to Toronto in two days."

Fingering my purse, I thought about the can of Lysol and the loaded gun buried deep inside my tote bag in the trunk of Raisa's car. Quite a change from the usual baby powder, tissues, and diapers. My two improvised weapons made me feel stronger, even a little powerful. I would not quit.

I stood straighter, my backbone stiff. "I only want to find the grad student who looks like the right suspect. Then I'll back off. I promise."

Was that like the promise I'd made to David, earnestly meant but made with crossed fingers behind my back? No matter. I was not about to let a small thing like guilt stop me now. I knew my objective.

Inwardly I chuckled. Such a pity I'd never dressed up as Wonder Woman at Halloween. I could have used that costume now. And her weapons.

#

"Wait, Raisa. I need to do something first."

We were in the hospital parking lot, ready to drive off, when I felt the urge to check the Makarov. "May I have the key to open the trunk please? I won't be a minute."

Once reassured about the gun—right where I'd left it when we dashed into the hospital—I climbed into the front seat and put Wy back on my lap. "Okay, all set. Let's boogie."

"Boogie?"

"Uh...never mind."

"Why not go to man's home? Thought of that?"

"I did, Raisa, but I'm rushed, with no time to dig up where he lives."

Raisa nodded, agreeing "*Ya ponimaiu*. I go to chemistry building and return hour later." Naturally, Wyatt would stay with her. Raisa and I agreed on that too.

Why couldn't my mother be like Raisa? Mother and I never agreed on anything. She never understood pursuits that mattered to me—only her own, centered on status, respectability, and bridge playing. Once upon a time I'd tried to please her, conforming to her standards, but David had helped me move beyond that.

Raisa accepted me as I was. What a treasure.

We had worked out our plan. If I wasn't in front of the chemistry building when Raisa returned, she would either call the police or take Wyatt to Mrs. Mirnaya's house and then return to find me, all the while keeping an eye out for the dark sedan sent by Mr. Jones. Raisa seemed confident she could handle whatever situation cropped up.

I was sure too. Her internal resources and fortitude appeared endless.

Traffic was busy as we moved west along Broadway. "Is slow going," Raisa said. "Many people shop on Saturday."

I tried to ignore the tension in my arms, back, neck. Everyone's advice—David's, Klimenko's, McKinnon's— increased my anxiety. Only Raisa had helped me prepare for battle.

"Mind if I turn on the radio? I need some distraction."

Raisa slowed the car to allow a pedestrian to cross the street. Her eyes flicked over at me, and I fancied she looked scornful.

No, probably she was only checking to see how my nerves were holding up. Yet if she thought my adventure was *nichevo*, nothing, then why should I get nervous in anticipation? I wished I'd taken the time to hear about some of her exploits in the Soviet Union. Chances were some of them were real doozies.

If she had fought her way out of tough spots, then I could too.

The news announcer was in the middle of a story. "Police say at least three hundred thousand young people have overwhelmed the Woodstock Music and Art Fair near Bethel, New York. The crowd is so large that few can hear the famous performers, among them Joan Baez, Jimi Hendrix, and the Jefferson Airplane. Cars jam roadsides twenty miles in all directions. Despite acres of mud and shortages of food and water, organizers say there are—"

Raisa chuckled. "Such a country, America. Not like Russia. Maybe is good, though. You miss your country? I miss mine."

I caught my breath. "Nobody asks me that. Of course I do. I try not to think about it, though, since I may never be able to live in the States again. That really upsets me."

"Me too. I feel same," she said. "But better in Canada. Less danger for me."

Shoot. Now I really craved hearing about her exploits in the USSR. Professor Klimenko and his sister-in-law had both managed to escape their dangerous pasts.

I tried to catch the rest of the news about the music festival, but the announcer switched to the war. I clicked off the radio. Anything bad from Vietnam would tip me over the edge. Who needed that—more gloom and doom?

We passed the clothing store on Tenth where I bought the skirt I wore. "I hope my suitcase comes before I fly home on Monday."

"Your visit has been, uh—*kak skazat?*—*strannyy*," Raisa said.

"Yes, *strange* is the right word," I answered. "Worse than that, though, I haven't been able to keep my promise to my husband."

"What was that?" Raisa's tone was sharp.

I chuckled. "I said I wouldn't meddle in the murder investigation."

Raisa's laugh was so loud that Wyatt jumped in my arms. "See? Even baby knows his mama is—*kak skazat?*—nosy. You curious *devochka*. Most I ever saw."

Hmm, many people had called me a curious girl since I'd come to Canada.

She drove in silence while I burped Wyatt on my shoulder and stared out the car window. Up ahead lay the green expanse of the University Endowment Lands with its towering trees. In a few minutes, we arrived at the chemistry building.

Raisa drove as close as she could and stopped the car. I gave Wy a big kiss, tugged the tote bag from the trunk, and synchronized my watch with Raisa's.

"See you in one hour."

She wished me good luck in Russian. I took it as a good sign that I understood her.

I sucked in a deep breath, hoping I wasn't being foolhardy.

That word kept popping to mind. Did it fit me?

Perhaps, but my anger at the killer propelled me onward. And I knew my skills. Ferreting out information was one thing I could do well. So I planned to see it through. I'd contact the authorities as soon as I had proof of who had murdered Shona—and maybe even Bethany—and nearly killed Larissa. And then I'd be out of it.

Chapter Thirty-Seven

I TRAMPED TOWARD the chemistry building. Inside the main door, I stopped to glance around the ground floor where Larissa and I had paused two days earlier.

How was that possible? Those days felt more like two weeks.

I remembered how Keith had rushed down the stairs, running from the fire in the lab. Later I met Frank, who had caused the accidental fire. I wondered if either was around today. My intuition had selected one as the killer, and there could be evidence upstairs to prove it. My job was to find that proof.

If my suspect was there—if too many students were hanging around—I'd simply leave and come back later.

Thoughts about the sexist grad students made me grind my teeth, and my jaw ached. I tucked my bag—with gun and Lysol inside—under my left arm and grabbed the handrail with my right.

I climbed, counting each step. I always counted when I needed to stay calm. After fifteen, I reached a small landing midway up and turned around to judge how far I'd come when *bang*, a wave of vertigo hit me. Even though I'd flown up the mortuary stairs in Seattle, this time I was going toward something that scared me, not running from it.

I was going to topple over.

But the handrail was my friend. It helped me up the steps to the next floor. Again, fifteen of them. At the top I took deep breaths and peered down the hallway ahead.

Stop being jittery. Nothing's happened yet.

Halfway down the hall, a janitor pushed a broom. Beyond him, a woman cleaned a glass case. No one in sight that looked anything like a student.

First I went to the office where Mrs. Carson worked. The door was locked. Next I walked a few paces to the lab. This door was unlocked. I pushed it open and entered quietly, then shut the door behind me. My nerves frizzled up and down my arms.

No one was inside, but I had to work fast. Students could show up at any time.

I scanned the row of work benches. I walked past study cubicles and eyed the memos and photos displayed there. I found Keith's work area, gave it a cursory glance, and passed it by.

I kept going until I found Frank's desk. He was my number one suspect.

The top of his desk was a mess. Good news. Maybe he wouldn't notice if I messed it up some more. I was still alone, so I systematically went through the things on the top. A rubber band held several snapshots. Stuck in the middle was one of a woman and three children.

It was Becky, the quiet woman who disliked the Rolling Stones song "Under My Thumb."

Here was the connection between the chemistry lab and Shona's women's group, but this wasn't evidence—I needed proof. Real proof that Frank could kill. That he *had* killed.

When I finished with the top of the desk, I started on the drawers. I found a letter from the departmental chairman, Dr. Adler, addressed to Frank. The message was jarring. Adler warned Frank that his attitude in the lab was disruptive and mentioned the possibility of disciplinary action.

Nothing else noteworthy in the other drawers. Curses.

But the wastebasket was full.

I put my bag down beneath the desk, squatted, and began sorting through the trash.

Halfway through my task, I felt the hairs on the back of my neck prickle. I looked toward the door and, seeing no one, returned to digging through the waste basket. I found a photo.

The crumpled photo showed Shona and Janet. An *X* was slashed across Shona's face. I only had a few seconds to adjust to this revelation before the picture was ripped from my hands.

"What're you doing? Give me that."

I whipped my head around. Frank towered over me.

"What're you doing, bitch?"

My eyes shifted rapidly left to right, checking to see if anyone else was in the lab.

No one.

I attempted to stand, but he pushed me back down. I crumpled to the floor. My heartbeat doubled, and my breath came in gasps.

Where was my bag?

Its handle peeked out from under the desk, slightly more than my arm's length away. My brain churned, working out ways to reach the bag while Frank stood over me.

He grabbed my hair and pulled my head up. "Pay attention to me, God damn you."

Wow, that must be the key to his actions. Becky's attention must have wandered off her husband, and his ego couldn't take it.

"You hear me? I'm talking to you."

Too terrified to speak, I merely nodded.

He moved back, shredded the photo, and flung the pieces at me.

"You know why I'm here, Frank." My voice wavered.

Get a grip, Austin. Be strong. Pretend you're Raisa.

"I pity your poor husband," he yelled. "And your baby. What kind of mother are you? Where is your baby anyway? Why aren't you at home where you belong?"

I opened my mouth to speak, but he motored right on.

"You're all alike these days. Selfish bitches, thinking only of what you want. Women used to know their place."

"Times are changing. That world is dying."

"Hog swill. You all have too damned much education. Mrs. Carson said you're in grad school. How bloody useless. You don't need it for keeping house and tending babies, washing dishes and cooking meals. That's what you're designed to do. Who said you should go to university? Look at you, groveling around on the floor."

He swatted at my head. I dodged the blow just in time. When he missed, he stepped back again and crashed against the desk next to his. He was breathing heavily now.

I determined to keep him talking until someone else showed up.

"Your wife is Becky, right?"

He nodded, still breathing hard.

"She strikes me as—"

"Who asked you, bitch? What do you know? You're just like that *stupid* Shiny Shona. Hell, what a laugh that was—everyone calling her *shiny*. She thought she knew everything, but I showed her. I fixed her so she'll never convince another dutiful wife to go astray. That's what—"

"That's why you had to kill her?"

"She did that to my Becky, lured her away from her duties. Becky had agreed to try for our fourth kid, and then Shona talked her into attending those God-awful meetings. Probably all a bunch of dykes too. Dreadful influences, the whole lot of you."

His rant stopped when he brought a hip flask out of his pocket and took a swig.

I sniffed the air. Was he drunk? That would explain why he got irate so fast.

"Where's Becky now?"

Frank put the flask down and squinted at me. "Becky? My so-called helpmate took the kids and moved out. I don't know where the hell they are. Do you?"

He was yelling now. I prayed he'd grow even louder and soon I'd hear the door to the lab open, but no luck. I wished I hadn't shut the door when I'd come in. I caught sight of a wall clock and saw that Raisa was due to pick me up in just ten minutes. If I could hold Frank off a little while longer, then she would get the police.

My fingernails dug into my palms, the slight pain something to focus on other than my rising panic about what this idiot would do to me. I spoke calmly. "What do you expect, Frank? Even slaves revolt eventually."

My taunt enraged him. He swung at me again, and this time his fist connected with my head. The blow hurt badly enough, but it turned into a double whammy by pushing me back against the desk.

When a yelp of pain burst from me, he cackled and did a dance step, taking another swig from his flask.

I rubbed my head and then my shoulder, tried to focus my thoughts and ignore the throbbing in my body. My right hand fell to the floor and landed near my bag. Leaning forward to block the view, I felt around the bag. The top was open. All I had to do was ease my hand in a little farther and pull out the Makarov.

And then what, shoot him? That thought sobered me up.

Could I actually shoot a man, even one as mean and crazed as this one?

My hand froze in place inside my bag while I tuned back in to Frank's tirade. Perhaps I could get him so worked up he'd stop paying attention to what I was doing. But not *too* worked up. I didn't want him to strangle me, as he had poor Bethany.

No, must not think about that. I only had to wiggle my fingers another an inch or two and then they'd reach into the bag and grab the gun.

Really?

That didn't seem like a viable option, or a smart one. What if Frank grappled with me and managed to use the Makarov to blow me away? A distinct possibility. After all, I was raised in Texas. Daddy had drummed into me how dangerous guns were, and he'd made me a true believer.

Frank continued to spit invective in a steady stream, raining curses down on my head. His harangue—full of a particular four-letter word based on the female anatomy—detailed things he'd do to as many "filthy libbers" as he could get his hands on.

"...and I'll make you another example. This time I'll have real fun. After I kill you, I'll chop you up and throw the pieces down a trash chute."

My stomach flipped over.

"I had to hurry out before I finished off Larissa, but I've got you now." His high-pitched cackle was unnerving. "At first all I wanted to do was get rid of Shona. I figured out how to do that. One death, fine, no problem. That's why I warned your little friend to—"

"The note on Larissa's windshield?"

"Right. I didn't have a plan for her. I left the warning right before I drove down to Seattle to take care of Bethany."

"Why'd you kill Bethany? You didn't even know her."

"Her? She knew too damned much."

"How did you find that out? You are smart." I knew he'd love flattery.

"Helene told me Shona was always talking about her."

"Who's Helene?"

He sniffed and drank from his flask. "She's Mrs. Carson to you. The only good woman around here. After she told me about Bethany, I knew she was a risk, so another libber goes down the drain. Good riddance."

Frank looked so pleased with himself that he gave me an idea. I'd heap on the flattery, just to keep him talking.

"You did a good job of fooling the Mounties. I hear they're still puzzled over the poisoned tea. How did you work that?"

I swear his chest puffed out five inches at my words.

"My plan took some time to put into place. First I stole a few inconsequential things, and then I stole some of that stupid Earl Grey tea that Adler loves so much. People started being more careful, thinking there was a thief around."

"Right, I get it. You obscured the fact that tea was your primary target. But how did you get the tea into Shona's thermos?"

His smirk was condescending. "That awful Shona was under my nose the whole day, every day. I studied her habits. Bought a thermos just like hers, watched when she took it to SUB. Her last day on earth, I tailed her to SUB and switched the thermoses when she left her lunch to go chat with some of her female sycophants." His laughter was triumphant, maniacal, awful to listen to.

But his tale of the thermos reminded me of the Lysol I had in my purse. I wouldn't have to use the gun. I had an alternative.

I snuck a look at the wall clock over his shoulder. Just a few more minutes and Raisa would be outside, ready to pick me up or sound an alarm.

I leaned my shoulder to the right and edged my hand forward a little. My index finger felt around inside the bag. Next it sought the smooth sides of the Lysol can.

Frank stopped to take another drink from his flask.

"Why did you set fire to Mia's van?"

His mouth hung agape. "What van? Don't know what you're talking about." He pulled on the flask again.

Okay, not his work. I'd think about that one later. Worry about Senator Simpson later too. If I lived that long. I had to find another subject guaranteed to keep Frank going.

"I bet your mother was really nice to you, wasn't she, Frank?" Meaning, I bet she was not.

His face contorted. His foot lashed out and kicked me.

I yelled. Then I yelled again, the second time louder than the first. With luck someone might hear me and come running.

Where was the janitor? Where was the lady who cleaned the windows?

Frank threw the flask across the room. He watched it bounce and slide across the tiled floor. "See what you made me do?" His scream was louder than mine had been.

Good.

He grabbed a glass beaker and brought it down on my head. It shattered, and pieces fell around me. Blood trickled into my eyes, but through the drips I managed to watch Frank suck blood from his thumb, then turn away from me.

While he lunged to pick up his flask, I thrust my hand all the way inside my bag and grabbed the slick can. When he bent lower, I drew the Lysol from beneath the desk and tucked it under my leg.

Now I was ready for him.

I had to bring him closer. But how close? I wiped blood off my face with the back of my hand. I needed to be able to see.

Frank returned and edged toward me, perhaps only a foot away, gulping again from the flask. Maybe his reflexes would be impaired from the booze. Whatever it was, I hoped the stuff was good and strong.

"Your mother," I began. "You were going to tell me about your mother. Why don't you sit down and tell me about her."

"You're crazy. Why would I do that? You're all alike. All miserable bitches and lousy mothers. All you do is leave us. Working women? What shit." At the end of this speech, Frank was blubbering. He put the flask down and rubbed his eyes with both fists.

I saw my chance. I took my chance.

I whipped out the Lysol and rose off the floor. My legs had stiffened, but they wobbled and held.

Before he registered my actions, I pushed forward and sprayed a steady stream of toxic chemicals into his eyes.

Frank crashed back against the desk, then collapsed at my feet. He rubbed his eyes, hard, frantically. His yells were terrifying.

A demon inside me danced with delight. Rubbing his eyes would spread the toxins.

I swung around, grabbed my bag, and brought out the Makarov.

When the janitor and cleaning lady ran into the lab, I stood over Frank with a gun in my hands. He was crying in pain and rage.

"What're you doing, lady?" The janitor shook his broom at me.

I backed up. "He wanted to kill me. He's already killed two other girls and hurt another. See where he cut me." Blood still dribbled down my face.

"It's *him*?" The woman flapped her wash rag and beat Frank about his head. "He was always nasty to me."

I gently pushed her away.

To the janitor I said, "Please stand by me. This guy is probably stronger than I am."

To the cleaning lady, I said, "Can you call for help? Next, after that, there's a woman right outside in a car, a lady named Raisa. She'll be looking for me. She knows what's what."

Without saying a word, the woman rushed to the phone on the other side of the room.

The janitor sprang to my side, and together we kept watch on Frank.

One of us brandished a mop and the other a gun.

It was a tableaux from a B movie crossed with a mystery.

It was a standoff for the ages.

Chapter Thirty-Eight

"AND THAT'S HOW it all went down."

I fell back into the armchair in Larissa's hospital room, drained of energy from my recitation. I'd talked constantly since capturing Frank the day before. The Mounties had quizzed me for hours—so much for trying to avoid them. DS McKinnon had vouched for me, so his colleagues in law enforcement had treated me reasonably well.

Professor Klimenko lowered his chin, remaining in that position until I asked what was wrong. He raised his head.

"Why did Frank attack these girls? What made him deranged? I don't understand his hatred."

"Frank himself gave me insight into his rage. He is, after all, a very smart man—well, book smart. Once the police came and put him in handcuffs, he calmed down, but wouldn't shut up. He spewed justifications for his crimes, fueled by the liquor he'd chugged.

"His life had been idyllic, just the way he wanted it. He buried himself in science while a nice home and three children were managed by a dutiful wife. All this he saw as his due. The first attacks on his cozy world came from Shona. She challenged him at work and then she led his wife Becky astray and into women's liberation. He couldn't abide women who weren't docile.

"His childhood had been wrecked when his mother took a

bookkeeping job at a shoe store and then ran off and left the family for a shoe salesman. That set the stage for his hatred of women who worked outside the home."

How many of us were happy with the mothers we got? I'd have given anything for my mother to have devoted less attention to me. A job for her would've been perfect.

Professor Klimenko said, "I see—a warped, disturbed man. Is there more?"

"Frank truly believed that if he got rid of Shona's pernicious influence, his wife would return to her subservient role. He didn't understand he couldn't put the genie back in the proverbial bottle."

"Terrible, terrible," Professor Klimenko muttered, absentmindedly patting Larissa's hand lying atop the sheet. Like the day before, she was comatose. I'd spent twenty minutes in the room and her eyes were shut the whole time.

The door opened, and Garrett burst in. "Sorry I'm late. My alarm didn't go off so I could come back last night. I slept the clock around, almost. Guess I was more tired than I knew."

Professor Klimenko had sent Garrett home the afternoon before, insisting that he get some sleep. Now he stood to shake Garrett's hand.

"Thank you for coming back, but you didn't need to. You've done enough for our family already."

Garrett shook his head vigorously. "I'm compelled to guard Larissa and must save her from danger."

What? He didn't know yet?

"The killer is in custody now," I said.

Garrett let out a cry of surprise.

"Far out. When? Who is he?"

"Austin caught the killer by using herself as bait," Professor Klimenko said. "One of these days her daring will get her into real trouble, but not this time."

Garrett danced a little jig. "Give me details, lay it all on me."

He sank onto the end of the bed, and Larissa's eyes flew

open. She moved her legs and wiggled her fingers. Her voice sounded stronger than when she'd spoken before.

"Hi, everybody. What's going on?"

Her father, Garrett, and I all answered at the same time.

"Stop. Please stop." Her hand grasped Garrett's. "You make my head hurt. Can't you take turns talking and then get me something to eat? I'm starved."

We all shut up. However, the quiet spell didn't last long. Stifling my sudden urge to whoop and holler, I contented myself with punching Garrett in the arm and hugging Professor Klimenko.

"I'll tell a nurse the patient is better. You tell Larissa about Frank."

I didn't wait for a response but rushed out the door.

I alerted the nursing staff and then ran to the waiting room to tell Raisa. I sat with Wy while she ran down the hall to see her niece.

When the visiting hour was up, the head nurse let Garrett stay alone with Larissa for a short time. The rest of us left, making a noisy group in the waiting room, but other visitors didn't seem to mind. Our joy and relief was so obvious that strangers congratulated us on Larissa's recovery.

"Are all the mysteries solved now?" Professor Klimenko asked after the nurse left us.

"Almost," I said. "Frank admitted he not only killed Shona and Bethany but also attacked Larissa. He would have killed her too if he hadn't been afraid of someone interrupting him in the ladies room. By that time he'd become irrational in his thinking and ability to plan. I don't know the event that pushed his wife Becky to leave with their children, but her actions enraged him further. When he saw me in the chemistry lab, he snapped completely and didn't seem to worry about getting caught."

"You said almost. But not everything?"

"There's the matter of the killing at Wreck Beach. I found out why it was such a distraction for the Mounties. It sucked up manpower because two wealthy Vancouver families were tangled up in the murder. The RCMP is still working on that high-profile case that threatens to become a major embarrassment for the provincial government."

"How did the RCMP officers treat you?" Professor Klimenko asked.

Raisa and I exchanged amused looks.

"I was there," she said. "They treated her like foolish little girl who stumbled into mess."

I shrugged. "I don't need any credit. I *know* what I did."

Wyatt had had his fill of grownups talking. He flailed his arms and legs and worked up into a big crying jag. It was time to leave anyway. Professor Klimenko walked us out of the hospital, gave me a big hug goodbye, and thanked me with great earnestness.

That was all the reward I needed.

The rest of the day sped by. I gathered up what few possessions I had with me, called Canadian Pacific Air to see if my errant bag had arrived in Vancouver yet—it had not, naturally—and ate Raisa's delicious pelmeni for one more meal. When we were settling down for the night, Raisa handed me a sheaf of typed pages.

"These are for you to read on the plane tomorrow. About my exploits in Russia. You are interested, da?"

"You bet I am. Dear Raisa, you are a true inspiration. If I'm ever in a precarious situation again, I'll imagine what you would do and then follow suit."

"Oh, you *will* land in mess again."

We grinned in sisterly satisfaction. Raisa went upstairs, and I stayed behind to make some last-minute phone calls. I called Mia to tell her goodbye and encourage her to keep in touch.

"I'm not much of a letter writer," she said in her characteristic sharp tone.

"Then pick up the danged phone," I said, replying in kind. "I like you Mia and hope we can stay friends. If you ever visit

Toronto, look me up."

I fancied the noise I heard in response was a veritable purr.

Then I called Mr. Jones.

"Have news for you," he said. "That minibus or van, whatever you call it, that you rode in to Seattle and back?"

"Right. What about it?"

"Don't know who did it, torched the thing, but have my suspicions. My man wasn't there when the fire started. He'd gone off to grab a sandwich, but when he returned and saw the blaze, he asked around. Students told him there'd been a tall, good-looking man in a dark suit near the van earlier. He dug some more and the trail led to Simpson's aide, Darrel."

"Well, damn it. But why would he burn a minibus that wasn't mine? Makes no sense. In any event, glad I'm flying back to Toronto tomorrow."

"Good to know. I'll have a word with our guys in Ontario. They can keep their eyes out for Simpson there too. Watch your back, Austin. Something—I don't know what—has got them determined to do you real harm."

I hung up the phone, feeling numb. Jones's news had dented my euphoria over catching Shona's killer. But it seemed surreal, hard to fathom. After pondering this new mystery, I decided there was only one solution. I would borrow the maxim of a famous fictional heroine of the old south. I would think about it tomorrow.

Somehow I managed to sleep well. The next morning Professor Klimenko drove Wyatt and me to the airport. Our spirits were buoyant because Larissa's doctors had confirmed her recovery would be complete.

Professor Klimenko helped us to our gate and left us, eager to return to the hospital. As I watched his figure march across the length of the terminal and disappear from view, a happy glow filled me.

I had accomplished my mission.

I sat on a bench, propped Wy on my lab, and flipped through

the Vancouver newspaper. Inside were photographs of the Woodstock music festival. Not my scene. All that mud didn't sound like fun, and besides, I disliked huge crowds.

When Wyatt started fussing, I laid aside the newspaper, held him against my shoulder, and that settled him. Staring off into space, I cast my thoughts back over the days we'd spent in Vancouver.

Two well-dressed gentlemen passed down the hall opposite my seating area. They wore dark suits, crisp white shirts, and ties.

A vice clamped my throat, and I felt strangled.

Senator Reginald Simpson and Darrel walked into the waiting area beside mine and took seats there. Thank heaven I was surrounded by people.

I should have angled away, but I couldn't help myself. I couldn't even avert my eyes, even though I feared one of them would notice me. Staring hard for several minutes, I was about to turn away when the former senator lifted his head and caught me watching him.

His forehead wrinkled, and a hard look came into his eyes. He raised his hand. His fingers formed a gun, and they pulled a pretend trigger. Then a lazy smile spread over his handsome, evil face.

How I wished I would never see him again. I hugged Wyatt tightly, recalled Mia's burning van, and said a small prayer.

Five hours later Wy and I exited the plane at the Toronto airport. David was there to greet us and smother us in kisses.

My husband's first words amused me.

"Raisa called this afternoon and left you a message. Your missing suitcase arrived at her house an hour after you left Vancouver."

I chuckled and burrowed deeper into his arms. "Oh, David, I don't care. I'm so glad we're home."

"Where you belong." His voice was strong and demanding in my ear. "No more exploits for you. This adventure turned out fine, but another one might not."

I handed Wy to David and linked my arm through his. "All's well that ends well. Larissa is safe. All is right with our world."

He couldn't see my hand behind my back, my crossed fingers.

It was true, almost everything was indeed right in our world. All except for one crooked senator.

Acknowledgements

WHEN I FINISHED writing the manuscript of my debut mystery, *Desolation Row*, the thought of thanking everyone who'd contributed to its publication overwhelmed me. I owed so many people a great deal of thanks for their encouragement and support that I feared the list would be endless and that I'd forget someone. Therefore I avoided the whole ordeal and skipped the acknowledgements altogether. Now I will attempt to rectify that lapse.

My unending gratitude goes to Ken Coffman, whose Stairway Press of Seattle publishes my mystery fiction. His support has been central to my ongoing writing efforts. He and his team are delights to work with: Stacey Benson, Chris Benson, and Beth Hill. Beth earns special thanks for her refined editorial sensibilities, intelligent suggestions, and nose for hunting down clichés. She is a joy of a collaborator, and her attention to detail is amazing.

My thanks also go to my critique group. Their ideas improved this mystery. Amy Sharp, Bob Miller, Dean "Miranda" James, Julie Herman, Kay Finch, and Laura Elvebak buck me up when my spirit flags. Our gracious hosts Charlie and Susie Hairston offer a restful atmosphere in which to chase our muses.

Two former journalists are long-time supporters of my writing efforts. Canadian Bob Parkins encouraged me from the beginning, and New Yorker Harold Ravis reviewed all my manuscripts in draft form. And the erudite William Leigh Taylor more than once pulled me out of a slough of despond on my march to publication.

Two famous authors took a chance and agreed to give blurbs to my debut mystery. My deepest thanks go to Hank Phillippi Ryan and to Norb Vonnegut. I recommend their masterful books to all.

Two traveling companions authors Laura Elvebak and Marjorie Brody—are intelligent, comfortable women to share time with when we meet other writers and court readers. Suspense novelists Jenny Milchman and Pamela Fagan Hutchins offered a wealth of supportive friendship and knowledge about the publishing process. My cheerleader Pam Fetzer Vetter provided oh-so-wonderful practical support.

My belated thanks go to Ontario Superior Court Judge Eugene Ewaschuk for reviewing *Desolation Row* in manuscript form. He ensured that my depiction of the Ontario provincial judicial system was accurate. However, I pooh-poohed his opinion that my description of Ontario weather was too harsh. Whereas he recalls formative years that included frigid winters on the Canadian prairie, Austin Starr remembers her fictional upbringing in balmy south Texas. My mysteries always reflect her views on what is "normal."

Another point about weather. As its title indicates, *Rainy Day Women* features an abundance of rain. Vancouver did experience such rain in the first half of August 1968, but not in 1969, the timeframe for this book. I confess to using poetic license.

My college friend Regina Kahn Miller and I studied Russian together and shared exploits at a language institute in the Soviet Union. She also checked this manuscript to ensure that my depiction of Jewish culture was accurate. My close friend Irina Mirnaya O'Neill, who hails from Moscow, shared her Russian family and friends with me, helping to keep alive, even in Texas, my love of Russian culture and history.

Canadian biologist and longstanding friend, Dorothee Josenhans Kieser, ensured that my descriptions of a science lab circa 1969 were correct, including details about the use of fire blankets. College friends Pam Herd Brink and her husband, Jim (a learned historian who earned his Ph.D. at the University of Washington), supplied the setting for the Spektors' apartment over a mortuary. The memories of their home from Jim's grad school days stuck with me until I could use it and make it the Spektors' own. Seattle writer Peggy Louise West described the campus of UW in the late sixties, backdating my own memories made during a visit in 1992. Seattle was also where I first saw the great Bob Dylan perform. The year was 1974, and I had to wait until 2015 to see him perform again, this time in Houston.

Two young Houston lawyers—both mothers of young children—refreshed my memory regarding the difficulties involved in maintaining a solid family life while advancing a career. Both these friends, Catherine Devore Johnson and Emily Wolf Schaffer, are also aspiring novelists. You will read their stories one day, I'm certain. Canadian business executive, philanthropist, and friend Florence Campbell has shown me for several decades how a strong woman can work to gain influence for the public good.

And then there are my girlfriends who date back to kindergarten and Sunday-school days. Carole Cour Widick, Glenda Jean Shoemake, and Nancy Higgins Lichtenfels taught me the depths of female friendship. They never fail to cheer me on, attending my book events when geography allows. I appreciate having dear ones from my Kansas days, including my cousins Ann and Mark Wagner and their mother, Lacy, attend my book events. Would that all my friends and family could attend. I mourn that my college roommate Anna Hegenbart Misak was never able to hold one of my books. Although she and her husband, Bob, helped me celebrate my first book contract, soon afterwards she passed away unexpectedly. I miss her and her keen intellect every day.

I grew up an only child, but living across the street were the McMillen kids—Janis, Mac, and Jack—who were like siblings.

While Mac has passed on, he lived just long enough to read *Desolation Row* the month it was published, and his online review never ceases to give me a pang. Janis attended my book signing in the Kansas City area, and Jack opened his gracious home to me while I was there.

Life has blessed me with caring friends, and I want to acknowledge them all. I also give thanks for my mother, Kathryn, who taught me how to be a good friend and how to keep friends despite the distance of years or geography. My father, Bill, gave me the love of language, reasoning, and different cultures. My son Hugh's careful attention to detail—so useful for an architect—has helped me moderate my slapdash tendencies. He and his wife, technical editor Jennifer, are raising Aidan and Madeleine as avid young readers. I know my grandchildren will keep the love of literature alive in our family.

Lastly I thank Bruce, my husband of four decades. I unreservedly acknowledge the crucial role his encouragement has played in my writing—a 100 percent cheerleading effort for Team Kay. He's always willing to brew another pot of coffee or listen to me rant about the anxiety of pushing a manuscript to completion. How lucky I was to run across him in the "wilds" of his native Western Canada.

To all these wonderful people, I extend my deepest gratitude. And to the countless others, here unnamed, who facilitated and encouraged me along the road to publication, thank you.

—K.K., Houston, Texas

CPSIA information can be obtained at www.ICGtesting.com
Printed in the USA
LVOW07s1659221215

467400LV00007B/1125/P